C0-AWC-233

Rumor Has It

ALSO BY CHARLES DICKINSON

NOVELS

Waltz in Marathon
Crows
The Widows' Adventures

STORIES

With or Without

Rumor Has It

CHARLES DICKINSON

WILLIAM MORROW AND

COMPANY, INC.

NEW YORK

This is entirely a work of fiction. Any resemblance to people living or dead is purely coincidental.

Recognizing the importance of preserving what has been written, it is the policy of William Morrow and Company, Inc., and its imprints and affiliates to have the books it publishes printed on acid-free paper, and we exert our best efforts to that end.

Library of Congress Cataloging-in-Publication Data

Dickinson, Charles, 1951–
Rumor has it / Charles Dickinson.
p. cm.
ISBN 0-688-10225-5
I. Title.
PS3554.I324R8 1991
813'.54—dc20 90-42502
CIP

Printed in the United States of America

First Edition

1 2 3 4 5 6 7 8 9 10

BOOK DESIGN BY BARBARA BACHMAN

For Donna, Louis, and Casey
and for my friends in the business

In a whisper: "Who's that ghoul?"

A face painted in the colors of decay edged into the bedroom of Rita and Danny Fain. It was a crusted haunt of a face, with mossy canines dripping flesh bits, a paste of rot under the eyes. The fiend departed when Danny waved. He switched on his reading flashlight and aimed it at the clock across the room. Time had moved back an hour that weekend. The walking corpse looked into the room again, hope and anticipation out of place in his returned-from-the-dead eyes.

Danny caught him with his flashlight beam. The ghoul regarded with impatience the figures in the bed, rolled his eyes, and slipped away.

Clark, the ghoul's younger brother, stirred. A toy steel ambulance fell from the upper bunk and hit the floor with a bang that Dan in his falling back toward sleep feared was a malfunction in the furnace. His hand felt for the register; warm air flowed. He began to lose interest in the source of the noise, tumbling down into the rare minutes of sleep remaining. Clark came down the ladder from his bed. The ghoul saw an opportunity and hid behind the bedroom door.

Rita ran a hand down her husband's body. She paused in the middle and squeezed. The night before, both of them sleepy, relatively ardent, they had taken care of him but not her. Deep inside she maintained an anticipatory itch. Danny rolled over and companionably nuzzled her breasts. Rita cupped his head with her free hand.

"Later," she said.

The ghoul pounced. The face of death was the first face Clark saw that morning and he screamed in unison with the alarm clock, which preceded by a half second the awakening howl of his sister, Tracy. Rita dropped her thickening toy, muttered, "Happy 'ween."

She got to her knees, then to her feet, then stepped over her husband to reach her robe. Clark buried his face in his mother's grasp. Rita held him until just before he was convinced the moment would last forever and then she turned him out. "Brush your teeth," she ordered. Stu in all his horrific getup jumped out at her and she caught the wall in a mock swoon. Tracy emerged from the bedroom, tiara in place.

Dan saw them all from where he lay in bed endeavoring to extend the night a minute. Everyone clustered around Rita. Stu removed his fangs and made a joke of brushing them, going so far as to work up a blue froth.

Tracy complained of the cold and got into bed with her father. Her mouth was already indistinct with lipstick. She had hidden it in her bed and applied it in the dark, and now her mouth had the smear of a woman who has been passionately kissed. She was a girl whose looks prompted comment from strangers. The tiara fell from her hair. A cheap sharp stone cut into her father's side. He stood up and Tracy rolled into the warm spot he left behind.

Rita carried a tray of juice from the kitchen to the sunroom. A ghost swung from a neighbor's tree. She began to assemble lunches. Eight slices of bread on the counter. Meat. Apples. Bananas. Cups of fruit sauce. Thermoses of ice water. Danny opened his robe and took her by the hips and ground himself against her fuzz-padded butt. She counterrevolved.

"I said later," Rita laughed.

"It *is* later," Danny said.

"Not ninety seconds later. Tonight later."

"I'm going to shower," Danny said.

"At least you have a hook to hang your soap on a rope."

The telephone rang. He took it in the office. Witches—snag-haired, toothless, laughing things—were in flight across his office window. The air smelled of pumpkin remains.

It was Marge from the *Bugle.*

"Mr. Derringer asked me to call all management-level personnel to alert them to a nine o'clock meeting this morning."

"I'm not due in until ten," Dan said.

"It's a mandatory meeting, Mr. Fain."

"How mandatory?"

"I was called in here early to make these calls."

"They can't struggle by without me?" Danny asked.

"They probably could, but would rather not."

"What is the meeting about?"

"Mr. Derringer did not inform me."

"Only editorial is invited?"

"All departments will be present."

"I don't take that as a good sign, do you?"

"I was asked to make these calls. I don't interpret signs."

The kids were yelling at each other in the bathroom, where Tracy was trying to use the toilet. He informed Rita of the meeting and she immediately looked for the balance in the equation, asking him if that meant he would get home early. He poured a little milk into a red Bulls cup and drank it to cool his stomach.

"Are you going to be sold again?" Rita asked.

"At the *Bugle,* you never know."

"Sounds like a good slogan for their next ad campaign."

The shower was upstairs, across a cold room perilous with toys: marbles, jacks, sharp edges of broken train track, bayonets of soldiers hiding on their backs in the high weeds of the carpet. The people who had built the house, whether through mischief or miscalculation, had positioned the room's only heating vent inside the room's only closet. The air was icy as he undressed. He turned on the shower. He looked himself over in the mirror. Needs a shave, something scaly at his hairline, a slack stomach, pencil legs, everything tight and shriveled in the cold. Nothing special as he came up on forty. He shaved in the shower, tracking his progress in a fogless mirror suctioned head-high on the tile. The mirror was a gift from Rita; it had come with a card expressing the desire that the mirror would save him precious seconds in his hectic life, seconds he might accumulate into a lump of time that he could spend with her.

The children were fighting again. Rita let them go on longer than he did. She had a feel for that sort of thing and she allowed the children the option of ending the fight themselves; he was apt to step in snarling the instant the battle began. Rita let things run their course; she understood the life of things, that events had their own momentum, their own desire to find a solution.

Someone knocked at the front door. A cluster of children stood on the porch. They were backed by a committee of moms. The sun was hardly up and already the children were out. A scuffed trail in the frost marked where they had crossed his yard. Ghosts. Fairies. A president. A raisin. They were out to have their fun before the perverts awoke, before the blades went into the apples, the urine into the cider. Dan remembered giving stones and crab apples to kids when he was in high school. It had seemed funny. Now he'd be arrested.

Then one mom came forward. She wore her husband's Bears stocking cap. "Tell Rita I was here," she said to Dan. "I told her we'd stop in early. She wanted to see the kids."

"I'll get her," Dan said. He was loaded with candy to pour

into bags, but there were no bags. The children stood shoulder to shoulder, befuddled by the hour and their empty hands.

"This is just a dress rehearsal," the mother explained.

He kissed his wife in the kitchen. "A woman is here with a bunch of kids," he said. "I don't know her name. Gotta go. Gotta go." He left his family with their disputes and their rapport. Two newspaper tubes were bolted to his mailbox: yellow Chicago *Bugle* on top, green Chicago *Morning Quill* underneath. Only the *Morning Quill* had arrived. Somewhere in the complex and bedeviling world of distribution, his *Bugle* had been lost. Three days out of seven it did not arrive, whereas he could not remember the last morning he had not found the *Morning Quill* rolled snug and dry in its green container. He stuck the paper—thick, crisp, and obscenely profitable—in his briefcase. One bitter consolation: He was the only person on the block with a *Bugle* tube, and thus the only person disappointed.

He opened his garage door and got behind the wheel of his car. He turned the key and the dash lights came alive like a billboard of malfunctions. Alternator. Oil. Brake. Seat belts. Door. He got out and pulled up the hood. Every belt had been sliced and neatly placed like a nest of snakes atop his air filter.

He ran to Rita's car but she kept her doors locked and the vandals had not been able to get to the latch to open her hood. Rita and the children came down the steps from the door. Atop Clark's head perched a colander, which he had covered with a layer of aluminum foil, shiny side out. His face was painted silver. Tracy's tiara was in place, and she wore a sash.

Now Dan was there.

Rita saw him and said, "What?"

"The train. Drive me to the train."

The train was in the opposite direction from the school. Stu lamented around his gory teeth that they might miss the grand march in the gymnasium. Dan expressed disbelief that someone would be so mean and thorough that they would get into his engine just to sever all the belts.

The train he needed was the 8:01. It was an express that

arrived in the city at 8:35. If he missed the express there was an 8:05, but that train made nine stops and arrived only seven minutes before the meeting was to begin. The clock in Rita's car read 8:54. All time cushions were gone. Rita slipped through the streets.

Danny Fain calculated distances while he turned Rita's car clock back an hour. She thanked him. "Can I stop hurrying now that I've been granted an extra hour?" she asked.

Two blocks from the station they were stopped by traffic. Dan kissed his wife good-bye again, waved to the ghoul, the alien, and Miss America, and exited. Rita would dodge down a side street against the current of people coming to board the train and perhaps get the boys to school on time. Dan saw the light from the approaching train, a bobbing rhinestone to the west, as he crossed the tracks.

He took coins from his pocket to buy a paper. The honor boxes were chained to a light pole; two of the polished green-and-silver boxes for the *Morning Quill,* one chipped yellow box for the *Bugle.* Two to one: the circulation ratio. The line story on the *Quill*'s front page was headed NEW GAINS IN WORLD DEMOCRACY. Bells, lights, and descending gates announced the arrival of the 8:01. Four commuters fed money into the *Morning Quill*'s boxes and removed papers. Dan found it interesting that the *Quill* readers did not hold the doors open so each person in line could take a free paper. They were used to paying their way. Dan put money into the *Bugle*'s box but there was no satisfying sound of coins falling into the latch release. He squinted into the slot; he saw the faint edge of his quarter stuck there. A man in line for a *Quill* observed, "I could have told you that thing jams every morning."

The *Bugle*'s front page, glimpsed through the box's scratched plastic window, was headlined in 120-point type: DEVIL'S WORK: *Halloween eve 'tradition' sends 7 homes up in flames.* Played beneath that story was a sidebar headed PUMPKINS: ENDANGERED SPECIES? *Drought, vandals thin local patches.* The entire package, including a picture of a burning house with a jack-o'-lantern on the front stoop, was bordered in thick black-rule tape decorated every half inch with a smiling pumpkin. Danny could hear Derringer rationalizing, "Pumpkins are fun. They sell papers."

Danny Fain was one of the last people to board the train. He took a window seat and opened his *Quill.* The paper *was* hard to maneuver in the train; he poked his seatmate with his elbow folding the big sheets open. The *Bugle*'s tabloid format was its major selling point. What always surprised and discouraged him about the *Morning Quill* was its color reproduction. Each copy of the paper looked individually painted. A candid of a notorious actress was the primary piece of art that morning in the Women & Children First section. She had come to town to promote her new movie and the *Quill* had reproduced her image with depressing clarity. Blond hair: Anyone could do blond hair. Skin tone: Skin tone was a little more difficult. They had even reproduced a tiny birthmark on the actress's chin, a fidelity she might not appreciate. But the actress was famous for the color of her eyes—a libidinous hazel—and the *Quill*'s picture had nailed that color perfectly. Dan could have cut out just the eyes from that photograph and most movie fans could identify the actress merely by the color.

The *Bugle*'s ancient presses had to be geared up for color by 3:00 in the afternoon. Any later than that and the picture wouldn't get in. The *Quill* could take a color picture at 10:30 P.M. and print pronto. The *Bugle*'s color came out muddy and indistinct. No edge. No jump off the page. It was such an obvious laboring to get color in the paper that the picture drew attention to its poor reproduction.

The door at the front of the car rolled open and a conductor came through. He was dressed in stripes like a prison inmate, jovial in his convict garb. Dan handed over his money.

He found a story by Julia Marx, who had at one time worked for the Chicago *Bugle.* She had been the finest writer on the staff for the twenty-seven months she was employed there. Her brain and talent tended toward involved stories that required time to develop. She possessed the gifts of organization and simplicity. She taught as she wrote. She transformed the mundane but vital subjects that the public should know about (for their own good, Danny could hear Julia say) into interesting and informative articles. She won some prizes: one for a series on mentally retarded adults living in boxcars at the edge of the city and another for a series of four stories about the life of a drunken driver who had killed a family of six. Julia Marx was a star on a paper that traditionally could not afford stars.

She seemed to understand the situation too well. She hinted at her desire for an office. Space was discovered in a cramped, elbowed corner of the newsroom to encapsule a desk, a phone, and a computer tube. Julia noted management's willingness to do this for her. She did not consider herself a greedy person, but she looked around and saw no one better than she was and that opinion informed everything she did.

Some time later Julia Marx was sent out in the afternoon to report on a Shih Tzu in need of a liver transplant. She followed orders, but the story she filed was sarcastic, nearly advocated letting the dog die, and was useless for the paper's purposes—the only Julia Marx story ever spiked, legend went. The next day she requested another reporter to work with her on a series about defective septic tanks. A suburb to the north, one of the wealthiest communities in the state, had had three hundred septic tanks installed by a single contractor in the early 1970s. From a tip, Julia had learned that the tanks had been defective when put in the ground; too-porous concrete, she was told, with a tendency to rot out at the bottom. The contractor, according to the tip, knew the tanks were bad but went ahead and used them because any delay would have thrown the work to another company.

Now the tanks were nearing the end of their lifespan; fifteen to twenty years, tops, the informant said. Human waste could seep into the private wells that served the homes in the community. The story had the weight and pop of a real scandal:

Hundreds of septic tanks buried under the perfect lawns of million-dollar houses would have to be excavated and replaced. Furthermore, the contractor was now mayor of the community, his power base built on the money he had made sinking three hundred substandard septic tanks. The story had money. It had politics. It had human greed and negligent moral fiber. It had beautiful symbolism.

The *Bugle* had the story to themselves, too, but they refused to assign a reporter to help Julia Marx. Insufficient manpower was the answer. They had animal drownings and lottery winners and defective children needing medical miracles to cover. Julia was put on the story alone.

Soon after, she was seen at lunch in the company of an assistant managing editor from the *Morning Quill.* She practiced no subterfuge; he was a friend from Princeton, in fact. But within forty-eight hours Julia Marx's new office, still smelling of paint and drywall, was devoid of any trace of her. The *Bugle* scrambled to build the septic tank story but Julia's notes departed with her and her personal queue in the computer system was empty. She might never have existed. Ironically, typically, the *Bugle* put three reporters on the recovery. Then the *Morning Quill* opened their behemoth Sunday paper (where the eternal 2-to-1 circulation ratio did not hold, but exploded to nearly 3.5-to-1) with the septic story and continued with it through eight daily main stories, a dozen sidebars, and enough reaction copy to give the story the feeling of immortality, a story that wouldn't die. Every word was written by Julia Marx: clear, sharp, captivating.

Nobody at the *Bugle* knew whom to fire when the series won the *Quill* a Pulitzer Prize. Julia Marx sent a fax to the *Bugle* newsroom: THIS COULD HAVE BEEN YOUR PULITZER. MARX. That taunt vanished from Derringer's desk. The folklore went that it was hanging framed in someone's house.

Now Julia Marx wrote occasional features for the *Quill.* Author interviews. People pieces. Color fill. But she had a staff of three reporters working for her and the *Bugle* kept careful track of her byline. If it disappeared from the paper for more than a week the assumption was that Julia and her team had found a story worthy of their time and effort. The *Bugle* could only wait and watch from afar. Her story in the Halloween *Quill* was about divorced men who brought their children to work on a regular basis. The story's art had been shot by a photographer who had gone from the *Bugle* to the *Quill* because he wasn't paid enough and his pictures weren't used large enough. The *Morning Quill* was full of that sort of person, people with the luxury of talent.

Danny Fain turned a page, creased the fold, felt a little cramped; tabloid had its advantages. His eye wandered out the train window to witness a ghost being struck by a car, this vision then abruptly blocked by an outbound freight.

"Hey!"

He looked at the woman to his left.

"Did you see that?"

She glanced up from her magazine. "See what?"

Danny Fain swiveled in his seat to look behind him. He half stood. The man directly to the rear was asleep, glasses propped on his forehead. Seated beside the man was a pretty girl reading *Vogue* and chewing a nail. She cooled him with a glance. The next seats back held four men playing cards. Dan crawled over the woman to his left and confronted them.

"Did any of you see that?"

They removed their attention reluctantly from the cards.

"See what?"

"A kid dressed as a ghost hit by a car?"

"We're playing gin here."

The freight had passed. He was far removed from the scene. Could other people have seen something? He was sitting in the last car in the train. People in the cars ahead would have had their vision obscured by the freight moments before Danny Fain's witnessing glance. He should have been paying closer attention to location. A street parallel to the tracks. But what about landmarks? What about street signs? And what about the car? What color was it? Make? Did it stop? What *exactly* had he seen?

His memory would not replay for him. He had looked into the scene too late. A short loop was all he possessed: a child in a sheet, arms spread, running hard as if with the promise that his costume bestowed the talent of flight, running in the same direction as the train, an automobile behind the child *launching* him into the air. Then the freight train moving the other way, coming across the image like a curtain, or a camera lens, closing, a screen going blank.

The loop ended with the ghost in the air. He played the loop again. He would send a reporter back to look for the ghost, but he needed an approximate location. More than that, he needed a seasoned hand, someone with discretion, reliability, poise. And what about the police? By the time he reached the office the accident might already have been reported; there might be no story at all.

The ride downtown stretched on. His fidgeting and his bizarre question made the woman to his left stand and walk the rolling deck down the train to the double doors. The kid might still be alive. The car, too, might have stopped and summoned an ambulance and saved the kid's life, limited his suffering to the bruises and scrapes suffered in his landing. Perhaps it was a young girl, head hidden in her mom's old sheet. The story was full of a range of possibilities. Danny would have liked to explore them all, and keep it all secret at the same time. If the kid was alive and unharmed there was nothing to report. If he was hurt or killed and the paramedics were on the scene, then it was a short. But if the ghost was the victim of a fatal hit-and-run and was now lying broken along the railroad tracks, then it was the kind of story that could turn nonreaders into devotees, occasional perusers into subscribers. It was a ticket story: a ticket to a better job, a ticket to a better tomorrow.

The train glided over the last tangle of rails and into the overhanging shadows of the station. People rose from their seats, gathered their belongings, balanced in the aisle against the small dips and sways of the final hundred yards of motion. They tumbled off the cars into a basement gloom. The long walk to the exits was a herding of people between the train's grimy flank and walls too filthy to touch. Cigarettes were fired up. Dan wanted to hurry but there was no room to pass.

He bought a *Bugle* at a newsstand in the station. The girl who took his money had a very realistic-looking bullet wound in the center of her forehead, like a red and puckered drill hole. The skin beneath her eyes was blackened and scabious. All in all, Dan thought, Stu's ghoulish features were more artfully applied. She laughed at him.

Danny called the office from a pay phone. Tim Penn was not in, he was informed. Dan asked for someone who could look up a number for him in the gang file. He was put on hold. In his brief history as a reporter he had made no friends with cops, cultivated no sources in the department who might look the other way while they did this one favor for him; it was a problem, one reason why he was no longer a reporter. He came off hold and asked for Stan Mansard's number at police headquarters.

Stan Mansard was the *Bugle*'s police reporter, a good hand with a weakness for secrets. He loved to spin tales around free drinks. *Quill* reporters on more than one occasion had wooed him with icy scotches until the hush project that occupied his days became theirs to beat him with. Telling Stan what he had seen was akin to putting it on the wires.

Stan Mansard was not in, according to the woman who answered the phone in the press room.

"What if I wanted to report a crime?" Danny asked, feeling safe in the anonymity he shared with the woman at the other end.

"Tell me."

"I want to keep it secret," he said.

"It can't be done," she stated.

He hung up the phone. This story would be his alone. Work was eight blocks away through bright, crowded streets. He followed a route along the river that he imagined cut down the distance as close to a straight line as possible. The anonymity of hurry was enjoyable. Nobody looked at anyone else. Everybody had a destination. To be taking the sun with a casual stride was to admit to having no place where one's presence was required. Such people existed, nevertheless. They were mostly men. Some picked through trash barrels for mistakenly discarded ten-dollar bills or shreds of lunch. Others pulled their coats around them as they jacked their spines up flat against the walls of commerce.

In the next block Danny saw a large man in rags tugging on the door of a computer store, trying to pull the door open while a girl inside tried to pull it closed. The man had a nutty little smile of mischief on his face. He possessed an idle, unconsidered strength, for he was using only one hand, the other in the pocket of his tattered coat. He didn't seem to want anything in the store. He probably didn't even want the girl, although she was quite attractive and prosperously dressed, and the growing uneasiness in her eyes may have appealed to the man. The store she was protecting was dark behind her. She was probably the only person inside, and therefore she did not want to lose this tug-of-war. The man's goofy smile remained in place. He had not brought the strength of his second hand into play; he bore no specific malice. She was only a pretty girl who had a job, a warm home to return to in the evening, enough to eat, and he saw the opportunity to impose a measure of his misfortune upon her. Make her think. Give her the creeps. She would tell everyone she knew about him. He would remain large in her memory for a day; he would never entirely leave.

The man teased the girl by letting her pull the door within an inch, a half-inch, of locking, before he exerted the strength necessary to pull the door open and begin the game again. She was biting her lip with the effort, and as Dan came near he heard her whimper in desperation. He stepped around behind the man and smelled sweat and alcohol. A fly roosted in his ear.

He wore three sweaters, two old shirts, boots without laces. Up close, he was enormous; wide across the back, tall, hungry. He let the girl pull the door nearly shut and then her eyes jerked hopefully toward Dan. The man looked his way. Dan added his strength to the girl's, pushing on the store's door as she pulled, and the lock banged home and the girl was safe. She disappeared immediately.

"But you're out here with me," the man said in a casual, intelligent voice. A sheen of education coated his words. "You miscalculated. You saved the heroine but you locked your own ass out in the cold with the villain. She'll be no help when I beat in your skull." The man's posture, hand in pocket, gave his threats a benevolent, professorial quality.

Dan started to walk rapidly away. The man followed, but almost immediately fell behind. His boots would fall off if he hurried.

"Give me money and I won't beat you up," he said, out of range already. "You smug asshole. I used to be a commuter."

Dan stepped behind a UPS truck and crossed against the light. He didn't look back. The man shouted deals after him; money in exchange for his continued good health, a quarter for a blessing. Dan was safe again in his anonymity.

He crossed the Irv Kupcinet bridge and went through a windy courtyard behind the *Bugle* building, skirting a piece of sculpture—a flat-black marble coin balanced on its edge, with thousands of holes in it for water to spurt—a piece of civic art disdainfully titled "Management Style" by the *Bugle* employees. Put up in the late 1950s out of burnished aluminum, plate glass, and thin slabs of black granite, the *Bugle* building was only seven stories tall. The skyscrapers surrounding it sailed up into the sky while the *Bugle* squatted on its prime real estate like a testament to meager ambitions. People were reminded of a tugboat. A wedge of cheese. A Roach Motel.

Dan saw people he knew moving toward the front entrance. A couple of reporters. An artist fighting against the wind with her portfolio case. Dan checked his watch. Coming to work had always pleased him. He had never been one of the mopes who infested the halls with their blatant desire to be elsewhere. He felt comfortable at work. He belonged. Although his job had periods of challenge and excitement, he did not require constant relevance in his work, or even stimulation on a day-to-day basis. He believed the *Bugle* possessed life, spirit, an air of rebellion, and feistiness. But these were qualities unappreciated by most people, especially advertisers and the demographically beloved with money to spend.

The front security desk was staffed by three men with walkie-talkies and takeout coffees. On the wall opposite the elevators was the building directory. Danny Fain's name was up there. He was still ASSOC. METRO EDITOR. This might have given solace, that he still had a job, but on two occasions terminated employees had remained on this public roster for a year after they had been escorted from the building.

Sam Lindsay waited for an elevator. He was a reporter who had once worked a few shifts as assistant city editor. He was not someone Dan had expected to be summoned to this meeting.

"What do you think it is?" Sam asked.

"A mystery," Danny said. "I'm called at the crack of dawn and told to be here. I'm here. I can read the writing."

"I'm just coming to work," Sam said. "I got a call from Woods this morning. He was all excited. What had I heard? I'd heard nothing."

"So you weren't invited to the meeting?"

The elevator arrived. "No. I'm just coming to work."

"Maybe they're changing the headline fonts again," Dan said. "Or painting the trucks and honor boxes dollar-green."

"The *Quill*'s already that color. Maybe a price hike," Sam Lindsay speculated. "Maybe someone is replacing Derringer."

"Maybe raises for the entire staff."

"Or a new contest!"

The *Bugle*'s last contest had boasted twenty-four cheap French cars as grand prizes, but so few people played the game that they only gave away three. One of the winners kept calling the office to complain of breakdowns. The radio didn't work. The seat was inclined to go horizontal at any moment. He got mad and hit the steering wheel and the top half snapped off. He made threats. He promised to visit the newsroom with a shotgun. This is our typical reader, Danny Fain thought. This is the type of person who gets his view of the world from the *Bugle.* By pure chance he has stumbled onto the largest piece of good luck in his life. Now something that he can't afford even when it's given to him is falling apart in his hands. It was explained to the man that taxes, insurance, repairs, upkeep, gas, etc., were the responsibility of the winner. He had been given an $11,000 automobile for nothing. The *Bugle* was not going to pay for every expense he incurred in the operation of that car. Another winner wanted to sell the car back to the *Bugle.* He wasn't even interested in sitting in the car for a publicity photo. A scuffle broke out when PR types tried to force him behind the wheel, loudly reading from the fine print the section devoted to winners' promotional responsibilities. "Just gimme the cash," he demanded. He was another typical *Bugle* reader: a hand-to-mouth guy, a bad credit risk, a man reluctant to be photographed.

Dan stopped to use the bathroom on the fourth floor. Eric Maas was combing his hair. Eric was a determinedly hip man in his thirties who wrote about the city's night life. Today he had on five earrings, a woven leather bracelet, shades with a neck chain, jeans, high-top blue sneakers, a smirk. He was assigned to Features, out of Dan's loop. Dan would have loved to get hold of some of his copy. He could never make sense of Maas's writing, which seemed doggedly incomprehensible, a late-hours code for the illiterate. A guitar was a *bat.* Women were *chickens.* To dance was to *bodulate.* A band's sound was *arrogant as a rumpy god high on hate.* Smoke in bars did not drift or rise, it *frescoed the night rhythms.* A drink was *fun punch.* Music was *killing, grinning, apocalyptic as a farewell finger bob. Smooth as the face on a heaving chicken's one-love one-glove bribe Rolex.* Dan was too polite and too intimidated to ask, "What *is* this shit? What does this *mean*?"

Eric Maas popped some Visine into night-burned eyes, put the bottle in his pocket, and lowered his shades into position.

"You just getting off?" Danny asked.

"I am always off. If you mean, 'Is my work day at an end?,' my answer is that it has just begun."

Dan pursued the conversation no further.

"Rumor is we're going to be sold," Eric Maas said.

"I hadn't heard that."

"Big meeting today. All the tip-tops required to attend."

"There is a meeting," Danny said.

"It can't be good news. Sold or fold is what I hear."

"From whom?"

"The air. The night. If you keep your hearing fork tuned you receptorize all manner of unrapturous notes. *Ciao.*"

The *Bugle* newsroom was noteworthy for its abundance of places to hide. Mountains of paper had been disseminated over the ranks of desks, forming little bunkers of privacy, and when a new office was added, usually three walls, glass from the waist up, tacked to an outside wall to form a cube, the new office opened a blind spot out of the view of the editors' desks that certain individuals were quick to adapt to their own uses: naps, long phone calls, chess, cards.

The newsroom's floor tiles were the color of ocean bottom. The walls were sneeze-tinted, furred with dust and printers' ink. The ceiling boasted a legendary look: Three years earlier a sprinkler system had been installed, necessitating the removal of ceiling tiles in selected spots so that sprinkler heads could be suspended. Dirty hands replaced the tiles when the job was finished, leaving fingerprints behind like animal tracks around watering holes. These smudge clusters were beloved by the staff. How long would they remain? What did the fact that no one bothered to wash the ceiling signify about the health of the paper? Danny Fain advanced the theory that the workmen who replaced the tiles had criminal records, and the police had asked the paper to keep their prints on file.

Dan had an office on the south side of the newsroom, a cubicle with a river vista, sun, and a good view of the staff at work. The only newsroom clock that Dan could see from his office had run amok in the spring, when the time was set ahead, and since then had been off by four hours and ten minutes. After a day, Danny could rapidly make the calculations in his head and tell the time. Now he'd have to take the added autumn hour into consideration. Requests to have the clock properly set became lost once they exited the newsroom and entered the Office of the Building, an infrastructural black hole of ready excuses and previous commitments that kept the newsroom enervatingly hot in the summer, bone-cold in the winter. Small typed labels began to appear beneath the errant clock: DERRINGER TIME. THE TIME YOU WISH IT WAS. TIME TO LOOK FOR A NEW JOB. NO TIME TO LOSE.

The newsroom was unusually active for that hour of the morning. Reporters had beamed the news of the meeting to each other, everyone flocking to the source of the heat. They stood in small groups, talking, worrying, updating their rumors. He made a call to Lucy Spriggs. He would need her permission to free a reporter to go hunt for the ghost. She was not in.

He looked in the computer for a phone number, then dialed that number without an idea of what he would say. He started out paranoiac, asking the man who answered, "Is this being tape recorded?"

"Would I tell you if it was?"

"You have to."

"Don't tell me what I have to do. Why did you call? And why don't you want to be taped?"

"Are you busy this morning?" Danny asked.

"We're always busy."

"Any unusual calls?"

"Just this one."

Danny felt his lack of a strategy betray him, so he hung up.

He looked up another number and called it.

"Any kids brought in hit by a car?" he asked.

They patched him through to another department, where he repeated the question. They asked for his name and he made one up. They put him on hold and kept him there nearly a minute, and just as he was set to abandon the attempt they came back and said that they had a minor auto accident with a child involved, but no one hit by a car.

Plenty to hang a story on.

Tim Penn slithered in and onto the couch, nudging the door shut in passing. He sat low, out of sight, hands stacked atop his crotch. He rolled his eyes: huge eyes, blue eyes. His face was ax-narrow, hollow-cheeked, killer-handsome. His wife—his third wife—suspected him of being unfaithful and her suspicions had a foundation in truth. Tim Penn could not resist the impact he had on women. He was a good reporter, a writer of some talent, but no one trusted him to cover anything of importance because he persisted in dropping out of sight for two or three hours while on assignment, waylaid by the women he inflamed in the normal course of his day. He had almost been fired twice, and was still employed at the *Bugle* only because his assignations had not become troublesome enough to reach the ears of Derringer, noted priss.

"What's the word, Scoop?" Tim Penn asked.

"A meeting. I don't know anything."

"My sources say a new day is coming. Fresh capital into the product. A new computer system. New presses. A Warbucks coming on board to finance a concerted run at the *Quill*," Tim Penn said.

"You have optimistic sources," Dan said.

Tim centered his tie by touch.

"What are you doing today?" Danny asked.

"Nothing. I'm waiting for Lucy. Something lame is planned, undoubtedly," Tim said.

"Talk to me when this is over. I've got something for you."

The meeting was not going to be held in Derringer's office,

with its tall windows and southern aspect, but rather in a small room off the back hall, next door to the smoking lounge, which Dan was startled to see was already so packed with reporters that most had to stand, their grimaces obscured by clouds. The meeting room had a gritty, particulate feel to every surface, a residue of secondary death that had sifted through the vents. It was where they met each afternoon to map the news of the day, and it gave Dan hope that this gathering would also be routine. The room was cramped, intimate, a chalkboard at one end wiped clean. Had the meeting been held in Derringer's office, with plenty of room and natural light, the atmosphere would have hinted at the ceremonial, at the possibility of a major announcement of great change.

Dale Busse, in charge of the photographers, took the seat to Danny Fain's right. Wearing a magnifying scope on a chain around her neck, an assignment clipboard on her lap, her gray-tinted glasses shoved up into her hair, she exuded the impression of having already been at work for half a day, of having only grudgingly made time for this meeting.

Dan asked, "Can you spring someone loose later on short notice?"

She gave him a wry look and inspected her assignment charts. "We've got one on vac and one sick," she said. "So no, I'm not swimming in shooters today." She touched a line on her sheet. "If Dunkirk gets back by lunchtime—and you have a *definite* place to send him, and he can get it done in twenty minutes—he could shoot you before be has to be at Field's for some brain-dead soap actress flogging her new aerobics video."

"I've just got something working," Dan said. "I'm going to put Penn on it if I can get him. I might need a picture."

Dale Busse shrugged under the pads on her shoulders. She wore silk blouses every day, buttons left strategically undone. Rumor had it she wanted Dunkirk for herself. "I can't promise anything," she said.

"I just wanted to get on record with you," Danny said.

The room was filling up. All the seats were taken except the one at the head of the table: Derringer's chair. His secretary had come in and set a cup of coffee and a black folder on the desk. Danny feinted toward looking inside the folder and a number of people laughed nervously. He was becoming troubled by the tenor of the room. Standing along the wall were most of the wigs from Financial, Features, and Sports. Strangers were present as well. Men and women dressed too fastidiously to be newspaper people. Advertising and PR types. Bean counters. Pea heads. Men in razored hair. Women in sensible suits. Halloween costumes.

"Who are all these people?" he whispered.

Dale Busse smiled at his question. "It doesn't bode well," she said.

"It's getting claustrophobic."

"*Das Boot,*" Dale Busse said.

"*Das Rag,*" Dan replied. She laughed and people overhearing laughed.

Constance Drane came into the room and treated everyone to a sour look. She was windblown, the bow on her blouse carelessly tied. She glanced around for a seat and frowned upon finding none. Dan gave her a low-key, one-finger wave. The line on Drane was that she had peaked at her current post of assistant city editor, had become a go-and-sin-no-more who would fill a niche and find the odd typo, but could not be relied on to push the paper forward with her aggressiveness or story ideas. She had let the loss of a promotion kill her drive, when in fact Derringer's management style was to withhold a promotion periodically from a deserving employee to gauge how that employee responded. Constance Drane had responded by folding her camp. She was at the meeting in her trim, dull suit and lobster lipstick, ready to take notes like a frosh.

Muff Greene arrived. Derringer could not be far behind. Muff Greene was the managing editor, the first woman to hold that post at the *Bugle.* She was married to a state representative she had met while reporting on his alleged official misconduct. Nearly forty-two, a prosaic woman who favored expensive suits, her hair cut the same way since high school (it was assumed), Muff was beloved by the staff for having ascended from beat reporter to being a heartbeat away. She worked long hours, unlike Derringer. One of her husband's campaign posters was taped to her office wall. Reliable sources reported she had risen to managing editor and now found the position lacking. She could be caught at moments disengaged from the deadline chaos around her, staring off across the busy newsroom, or merely into her tube. Her sighs could rustle papers at the far end of the room. A friend of a friend alleged that Muff Greene desperately wanted a baby.

Financial Editor Jack Lustig gave up his seat to her. She thanked him and patted his shoulder. Another clue of doom, Dan noticed. Muff Greene subdued, her optimist's gleam missing. She touched an eye with a wad of Kleenex hidden in her fist.

A phone rang in the smoking lounge and Phil Blick, a loudmouthed, one-lunged reporter, was heard to yell, "Yeah? No. Nothing. Derringer isn't there yet. *I don't know.*" Phil coughed, an explosion of such raw, windbag force and moisture that Danny Fain mimed the knocking of phlegm out of the receiver onto his hand and got a big laugh.

Metro Editor Lucy Spriggs arrived, apologizing. The room was now uncomfortably packed. Dan offered her his seat and she declined. She slipped between two people and perched on the arm of Derringer's empty chair. She was a sharp-witted, petite woman of thirty-eight, her small, oval face topped with a whirl of dark brown hair. Her figure was an incongruous, startling mix of stick legs, bony butt, and disconcertingly large breasts. Her rapid, sexy walk through the newsroom was always the first thing imitated at *Bugle* parties. Every Friday she wore some provocative style—usually in black—that paid heed to the chest she kept under wraps in business jackets the rest of the week, as if in signal that the weekend was upon them. There was a tiny hole in the stocking stretched around the back of her skinny calf. She drummed a long red nail on the chair arm.

Everyone watched the door for Derringer.

Danny said, "I have a project and I need Tim Penn to work on it with me."

Lucy Spriggs shifted her attention his way. Everyone seemed to listen. His project gave them something to focus on, took them into a future beyond this room.

"What is it?" Lucy asked.

"On the train to work today I saw a kid get hit by a car," Dan said. "A kid dressed as a ghost."

"Are you sure of what you saw?"

"Pretty sure. I have an image of it. I made some calls and nothing's been reported. No bodies found."

"Did you tell the police what you saw?"

"Not specifically. I asked them if they had reports on anything resembling what I saw—without telling them I'd seen it. With nothing reported, that says to me the driver didn't stop."

"You should tell the police," Muff Greene said.

"I'm not sure where it happened," Dan said. "The police wouldn't send a car to look for this kid unless I could tell them *precisely* where to look. But if I send Tim he can do some scouring. He'll be on assignment."

"Until he meets someone," Lucy Spriggs remarked.

People laughed. Muff Greene did not. She asked, "Why him?"

"He's dogged. He needs a change."

"Let him change wives," Lucy said.

Again, laughter from the initiated, nervous chuckles from the people along the walls.

Someone shifted position and brushed the light switch and the room went black. No one made a sound. Then someone said, "Maybe Derringer won't see us in here."

The lights returned. Muff Greene, regarding the wall when the lights went off, was regarding it still when they came back on. Dan felt a pain in his stomach. He thought of Rita. Time was frozen. It was not good news approaching.

Muff Greene spoke with some of the enthusiasm that had eased her through her life. "This sounds like a good *Bugle*-style story. Make a crusade of it. A newspaper out to do good for the community. Find the kid. Talk to his family. A plea to the hit-and-run driver, if it is hit-and-run. One of our own an eyewitness to life's real pain. TV and the *Quill* will have to play catch-up with *us* for once. Do you have a shooter?"

"Dale said Dunkirk might be available for twenty minutes at lunchtime," Danny said. "If we know where to send him."

"Why so brief?"

Dale Busse said, "He's got Suzy Slutmuffin at Field's at one. Pelvic thrusts. Powdery sweat in the cleavage."

Everyone laughed.

"Send Tim," Muff ordered. "Send Dunkirk when he gets in. Forget Suzy."

Danny Fain's dread intensified. Managing a wan, scared grin, he was now waiting for the ax to fall. Muff Greene had not become managing editor by killing photo shoots that placed major advertisers in a hip and loving light. Why start now, unless it no longer mattered?

An ad salesman standing along the wall read from the day's front page: "Seven houses set on fire last night." A grunt of disbelief circled the room. Old news to Dan; he was barely concerned.

"My sister-in-law was burgled two nights ago," said a man Dan couldn't name. "They took her stereo, her VCR, her CD player, and her TV. They left a copy of the *Bugle* on her table."

People at the door looked behind them. A commotion was approaching. An opening was created for something or some-one who commanded a mindless respect; Dan knew it must be Derringer. He had made them wait ten minutes; it was known among the staff as his power pause. The lights went out again and a woman screamed. When they came back on Lucy Spriggs was off the arm of the chair. She had taken a position, arms folded like armor across her chest, where she would be out of Derringer's line of sight after he took his seat.

Dan waited, breath held, looking for clues. He loved to sit and watch a room full of people for what they revealed. He tried to read looks, words, whispers, glances, angles of approach, touches, reversals, shrugs, stares, for the messages they conveyed. He had once witnessed Hagen Manley, a tall, handsome sportswriter, flirting with Claire Soames, the comely assistant food editor. A month after witnessing this flirtation, Danny heard Claire Soames whisper viciously to Hagen Manley, "Go fuck *your*self." A month later Claire Soames and her husband separated. The divorce left her hollow-eyed and incompetent. She lost custody of her son. Dan, working late, snooping through her calendar, saw the days she was allowed contact with her little boy highlighted with red marker hearts around his name: *Sean.* She ran away with him and became an object of news. Dan joked at the four o'clock meeting, "Call Hagen Manley for react," and from the blank, disbelieving looks he got he realized he was alone in his assumptions.

But from those gathered this morning Danny could take no clues. Everyone present was at the mercy of the man coming through the door. They had no secrets to hide about what was about to happen. A bad sign: Derringer was wearing his suit coat. He had reknotted his tie. A man who teetered as close to dishevelment as executive privilege allowed, this fussing with his appearance turned the air funereal. He, too, had risen from reporter to editor-in-chief, but without accruing the respect Muff Greene possessed. Whereas she was promoted because she mastered and outgrew each job she was given, Derringer ascended because he understood that his strength lay in conveying a shallow, impersonal bonhomie to everyone he met and he adhered strictly to that talent over his long and prosperous career. He was the man who never came down on the wrong side of a power struggle.

He made his way to the head of the table. He handed a folded note to Muff Greene but she declined to open it at that time. A woman opposite the door screamed when a witch doctor's mask popped in. This creature had slashes of blood on his coconut visage, a bone dripping gristle jabbed through his nose, a jaunty necktie, penny loafers. He shook a pink baby rattle ornamented with black feathers over the staring heads of the group. No one laughed. He saw that the moment was bad, shouted "*Booga!*" once, and withdrew. There was no curiosity as to his identity. Derringer was the source of the only mystery of interest in that room.

He flipped open the folder on the table. A single sheet of paper was contained therein. He took a moment to blow his nose. Lucy Spriggs leaned forward an inch to read over Derringer's shoulder. Danny Fain saw her eyes move over the text, a furrow of rage dig across her brow. Derringer made a production of folding his handkerchief, yet everyone now was watching Lucy, understanding that the word would come from her long before Derringer could get around to it.

"We're *closing*?" she gasped.

Derringer's head whipped round toward Lucy Spriggs so violently that his tie flew like a blade with the motion and wrapped around his neck. Muff Greene whimpered in her fist.

"Please, Lucy," Derringer said.

"We're closing? We're *ceasing* publication?"

"It's not as bad as it sounds," Derringer said. He turned back to the room, seeing that he would not win Lucy Spriggs over just then.

"What could be worse than that?" she demanded.

He ignored her. He lifted the statement and began to read in a constricted, infuriated voice, "The owners and editorial board members of the Chicago *Bugle,* taking into account the paper's decreasing circulation, diminishing advertising linage, reduced market share, and increased expenses, have regretfully decided to cease publication following the edition of Tuesday, November 15."

A number of people fled the room. Muff Greene was one. Marv Urquhart, head of the ad sales force, also tried to depart, but he was detained at the door by Puncher Mudd, the *Bugle*'s immense, hulking associate sports editor. Puncher put a hand the size of a pay phone on Urquhart's chest and drove him firmly back. Urquhart favored pastel shirts with white collars, gold collarpins, ties with tornado knots the firmness of diamonds, joke cufflinks: artificial eyes, the state of Texas, dice rolling seven and eleven, Roman coins, TV sets. He went where Puncher Mudd pushed him, back against the wall. "I'm not the *only* one who killed this fucking paper," Marv said in his own defense.

Derringer mumbled, "I'm sorry," stood, and started to depart. The witch doctor returned with an X-acto knife. Derringer fell away, fearing assassination. The witch doctor swiped the knife beneath Derringer's chin and sliced off his tie an inch below the knot. He danced out swinging his trophy like a scalp into the clangor of the hall. The crowd was sour and nasty. A plug of people clotted in the doorway. Derringer, touching the knot of his tie in a stab at dignity, waited patiently for an opening and when it appeared he went through it.

Lucy Spriggs fell into Derringer's chair. More people disconsolately walked out of the room. Danny thought: I hurried in early for *this*? Constance Drane was looking through her checkbook, as if the clues to her survival were contained in the balance.

Lucy Spriggs lit a cigarette. "Maybe the employees could buy it," she said, staring into the distance. "We should talk to Larry Mock. He could tell us how to set up an LBO. Can you look into that, Danny?"

He sighed. "Buying this paper is not something I'm encouraged about," Dan said.

"Are you encouraged about having no job? Are you going hat in hand to the *Quill*? What about you, Constance?"

Constance Drane looked up from her figuring. She had taken out a pen and a calculator and begun to work in earnest. "*Pardon?*" she said in a fake French accent.

"Would you be interested in helping the employees buy the *Bugle*?"

She tapped some numbers and wrote the answer down in

her checkbook. "I'm married," she said. "I can use the time off."

Dale Busse was examining Lucy Spriggs through her magnifying lens. "I'm not married," she said. "I've saved nothing. Count me in."

Puncher Mudd, who had waited by the door while people departed, spied on Constance Drane, then exclaimed, "You have seventy-two hundred dollars in *checking*?"

She snapped shut her book. "Mind your own *fucking* business!" she hissed.

Dan stood up. Dale Busse followed his progress with her lens. Her watching eye was grotesquely enlarged and sad. "Still have to put out a paper," he said.

"*Why?* Why should we hang around for two weeks just so they can pull in a little extra revenue?" Lucy Spriggs demanded. "They'll make a bundle on the last editions once this news gets out. But if *today's* paper turned out to be the last one, they'd lose. There'd be no final burst of circulation. Why help them? We should just go."

Dale watched Lucy's speech through her glass as if filming it. Lucy's eyes were full of tears. Ten years she had been at the *Bugle.* When she had taken the job she was engaged to a man who had grown shadowy in her memory. He traveled in his own work, then was transferred to a distant city, and she refused to give up her job to accompany him. She began spending more time at her desk, making calls, writing stories and memos of suggestion, and this manner of grieving was misconstrued by management as commitment and ambition. In this way, she fell in love with what she had become.

In the newsroom, reporters were standing in the aisles and on their desks shouting curses at each other and the fates. Newspaper clippings sailed like snow. A flaying of the walls had begun in an effort to remove the pictures, notes, signs, and other attempts that had been made to give the place some touch of home. The coffee machine was cracked like a big, square-shouldered safe. The door hung open, the coin bin emptied, the coffee free. Danny Fain took a cup on the way to his office. "This is a moment in history," he said to no one. "This is something we'll brag about surviving later on."

A fire began in a wastebasket. It tickled up through the papers and damp cups as if seeking permission to catch hold. Smoke feathered out over the nearby desks. Nancy Potter, working the phones, was a reporter nearing the end of a pregnancy that had remained cinched and mysterious behind stylish clothes. She kept a vase of yellow roses on her desk. She was an enigmatic dynamo, a passable writer but a voracious collector of facts. Potter was reserved, contained, punctual, *perfect,* and no one knew where she had found a couple spare minutes to conceive. The act struck those who knew her only glancingly as too messy for her tastes.

She talked on the phone through a headset, typing every word she heard into her tube. Her eyes were dry and clear. Early in her pregnancy her face had broken out in star-shaped spots and she took one day off, returning the next day clear-skinned and prepared to carry on. She extracted her yellow roses from the vase, then rolled in her chair as far as the phone cord would allow and poured the water from the vase into the smoking wastebasket. Nothing in her manner betrayed the least haste. When the fire was out she rolled back to her post and replaced the roses in the vase, taking a moment to fluff the blooms.

Lucy Spriggs returned to the newsroom at full gallop, her hurrying body even in the midst of degradation and ruin drawing admiring looks from the men. She towed a befuddled Larry Mock, Lawrence K. Mock to the readers of his investment advice column, and when they were safely in her office she slammed the door shut so hard that people thought the presses had started. Lawrence K. Mock's column appeared five days a week and was syndicated in 244 newspapers. He had been profiled in *Time, Fortune,* and *Money.* He wrote with the certain assurance of one privy to the answers, and his mail volume was eight times heavier than that of anyone else on the paper, even old Abe Skinback, the saurian gossip columnist who worked so exclusively out of his home that no one had seen him in months. People trusted their financial futures to Lawrence K. Mock.

"Do you think he'll survive?" Dan heard Tim Penn ask above the din. They both watched Lucy Spriggs pacing in her office, doing all the talking.

"Do you think Lawrence K. is thinking what it would be like to bury his face in those?" Tim Penn speculated.

"Tim! Did you hear the paper's closing?"

Tim Penn gave Danny a dismissive look. "A ploy," he said. "A shit screen. We may be *sold,* but we won't be *closed.* I've talked to people who've talked to people upstairs who've talked to investors who are putting together a package. Can you imagine this town with just the *Quill* to cover it? Sleep city. *Snooze control.* Am I still going to do that thing for you? I should get started if I is."

"You is," Danny Fain said. "But I need a moment to make a call."

Tim Penn said, looking around, "We are on the brink of a riot. Someone should make a speech to bring this place back to order."

"You're the man," Dan said. "Start talking."

Danny closed the door to his office, took his seat, kept his back to the door. The windows in the buildings across the river were flat and empty. He never saw anyone over there. Wasn't anyone as curious as he was? People moved in the street. He would have preferred some roiling pain, some sign that the people would be sorry when the *Bugle* was gone. But perhaps word had not gotten out. The news would have reached the *Quill* already. It might have been old news there even before the meeting began. The TV stations would be calling. They would take shots of that morning's front page with its ludicrous pumpkin-bordered package and run it over the shoulder of the newscaster, perhaps with a skull and crossbones or a gravestone superimposed. Something Halloween. Something in the mood.

He called home. Maybe Rita would surprise him with the news that she had gone out and gotten a job. A mystery career, a hidden talent. She picked up the phone. She sounded happy to hear from him.

"Who's there?" he asked.

She laughed. It was an old joke; he had learned to guess when she had company by the charge of excitement in her voice. When she was home alone with the kids her tone was cooler by a notch, as if she were in constant need of cheering up.

"It's just me and the Pretty One. We're drawing on the chalkboard."

"Who else?"

"Oh, yes. There's Pablo the gardener. Oh, Pablo! It's so *big*! What was the meeting about?"

"They're closing us."

"Come on," Rita said.

"They're closing November fifteenth."

"Danny, what does that mean?"

"It means deep shit. It means no job, which means no money."

"You should call the *Quill* right now. Before everyone else does. Everybody is gonna try to get over there—you should beat the rush," Rita warned.

"But I don't want to work for them," Danny said.

"What choice do you have?"

"I just wanted to tell you," he said. "I don't feel like a lot of career counseling just this moment."

"Sure, I understand," Rita said. She hesitated a second, then said, "But waiting can be fatal. You know people over there. If you get your balance and react before everyone else—that's what's important."

"I just can't right now, Reet. The time is bad, *mentally.*"

"What about severance?"

"I haven't heard."

"You've been there nine years, you deserve some sort of parachute."

"Nobody's said anything. The company's folding. Why

would they care about their employees landing on their feet?"

"They must be planning something," Rita said.

"Not necessarily."

"Go *talk* to someone," she commanded. "You've earned it."

"I will."

"No, you won't. You'll take what they give you. I know you."

"I'm so glad I called."

"These are the facts, Dan. We have thirty-six hundred in the money market," she said. "I've got the statement right in front of me. Eighty-four sixty-one in checking. Talk to Muff, at least. You can talk to her."

He held the phone between his ear and shoulder. Rita's numbers had frozen his brain. He could not think of anything but money. He said, "This is the sort of reversal that puts men out in the streets."

"Don't talk nonsense," she said. "You'll get another job. We can borrow a little from my parents. Or maybe yours. Everybody goes through this once in a while."

Someone tapped on his door. He swiveled around to look. Tim Penn stuck his head in. "They're starting to pass out assignments," he said. "Are we go?"

"Yes," Danny said. "If they ask, tell them you're with me today." He turned back to the phone. "That was Tim Penn. On the train today—say, could you call Amoco and get my belts replaced?"

"I already did," Rita said. "They'll be out later."

"Will that dry up our savings?"

"Just about."

"Can we afford candy tonight?"

"Just barely," she said. "And you better get home early, too. I don't want to see you busting your ass for those people if they're going to leave you up in the air."

"Yes, dear." He loved her spine, her bravado in the engineering of his affairs and emotions. "On the train this morning I was riding along and I saw a kid get hit by a car."

"Oh, Lord," she whispered.

"At least, I *think* I did. He was dressed as a ghost," Danny said. "I saw him the instant he was hit—and then my vision was blocked. I think the car kept going."

"Did you try and stop the train?" Rita asked.

"Are you kidding? A commuter express?"

"Did you call the police?"

"I'm not sure of the location."

"You should do *something,*" she said.

"I'm sending Tim Penn out."

"Think of that kid's parents," Rita said.

"We have," Danny said. "We've thought of every possible angle. We want this story so we can beat up on TV. If TV gets this, they'll murder us with footage."

"What a horrible way to go," she murmured, and he made the mistake of laughing, thinking she was making a joke. "You're a heartless prick, Fain."

"I've gotta run, Reet."

"Talk to someone about severance," she said. "Talk to someone for your family's sake."

"Will you stay with me now that I'm a failure?"

She gave him a scolding laugh. "Don't talk nonsense. Of course I won't." And she hung up.

He waved for Tim Penn, who entered and dropped to the couch. "Madness, Fain," he said. "Madness and panic and fear. You can smell it. Nobody's listening to anyone else. Nobody's working. Everyone's looking for someplace to jump to."

"I can't blame them," Danny said.

"Derringer's getting bought out. Three years' salary. Muff is getting two years' pay," Tim Penn reported. "How about you?"

"They haven't talked to me."

Tim Penn recounted authoritatively, "Reporters are supposed to get a week's pay, plus pay for any accrued vacation. Rumors, though. Strictly rumors."

Danny Fain shook his head to clear his mind of its dispiriting calculations. "Let me tell you about this wild goose chase I'm sending you on," he said. "Coming in to work today on the train, I saw a car hit a kid dressed like a ghost. I don't think the car stopped. I can give you only very rough coordinates—nothing very specific."

"And you want me to find this kid on the side of the road?"

"Find *him,* then find out who he is, talk to his parents. His neighbors," Danny said. "Look for witnesses. Solve the case."

"It has potential," Tim Penn said.

"Page One potential," Danny Fain said.

"We can put borders with little kids around it."

Dan smiled bitterly. "Yeah, something like that," he said.

"By the time I get it together," Tim Penn said, "the paper will have folded."

"We need this *tonight,* Tim. We need to splash with this before TV gets hold of it. Once they hook into the story, we're in the dust," Danny said. "So don't talk to anyone about this. No midday assignations. Okay?"

"I'll make some calls," Tim Penn said.

"No calls, Tim. This one is done on foot."

"But what if the kid has already been found?" Tim Penn asked. "I could shoot the day looking for a story that's already been bagged."

"I made some calls this morning before the meeting. I called Jefferson Park and Lutheran General," Danny said. "They didn't have anything even remotely resembling a kid hit by a car."

"Then the driver must not have stopped."

"That was my thinking," Dan said. "The kid's still out there."

"Who did you talk to at Jeff Park?" Tim Penn said.

"I didn't get a name."

"I know a million cops," Tim Penn said. "Some of them will even talk to me like I'm a normal human being."

Dan leaned forward, raised a finger. "I don't want this spilled."

Tim Penn grinned. "Me, spill a story? Hey, I know Satchelson who works the day desk at Jefferson Park. I've gone drinking with him. He's not ambitious enough or curious enough to check anything out that isn't placed directly in his path."

"Okay," Danny Fain said. "Then I want you on the street."

"So give me some bearings, chief."

Dan raked his hands through his hair. "I wish I could give you an address, but it happened so fast. I saw what I saw, then this freight going the other way cut off the picture. I spent about a half minute trying to verify what I'd seen with other passengers. By then, of course, we were way down the line."

"Good reporting skills, Fain."

Danny removed a map of Chicago and its suburbs from his desk and spread it open. He ran his finger southeast along the route of the train. He recalled, "It's before the tracks meet up with the Kennedy. That I know. It's northwest of Norwood Park. *And* it could be north of Devon. But I'm not sure. I just remember this kid flying, me looking around for someone else to back me up, and then we're meeting up with the Kennedy."

"Avondale?" Tim Penn asked.

"I would start on Avondale, yes."

"North of Devon is close to Park Ridge," Tim Penn said. "If it's a Park Ridge kid the *Quill* and TV will be very keen for this story."

"I'm pretty sure we were beyond Park Ridge," Dan said.

"Maybe it was an ambitious Park Ridge kid," Tim Penn rhapsodized. "An *adventurous* Park Ridge kid. Scion of a wealthy executive."

Danny kept his finger on the map until Tim Penn finished. "Give me that story" Dan said, "and I'll support you for a day after we fold."

"What side of the train were you on?"

"Right hand side, facing inbound. So you only have the south side of the tracks to worry about," Danny said.

"What about the car that hit him?"

"Nothing. A color. Maybe red. Maybe American."

"No wonder you didn't go to the police," Tim Penn said. "They'd laugh in your face."

"Go make your *one* call. Report to me before you leave." He followed Tim out into the newsroom.

A woman greeted Tim, the hitch in her progress indicating a willingness to be engaged in conversation. Tim Penn, out of habit, obliged. He put on a sympathetic grimace, the woman's concerns the only thing on his mind. Her name was Debra Foster, Abe Skinback's new assistant, a tall girl of twenty-two, exemplary legs, professionally tended nails, honey-blond hair kept short and upswept. Skinback had worked his first assistant, the legendary Marjorie, to death over the course of twenty-seven years. She passed away taking corrections from Abe over the telephone. She was in her office typing in his column changes, people saw her working, phone to her ear, left profile to the door. Then ten minutes later Skinback called the city desk to complain Marjorie was refusing to read back his changes and he wanted her fired. Abe's voice was affronted, irate, phlegmy. The phone had fallen into Marjorie's lap. Her hands in death remained on the keyboard, her head gracefully bowed forward in a final thought. The last word she had typed was *Sardine.* They informed Abe Skinback, who was peeved he had dictated his final four changes to a corpse, and now would have to repeat them.

Marjorie was replaced by a succession of pretty, energetic young women who stayed on the job as briefly as three hours and none longer than eight weeks. The ordeal of being dictated to and criticized by a man they never saw, a cuss of a man who was nothing more than a pissed-off mosquito voice in their ear each day, always proved to be too much to put up with. Tim Penn touched Debra Foster's arm. A slim arm, a gold watch, a small opal ring.

"How's Abe treating you?" Tim Penn asked.

"He's a turd. I almost quit yesterday."

"You wouldn't be the first."

"He called me on my lunch hour and gave me a spelling test!

Twenty-five words," she said. "I knew most of them. The others, I stalled until I could look them up."

"Very clever, Deb."

Danny Fain circled around this conversation until he caught Tim Penn's eye and pointed to the clock.

"Let me walk you back to your office," Tim Penn said. He guided her like an usher, even putting a hand in the small of her back. Tim Penn succeeded with women because he had the nerve to do what they didn't expect: the quick, private touch in public, the brush of the cheek, the glance at the breast at the perfect moment. Tim had an instinct for these things.

A white-lit uproar came down the hallway leading to the newsroom. A tumult like a train approaching. Scurrying ahead of the fierce illumination and the noise were reporters and other *Bugle* staffers, then a red-headed girl in Scottish drag accurate down to the bagpipes that squeaked and honked as she ran. People caught in the light covered their eyes. Danny Fain stepped behind a partition just as a Channel Eight camera with an unfiltered Frezzi light burning swung into the newsroom, sound man in tow, followed by a petite fellow in a robin's-egg blazer and magnesium hair, holding his microphone like an erection. The black camera eye swept the room in search of tears, heartache, fisticuffs, the rumored fire, the alleged staffer on the window ledge. The lens locked on a woman on the phone. It zoomed close to catch her wet eyes and running makeup, but she was laughing. The sound man's mike registered clearly her command to the other party: "Take off your pants." The camera swooped elsewhere.

Danny backed around the partition, trying to stay out of sight. "Someone should point them to Derringer's office," he said. "Let him put the company spin on this." But he understood that Channel Eight would not be interested in a guy who was being set softly free with plenty of money. They wanted to talk to the people dumped on, wallets empty of everything except baby pictures; people facing imminent devastation; people full of anger, confusion, and hate. *Photogenic* people.

People like Goop Traky, a general assignment reporter whose infant daughter had been born three weeks ago with spina bifida. Goop was sitting at the assignment desk, tie askew, pencil in mouth in lieu of a smoke, his look desperate and infuriated. He was a week short of thirty, presented with a malformed child by a wife he no longer loved. His actual name was Robert, but he had been called Goop all his life in honor of a talent for making a mess of things. For his first week at the *Bugle* he had been Robert Traky and he had done a solid job, writing tight and on time. His stories didn't come back to haunt him or the paper. One evening he brought in his sister to tour the paper. She innocently referred to him as Goop. Someone heard the name and laughed. An explanation was requested and Goop's sister readily complied. He was Goop forever then, and soon after he began to misquote people, leave out salient facts, miss deadlines. He was entrusted only with the no-brainers: parades, fireworks, name-the-oryx contests at Brookfield Zoo. By and by he forgot why he had married his wife. She became pregnant, another Goop-up, and the baby emerged with her backbone exposed, a necklace of tiny vertebrae floating in a leaking sac of spinal fluid: *meningomyelocele,* the very worst. He was given the bum's rush out of the delivery room, but not granted further permission to depart the marriage.

A hot light was beating on his back. He bit off pieces of eraser and spat them absently into the dusty space behind the tube's keyboard. The camera ground away at his back. He was not writing, merely typing. He typed and spat eraser and nodded over his notes. He kept hearing that word. Not *closed.* Not *folded.* Not *unemployed.* But rather, like a chanted curse, *meningomyelocele.*

The TV reporter's microphone entered like a slow bullet into Goop Traky's consciousness as it floated across his right shoulder. He yelped and pulled away. He had eraser in his teeth. The TV light washed out the green letters on his screen. Goop squinted, shaded his eyes. He was asked his reaction to the imminent demise of the *Bugle.*

"I think it's great," Goop said. "Great for me and great for the city in general. The *Bugle* hasn't provided any substantive journalism for several years and now the facade can be torn down and the truth revealed. All the people in this room are only in journalism because they can't support themselves doing what they really love—or because they don't have the courage to try. This will be a perfect opportunity for them to try to be the screenwriters, poets, novelists, filmmakers, biographers, ballerinas, and pro football players that they really think they deserve to be."

The TV reporter was uncertain whether he should pull the mike away. No question, they were burning tape with this guy. None of this would get on the air. But Goop Traky's crazy eyes and lucid speech were made for TV. For the first time in his life, he was electrifying.

He continued, "They won't have to come down to this dusty old office every day and pretend to be interested in what they're doing. The public won't have to pretend to be interested in their brand of news anymore. The editors and owners won't have to pretend to be interested in the *Bugle* staff or the citizens of Chicago. The *Bugle*'s closing will be the death of pretense. Me, I'm going to pursue my dream of being a colonic irrigator."

Someone laughed off-camera. *Colonic irrigator* struck the reporter like the trip words planted by a hypnotist to free him from a trance. The microphone drooped. The light went out. The reporter was informed that Derringer would consent to be interviewed. A clerk shouted that another camera crew was on its way up. The Channel eight crew ran for Derringer's office. Now there was competition. Now they had someone and something to fight over.

Fred Tobin rolled his chair up alongside Goop Traky, who had returned to his story, his head buzzing with the echoes of his little speech. He was thrilled with the sound of it, and how the words had come together in his mind, then moved smoothly onto the public record. Fred Tobin's lenses were a muddy rose color. He could no longer clearly see the screen or keyboard; this was his secret. It was all touch now with Fred. He set his hands in place on the keyboard and proceeded to stab from memory. On bad days he put his hands in the wrong position at the start and was always one or two keys to the left or right and his stories came into the city desk like coded messages and someone, usually Danny Fain, would decipher them. Dan had become proficient at this breaking of the messages. He scanned the gibberish, and if it was heavy on r's then Fred had lined up one character too far to the right. All the r's were supposed to be e's. So s's were a's, l's were k's, commas were m's, and so on. He would dial Fred's extension and tell him without a word of identification that he was lined up one key too far to the right. Fred thanked him and hung up. His wife got him to the building's front door in the morning and then he found his way to his desk himself. He didn't leave the building until it was time to go home. He worked the phones like a terrier, calling home for his wife, Bernadette, to read the number that he needed from the Rolodex he kept there. As he conducted a phone interview, he memorized at the moment of their utterance the quotes and facts he knew he would use in his stories. He had a red upholstered chair on black casters (labeled FRED'S CHAIR on the back, though he never knew; if Fred was not sitting in the chair it was not to be moved from its place at Fred's desk) and he moved around the office in the chair like an ex-president in a golf cart.

He rolled up to Goop Traky's side and put a hand on his arm. Fred said, "*This* is all I ever wanted to do, Robert. I'm happiest when I'm in this room. Just because you're unhappy here, it's unfair to include the rest of us in your unhappiness. This is the end of my life as I know it. And you made a joke out of that."

Goop blinked into Fred's red glasses. He said hotly, "If you feel that way, then *you* talk to them, Tobin. They're interested in the thoughts of people like you: the crushed."

The Four-Square News camera crew entered the newsroom. Lights out, mike off, camera at rest, the reporter saw the power glow coming from Derringer's office and raised his arm like a field commander. The Four-Square News light blazed on. The sound man punched a button and brought the mike to life. The camera came up. They hustled in a pack, linked by cables for Derringer's office.

Fred Tobin rolled back to his desk. He hadn't called his wife to tell her, but she would not hear about it on TV. She was so loyal to him that she refused to get her news from anywhere but the *Bugle.* She would remain ignorant of their circumstances until Fred told her. But he phoned her anyway and asked her for a couple of numbers he didn't need, because it was still a work day, after all, and she would be waiting by the phone to help him.

"Diana called," she said.

Fred Tobin closed his eyes.

"She had a radio on."

"Did she hear a song she wanted to share with you?" Fred asked.

"She heard the *Bugle* is ceasing publication."

"That is the rumor."

"Fred! Weren't you going to tell me?"

"Of course. But I thought: What's the hurry? If you found out this morning or tonight, what's the difference?" Fred said.

"I could start worrying sooner," Bernadette said. "I would have an extra eight hours for planning."

"So now you know," Fred Tobin said. "Our modern-age daughter foiled my plans to tell you myself."

"Oh, yes. The radio. Diana and her high-tech devices." His wife laughed. "You're fifty-six years old, Fred. We could swing a retirement package for you. We have savings."

"I have work to do, sweetie," Fred said. "I didn't tell you, I now realize, to avoid just that sort of crepe-hanging talk. We'll talk tonight. Feel free to make plans in my absence."

"I'll pick you up early."

"No. The regular time."

"All right."

"I feel better having you on the case," he told her.

Danny Fain dialed a number from memory, again with his back to the newsroom, his office door closed. She usually answered after no more than two rings. A stranger answered; a man, bland of voice, with no hint of ever having hurried after anything. Danny asked to speak to Dana Viola and was put on hold without another word. After a minute on hold the connection was broken. He called back. The same man answered and Dan explained what had happened. Back on hold. No apology. No warm promise to try harder. He timed the hold with his watch. He swung around in the chair so he faced his window onto the newsroom. People walked past and glanced casually in. Danny always felt comfortable on hold. The phone to his ear gave him some time to himself. He was *busy.* People could see that. A reporter named Becky Fudge went by crying. She was barely twenty-four years old, at the *Bugle* less than a year. She would be out of there unencumbered and young, with some experience at a major metro and no ties to the ground she occupied. In two years she would have forgotten all about the place. The last days at the old *Bugle* would be a battle star she could wear at parties, a war story.

He leaned into the phone, listening into the void of the hold. Lucy Spriggs appeared at his door. Her hair was a mess, a pencil lost in there; she looked excited, as if she had just broken off a kiss.

Dan raised a finger: *Wait. I'm busy.* He was not in the mood to hear her plans to have the employees buy the paper. He did not want to hear the notions Lawrence K. Mock had inserted in her brain.

"Viola," she said.

He whirled away from the door, afraid Lucy would see the blush that sprouted at the deadpan thrill of her voice. "This is Danny," he said. "Can you talk a minute?"

He kept expecting her to ask, "Danny *Who*?" It was always six months between calls. Their last kiss had been cheek to cheek, and that more than eight years ago. "Wait," she said. He went back on hold. She might be giving instructions to have the call transferred to her office. He had never seen it, but reliable reports placed it high above the city, shaped from glass and full of plants and a trio of ceiling-mounted Sony monitors, with a desk as large as a queen-sized bed, three phones, a coffee maker, an exercise bicycle she rode hard for fifteen minutes in the dark at midnight after everyone had gone home.

Dana Viola had been in Chicago while her husband, a pretty boy with anchor possibilities, worked at a station in Miami. They saw each other for thirty-eight hours every three weeks, sometimes in New Orleans, sometimes Nashville, someplace roughly equidistant between their two careers. Then he was fired for lacking Hispanic features and he came north for sixteen weeks before landing a job in San Francisco. Dan was in love with Dana by then.

They had met on a story, a winter fire that turned three babies into cinder dolls. She was doing sound, her headphones clamped on under a big woolly cap, wearing a fur-collared leather jacket, jeans, knee-high leather boots, and rainbow legwarmers. She gave him a handkerchief, saying she hated the sight of male snot untended. For a long time he didn't know she was married. Then her husband lost his job and she told Dan he couldn't drop in at all hours and "force your attention on me." Nor was he allowed to call. She slipped him her card: her work number. Very secretive. She showed up at his apartment in the darkness after the broadcast, her breath raw and white, her skin frozen. She was like a pillar of ice getting into bed with him. Talking all the while about the idiots she worked for, her plans for advancement, the warm feel of his skin, how she couldn't go home just yet, how she loved when he pushed against her right *there.* She moved off sound onto the assignment desk. She spent a year there, then another in editing, then returned to the assignment desk as its chief. She got to work at 10 A.M. and stayed until almost midnight. Her husband was in San Francisco by then, a full-bore anchorman with a national look, and Dana saw him one weekend a month, usually in a motel near the Kansas City or Denver airport. She fell into bed with Danny Fain three or four nights a week on her way home from work. They occasionally made love. More often, she just fell asleep in his arms. He disliked kissing her much because she tasted of cigarettes. One day when she was out of sight (though he still loved her, he was no longer desperate to be in her presence) he met Rita. The first time she spent the night with him he awakened in a panic at ten minutes to midnight and stumbled in the dark for the phone. He had to reach Dana before she left, arrived, opened his door with the key he had made for her, and surprised him with this sleeping woman who was not quite as beautiful as Dana but who had in his three days of knowing her set something in motion in his heart. He caught Dana as she was leaving. She sounded pumped up. No, she hadn't been planning to stop over. She was going out for drinks with friends from work to celebrate that she had been promoted that day.

She asked if anything was wrong. He said no. He asked if she could call next time before she stopped over. She said she certainly could. Dana never visited again. Within two months Rita had moved them from his ratty studio into a two-bedroom within walking distance of the lake. He went weeks without thinking about Dana Viola. He heard she got a divorce. He heard rumors about her salary after she became executive producer for the Channel Eight news. Abe Skinback liked to use her picture in his column as a "go-get-'em gal who is a credit to her sex."

"Hello, Danny Fain."

"Do you have your feet on your desk and your shoes off?" he asked.

"No, I'm management."

"That's not a managerial thing to do—show underlings your toes?"

"Did you just call to flirt?" Dana asked. "We heard you're folding."

"Unfortunately, that is the case."

"Has the mourning begun?"

"Oh, yes," Danny Fain said. "You should be proud. Your boys were the first ones here. They got the genuine tears. Everything since is third and fourth takes."

"Are you calling to ask me for a job?"

Dan paused. The thought had not occurred to him: a life in TV news. "Do you see me as anchor material?" he asked.

"No." Dana laughed. "You're not quite handsome enough, hon. Definitely back-camera. Unfortunately, we are cutting good people loose left and right. Family men. People with bills to pay. *Poof!* It would look unseemly, me hiring an ex-something or other of mine."

"I can't run any of those machines you use," Danny said.

"Oh, we can teach you that. Some people have been here ten years and don't know how anything works," she said. "People annually lauded for their professionalism." She let a pause run on. "So, why *did* you call?"

He heard something new in her voice, a deepening in her throat. An anticipation of his getting personal? He remembered warming her icy body in his arms. The way she wanted to rush through everything until he talked her down like a jumper on a ledge. The distant, pained anecdotes she shared with him about her husband, and the sad little stories of reunion after each weekend in a layover motel. He liked to watch her on-camera. For two years she wrote and broadcast editorials to close the 5 P.M. news hour and he made a point of taping them, or having Rita tape them; getting the entire newscast ostensibly to keep an eye on the competition but paying attention only to the ninety seconds she was on the air. She won some big award and then quit, bored, he supposed, as always, with anything that became too easy to do.

"I'm calling, actually, to share a tip with you," Danny Fain said.

Dana Viola scoffed. "My ass! Why are you calling, Dan? I've got work to do." She was the news bitch again, all brass and deadline. That personal softness in her voice was gone at the first mention of a tip, at the first hint he was not calling with an express interest in her. "Since when does the *Bugle* share a tip with TV?" she demanded.

"You're right. I was laying smoke. I was calling to see what you had on a certain story," Dan said. "And now I realize if you didn't have it I would be alerting you to it."

"You've got a story?" Dana said.

"We *always* have stories."

But if you *really* had it—had it bundled and wrapped—you wouldn't be calling me to see what I know."

"Very true, Dana. It's developing."

"You've got an ongoing. Tell me. We'll share."

"You'd kill us on this," Danny said. "It's a made-for-TV story."

"It couldn't be a murder," Dana mused. "The police would have told us. It isn't a fire."

"And no sex involved," Dan said.

"There's *always* sex involved, Danny."

"I've gotta run. I've given myself away, haven't I?"

"*You* called *me.*"

A jolting light poured into his office. Beyond the glass a camera worked, aimed at him. "Hey," Danny said, "I'm on TV. It's your crack crew."

"Give them the finger. They can't use it then."

He followed her instructions. The cameraman returned the gesture, but pulled the camera away.

"It worked. They're gone. We're alone again."

"Tell me about your story." Her voice was seductive, conniving. Dan laughed and Dana laughed along with him. "Give me a direction," she said. "North side? Is it north? If it's south or west I can live without it. But north side? *Please?*"

"Gotta run," Danny Fain said.

"It *is* north, isn't it? Have you called the *Quill?* You won't risk tipping them to see what they know," she said.

"This is a TV story, Dana. The *Quill* couldn't do anything more with it than we could."

"Those crews over there?" she said. "Be careful. They're

trained to tape everything. We don't just listen to the schmucks we're interviewing. They're usually saying the *least* interesting things."

"We'll be careful," Dan said.

"Did I tell you about the time we picked up two men discussing a murder when we went to film a car wreck?" she asked. "That tape is like an heirloom around here. Everyone wants to hear it, it is *so* chilling. Unfortunately, our camera didn't get any pictures of the guys."

"That's too bad. Gotta run."

"It's north side. It's *big.*"

"Did I say big? Does everything on TV have to be big?"

"Okay, small. But small in a way that is perfect for TV. *Kidnapping!*"

"Gotta run, Dana." He winced, rubbed his eyes, felt himself begin to sweat. But he admired Dana. He didn't fall in love with brainless women. If he stayed on the phone much longer she would guess everything. She was already pointed in the right direction. He had been happy to learn that she didn't have anyone on the story and now she was a small deductive leap away from figuring out everything he had.

She asked, "You got a hysterical mother over there? Is there a ransom note? Have they told her not to contact the authorities?"

"Gotta go, Dana. News to schmooze." He hung up the phone. Let her believe it was a kidnapping. She would be diverted long enough to let Tim Penn find the ghost. She would be on the phone at that moment calling around to the cop shops. She knew people in every station, people who liked to see themselves on TV, liked the idea of being needed by someone in TV. She would ask about hints of a kidnapping. Eventually she might stumble on Tim Penn's source at the Jefferson Park District and he would say, "That's funny, I just got a call from a pal of mine at the *Bugle* [though print lacked the panache of TV, they were also proud of being tight with newspaper people, because there was a greater chance of seeing their name in the paper than their face on TV] and he was fishing around about a possible hit-and-run. We've got nothing, but with you calling, maybe there's something to it." So then they would be bucking Channel Eight *and* the police, and in that race the *Bugle* was going to finish third. And if the police were in on it, the *Quill* would be, too, soon enough. From there, the other TV stations would feel the warmth and it would be all over. The hunt would have begun in earnest, the *Bugle* outgunned.

Danny Fain jumped up from his desk. Lucy Spriggs was sitting outside his office. He asked her to wait. Tim Penn, across the office, was on the phone.

"Tim!" Dan danced sideways between the rows of desks. He saw burn rings where fires had been attempted, sputtered, and refused to catch. He witnessed Dirk Flester, legal reporter, taking an X-acto to *Sullivan's Law Directory,* slicing each page off clean at the binding, then slashing the freed page once diagonally and letting the two rough triangles fall to the floor. Dirk Flester had been a reporter, quit to go through law school, passed the bar, then returned to cover law for the *Bugle.* He always struck Danny Fain as a man lost and afraid to choose between two distinct worlds. "Anarchy, Dan," he said. "They won't get a paper out of us today. Who will work to the end except Tobin and Potter?"

Tim Penn was still talking. Dan hesitated over Dirk Flester's question. Who, indeed? He would work. Work until the end. Work until dismissed. It was his nature. He would want his children to do the same when they were confronted with the death of their livelihood.

He raised a finger to Tim Penn, who covered the phone. "No calls, Tim," Danny said. "Even one call to the police might tip somebody."

"I already called."

Dirk Flester leaned close, knife poised. "Something clandestine brewing?" he inquired. "Need a lawyer?"

"No, Dirk. Go back to your vandalism."

"This is company property," he said haughtily. "It's my *duty* to destroy it. This is one thing they won't be able to profit from by auctioning it off."

"Who's that on the phone, Tim?" Danny Fain asked.

"It's personal, Dan. I made my call and fished around. My boy knows nothing. It's our story."

"Then get going!" Dan said. "I want to be able to sell this as something real at the four o'clock meeting."

"Okay. *Okay.*" He returned to the phone, said he would call back, then hung up.

"This is a work day, Tim. I'm being an asshole because this is important to me. So no little side fucks, understand? I want you looking until you find the ghost or I call you in, understand? No hour off in some woman's hammock."

Tim Penn gave Dan a small, proud *who-me?* grin. He loved his reputation. Men were not comfortable in his presence because of it, and women were wary, curious, orbiting the flame. He swept a hand through his hair, gave Danny the blue-eyed gleamer. "I am on the case," he said. He stopped at his locker for his jacket and then he was out the door. Danny Fain followed. He guided Tim Penn by the arm down the hall.

Dan said, "Call. Frequently." He pushed a scrap of paper into Tim Penn's pocket. "My office number. Don't go through the city desk. Spies are everywhere."

As evidence, the Channel Eight camera crew exited the men's room. They made a production of checking zippers, adjusting belts, tucking in shirts, but Dan saw the volume-level needle jumping on the sound man's box and he swept Tim Penn past. He pushed him into the elevator when it opened. "Call," Danny ordered, waiting to make certain the doors closed.

Two people were in the men's room, occupying adjoining stalls. By their voices, Danny tagged them as Tom Woods and Les Burkin, reporters exchanging cynical, nihilistic observations on their respective futures. When he returned to the newsroom, the Channel Eight crew was filming in his office, the cameraman blocking the door, panning across the contents of his desk.

Dan came up behind them. "Get a call from Dana?" he asked. "Tell her nice try."

The cameraman swung the lens up in his face. The light made Danny draw back. "ID yourself, please. Spell first and last name, and state job title."

Dan gave them the finger again. "For you, too, Dana. She taught me everything I know about TV news."

They taped him going to his desk. He didn't touch anything. Were clues to the story present? Something telltale for Dana to uncover in her examination of the footage? No notes. He had written nothing down. Nothing *existed* to write down. The day's paper. A can painted with glitter by the Pretty One to hold his pens and pencils. A memo about rental cars. A computer printout about the day's story prospects, dropped on his desk by a clerk in the time he had been escorting Tim Penn to the elevator. Reading upside down, he saw little of interest. Also, the printer needed a new ribbon, and Danny doubted the print would be visible to Dana Viola. But she was very clever. She understood the technology, and no doubt had ordered the cameraman to shoot a tight focus so that she could enlarge the images enough to make out the stray phone number or name written on a memo pad. He took his seat.

"I've got work to do, guys. Please?" Danny Fain said.

"Just a comment on the demise of your paper?" Yet the camera wasn't even trained on him. He picked up the phone and punched Dana's number. The station answered. While he was on hold he glanced down the story list. His story was not listed. The others, however, were a reminder that he still had a job to do.

"Dana Viola."

"Your crew is here bothering me, Dana. They're standing in my office door refusing to leave."

"Give them the finger."

"I did. It didn't work." Dana laughed. "And there's nothing

on my desk that will be of any use to you," he continued. "In fact, I'll sell the contents of my desk to you for one thousand dollars. Then you won't have to look at their tape."

"Do you think I sent them to spy on you?"

"I'm sure of it. They recorded two guys talking to each other from one stall to another in the john."

"They *didn't*!" Dana said happily.

"They did. This is journalism at its finest. You should be proud."

"You called me, Danny. None of this would have happened without you alerting me to it," she charged.

"Can I tell them you ordered them back to the office?"

"Have they spoken to Derringer?"

"I think so," Dan said.

"If they have Derringer, they can come home. Unless you want to make a statement."

He saw the map of the city then, pushed toward the back edge of his desk, closer to the camera. The map was folded open to the area of the city where he thought he had seen the ghost. A large area, granted, but he had helpfully drawn a black, pencil oval around the triangle formed by the Kennedy, Avondale, and Canfield.

"I'm waving good-bye to you, now," Danny said. The camera whirred on. He didn't move the map or cover it. They already had a mile of tape with the map out there for examination. Dana would see immediately there was nothing to be learned from anything else on his desk. She would be left with only the map to peruse and the map would reward her efforts with a more specific part of the city to focus her hunt.

"Good-bye." He hung up. "She says to get Derringer, then she has a refinery fire in Whiting. She said the smoke will be visible for miles."

The sound man winked, unfooled. The cameraman killed his light and backed off.

"Thanks, boys," Danny said. "We'll cover your funeral, too."

The sound man held a walkie-talkie. "No, you won't. You won't have a job."

"I'll get a new one just for that moment," Danny Fain said.

"You paper people are all alike. So fucking self-righteous. So fucking smug," the sound man said. "If you had paid attention in school maybe you wouldn't be in a dying field now."

"Are you taping this?" Dan asked.

"No. Say whatever you want."

" 'Bye. Good-bye. Thanks for coming."

His phone rang. It was Tim Penn. The sound man stayed at the door, as though waiting to resume their discussion. His microphone was tucked under his armpit, head pointed at Danny.

"Where are you?"

"I've made it to my car. I'm reporting in."

"*You* have a car phone?"

"Sure. They're like radios."

"Give me the number," Dan said. "Wait a sec." He put the phone down. He said to the sound man, "I've got work to do." He shut the door on him, but the sound man remained standing just outside. In this day and age, what impediment would a door be to the proper technology? Another notch up on the dial and whispers might flow through the door as clear as a song in a shower. The secret was to talk about nothing of interest to anyone else. Invisibility through boredom. He told Tim Penn to wait to give his number. "Call me in a half hour," Danny said. "If I'm in a meeting, call back. No messages. Talk only to me."

"Why the cloak and dagger?"

"This is a hot story," Danny said. "We are still competing, pointless as it may seem to do so. We don't want anything overheard that might cause us to fall off this story."

"Right, chief."

Danny Fain put the phone back. He gave the finger one more time to the sound man, who shrugged and walked away. Dan folded up the map. He glanced down at the A.M. story list.

VOTE. POLL. SCAR. DEV. DANC. LEFT. DEAD. MAC. STING. CTA. VEGAS. XOBE. Little he would read if he wasn't paid to read it. The same slugs repeated, only the number changed to reflect the next day's date, but the number was the only thing to separate the story from others that preceded it. The writing had lost its snap. The paper's best writers were about all gone, their talent allowing them to launch free of the *Bugle*'s tenacious suck of ennui and acquiescence: Julia Marx. Todd Kraft. Virginia Allen. Art Haig. Rick Blasingame. Anita Watts, Doug's wife. Anita put up with Doug's low opinion of himself throughout a long engagement, married him, then left him after a year to go to the *L.A. Times.* Divorce was an option, but the issue did not seem to trouble them unduly. Married or divorced, Doug Watts was never going to be a hard worker, or of much interest to other women. Anita Watts had no time even to give thought to her situation. In busyness, in crammed days, in unstinting work, she found her peace. The *Bugle* had some good writers remaining, but they were husks, dinosaurs of special projects who stood in the halls or slouched in the smoker all day or doodled at the keyboard for an hour now and then to produce every month or so one medium-length jewel on something assigned to them that never quite grabbed their attention. They had become soldiers of the word. Obeying orders. Enormous Bubb Cook, fingers fat and delicate, his shirt pocket full of fallen cigarette ash, was almost sixty years old, his teeth shot, his breath murderous, but he could perch on the tube in the chamber with a fire going in his mouth and in ten minutes tap out something beautiful from the thin bird-bones of a half page of some kid's notes. He farted while he wrote. He screamed into the phone, charring some reporter's ear for the sin of the wrong question asked. Where would Bubb Cook go? Where would that talent be welcome? Maybe at the *Quill,* if he could swing entry through the auspices of someone with some time in the business and an appreciation for the newspaperman Bubb Cook represented. If he tried to get hired by one of the corporate hounds rumored in ascendancy over there, a three-piece guy in sparkly shoes with a degree in newspaper economics, then Bubb Cook had no chance.

And what would become of Nat, short for Natalie, LaRue, a woman so pushy and full of ideas she had alienated just about everyone who came into contact with her? She had a desk in Siberia, a nook distant and hidden, so far away from the city desk that she could sit and polish her résumé all day without anyone knowing she was back there. Her aggressiveness and energy made people feel sluggish. In her presence, people felt bad about themselves. But rather than being inspired to work to her pace, her editors tried to pull her down to theirs with groaning, dead story assignments and grim night shifts where she would be bogged down and out of their consciences. Nat LaRue's problem was she couldn't write; her fatal flaw was that she thought she could. This discrepancy in vision, combined with her drive and her provocative personality, touched off fights and tantrums and screaming fits behind office doors that set the newsroom to humming like a hive under attack. She was a sucker for one too many adjectives, for transforming nouns into verbs, for the phrase turned hopelessly colorful. She reported so hard on stories, talked to so many more people than necessary, accumulated such bargeloads of material, that she felt compelled to use it all. Her sentences became leaden with their responsibility to carry more information than was helpful to the reader. Dan had once gone around with her for an hour over the lede: *The green-shuttered house on the softly rising hill at 439 W. Oakmont has weathered and witnessed the sun and rain and snow and memories of a dozen inhabiting families—the Crowns, the Zumbachs, the Townings, the Brachens, and all the rest—families that must now in this hour late in the century be crying at the knowledge that their former home constructed of red brick and bounteous love now faces its mortality because it squats unwanted in the path of a sinuous ribbon of freeway that even the public isn't convinced overwhelmingly must be built at a cost of $310 million and one dear old house.*

Dan actually kind of liked the sentence. He told Nat so. It had a rhythm, an eccentricity. But the sentence called attention to itself by its very weight and flow, and that was why Dan had a problem with it. He believed it was likely to stop readers cold, either in admiration or disbelief that such a sentence had found its way into the *Bugle.* And if the sentence stopped the reader's entry into the story, then the sentence was a failure. Nat LaRue, sitting in Dan's office holding a printout of her story, argued that the lede imparted a sense of the history of the old house as well as the callous abruptness with which it would be destroyed by the builders of the freeway. The sentence, she said, contained facts and feelings, in her opinion the ultimate components of the perfect sentence. She snapped the printout angrily between her hands, as if in freeing the paper of wrinkles she would remove what others found problematic in her work. Dan made some marks with a pen on his copy of the printout. Nat LaRue leaned forward to see what he was doing. She had enormous black eyes plunged deep into a face of classic triangularity, high cheekbones, pointed chin. Bad skin kept her from being a beauty, but her energy and fierce burn kept her body taut, her weight down, her eyes lively and demanding. The idle, joking sexual speculation about her imagined a woman driving her lover, goading him to fuck her, to come again and again, to keep up with *her.*

Sarcastically, she said, "Let me guess: 'A house occupied by many families in the past faces an uncertain future because it is in the path of a projected freeway.' "

"A projected *$310 million* freeway," Dan said, smiling at her. Her eyes blazed, her mouth was squeezed down to a button of disgust and loathing for his judgment. Dan continued, "Say that is the sentence. Why do you object to it?"

"It's *boring.* It's like every other sentence ever written in this paper."

"That sentence states the case," Danny said.

"Mine, too. And with a little style. Does everything have to be point A to point B to point C?"

"You can write with style and not put everything in the first sentence," Dan said. "People will be tired by the time they get to the end of this sentence, *if* they get to it. Give them a taste of the story, then put in what you know as you go along."

Nat LaRue remarked derisively, " 'House periled by freeway.' That'll be the headline."

"I don't write the heads, Nat."

"Well, the lede shouldn't be more boring than the head."

"This sentence has merits," Dan agreed. "I even kind of like it. But if we don't come up with something to satisfy both of us here, it will get chopped into something neither of us recognize further down the line."

"Run it as is," Nat LaRue said defiantly.

Danny Fain sighed. "How do all these families know the house is going to be razed? Telepathy? What? If we removed that section and a few of the adjectives, you'd have the start of a nice opening sentence. Drop 'softly rising hill' and the weather references and the family names and 'sinuous ribbon of' and we can send the rest along with our blessings. It sure ain't going to run as is."

Nat LaRue thrust her lower lip above her upper and exhaled. Her eyes were smoking. "Run it as is, or spike it," she declared. "And if you change one word, my name comes off. Understand?"

Dan tapped the point of his pen on the printout. He tried to read the sentence again, seeking a way to get through to her, but he kept getting lost, not in the twisting sentence but in the implacable arrogance of the untalented. "The copy desk will rip it apart," he predicted.

"My name comes off."

"Nobody's copy is untouchable."

"Nobody's copy isn't boring, either," she said.

"Are you going to pull a Bernie DeVille on me, Nat? This is his favorite stunt. Write shit, then pull his name off when someone has the temerity to improve it. Nobody respects Bernie. He's a joke. Don't pull a Bernie on me, Nat."

But changes were made and the story ran deep in the paper without art, the lede twenty-one words long, three inches trimmed for fit. Nat LaRue remained exiled at her desk, disdainful of the surroundings she saw as unworthy of her work. She did not grant Dan even the respect of openly loathing him. She would survive the paper's closing, being barely thirty-two and retaining a grasp on the coin of youth. Her next job would have to be her best shot, though, because four or five years at that job and she would be of less interest to subsequent employers as she neared forty, unable to write.

Lucy Spriggs was at his door. She rapped his window with the cap of her pen. He waved her in.

"Your story is all over the building," she announced. Lucy slammed his door.

"*My* story?"

"The hit-and-run. Promotions is working up a radio spot for tomorrow morning."

"It's not a story yet." His mistake had been opening his mouth at Derringer's meeting. If the story was all over the building it would be outside the building almost immediately after. Worse, it was a piece of information someone might use to buy a place in another organization.

Lucy Spriggs said, "Actually—can you keep a secret?—I suggested the radio spot. You'll get the story—I know you. And we need the paper to run strong while we arrange the employee buyout."

"Lucy, if we advertise this story before we get it, somebody else will beat us on it," Danny said. "TV is already sniffing around. The camera crews are all over with their tapes running, lifting conversations that they can search for clues."

Lucy gave him a worried look. "That's pretty paranoid, Danny."

"Jesus, Promotions," Dan said. "They're *paid* to disseminate secrets."

"It's only a story. It's not the Pentagon Papers."

"Stories are all we have, Lucy. *You* know that. It's like throwing money away," he said.

She picked up his phone and pressed four numbers. "This

is Lucy," she said. "Kill the radio thing I ordered. No story. . . . Yeah, a false tip." She watched Danny Fain for his reaction. "No. . . . Nothing comes to mind. When the day's budget firms up I'll call you. . . . Right. . . . I know. We'll plug something, promise. Bye." She hung up. "He's worried," she said to Dan. "We bought a quarter minute on six stations tomorrow. We've paid for the time, we should put something in it."

"What did Lawrence K. tell you?" Dan asked.

Lucy Spriggs removed a sheaf of notes from inside her jacket. "He's not confident," she said. "He says it might be done, but he questions the wisdom of doing it." She regarded Danny earnestly. "I want to ask you something. How important is this paper to you? And I don't mean just as a source of income. We all need it in that respect. But how important is it to you as a journalistic entity? As an instrument for the public good?"

Danny Fain felt cornered and unworthy. The *Bugle* had always been a job, something he enjoyed, something he was good at, a talent they paid him well to use. But he never thought of himself as a crusader for justice or the public's right to know. He was almost surprised in the morning when he saw his work on display and for sale. A front-page story that people bought and read and felt some emotion about remained in Dan's memory a series of conversations, arguments, negotiations, phone calls, word changes, fine points, nits picked. He was engaged in this work strictly for himself and for his family. "I'm in it for the money, Lucy," he said. "I'll be sorry when we close, but I expect I'll work somewhere again."

She looked away, sighed with disgust. She was missing an earring in her right lobe; he was positive something hung from her left. She was the type of woman who drove men to memorize such details. She said, "Maybe I should talk to someone else. I need someone to push this through with me."

"I'm not good at asking people for money," he said.

"You're not asking them *for* money. You're asking them to save their life as they know it."

Danny said, "Here's how I see it, Lucy. For a variety of reasons, the city of Chicago has rejected the *Bugle.* The people have voted us dead with their lack of support. Maybe it's poor management. Maybe it's lack of promotion. Maybe it's nobody reads anymore. Maybe the *Quill* is just that much better. Maybe the *Bugle* just sucks—we're a lousy paper. *Maybe.* But for whatever reason, we failed. The people who run the paper—and I assume they had an interest in succeeding and did their best—have declared us a failure. If someone now came to me sitting here at my desk scared to death because my job soon won't exist and asked me to invest what savings I had to support my family on in the near future—just to keep the paper struggling along—I would be very reluctant to hand over my savings. Say the employees do buy it. We'd have a huge debt. *And* we'd have journalists running a business. Why, I'd ask myself, do they think they could succeed where businessmen failed?"

Lucy Spriggs seemed relieved to be asked a question she was prepared to answer. "Because we could turn out a real newspaper," she said fervently. "Real news. Not contests. Not car giveaways. A real *headbutt* paper." She got to her feet, began to pace in the restrictions of his office. "It would be hard," she admitted. "We'd have to make cuts in staff and salary. But as it stands now, we've got nothing."

"If I don't invest, will you fire me?"

Dan had meant to joke, but Lucy Spriggs stared at him. "Yes," she said. "Why keep people around who didn't believe in us?"

"I don't have much money, Lucy."

Lucy Spriggs relaxed. She put the pen point to her notes. "Here's how Mock explained it," she said. "We would need to get up ten percent of the purchase. He thinks that would be at least three million. Maybe as high as five. This building is worth something. The land is worth a bundle. Then we have to borrow the rest against the paper's assets." She flipped a page in her notes. "I've called some bank friends. They're tepid. They want to talk to me about upping my Visa limit to see me through this tough time. When I ask for millions, they cool right off."

"Hey," Dan said. "We pool everyone's Visa ceilings and charge it."

Lucy Spriggs did not share the humor. "If only these assholes had come to us before they announced we were folding," she said. "We're already dead in the public eye. If we get the loan—at prime plus one—then we have to start streamlining. I've got some ideas. There's plenty of deadwood in this building. We all take a twenty-percent salary cut. We talk sense with the unions. We should also begin a fund to save for new presses. Or work a deal with the *Quill* to print over there. It would be worth the shit we'd have to take to get the product improved. After a lean year or two, we'll be in good shape."

"Have you talked to anyone in-house?" Dan asked.

"I have waffling promises of about seventeen thousand dollars," she said.

"Can we borrow the ten percent we need for the downstroke?" Danny asked.

Lucy Spriggs gave him a contemptuous smile. "No. They frown on borrowing *everything.*"

"What about Derringer? Maybe he'd invest his parachute. He must know he'll never be hired by another paper."

"Don't bet on it," Lucy Spriggs said. "Guys like Derringer have made a point of making friends in the business. They provide jobs for each other in exchange for rhinoanal massage."

Danny Fain laughed. Lucy Spriggs stretched, arms out wide, rising onto her toes, her eyes squeezed shut. Dan watched her closely. She was a spectacle he would miss. "One of your earrings is gone," he said.

She touched her empty lobe. "Shit. I've got others." She removed the one and flipped it onto Dan's desk. "A keepsake."

He picked up the small crescent of dimpled gold, the post moist and warm with the inside of Lucy Spriggs. Muff Greene appeared. "Let's meet," she said.

"I'm busy," Lucy responded caustically.

"This is still a paper," Muff said.

Lucy Spriggs turned on her. "I'm looking beyond tomorrow's tripe. I want this to be still a paper a year from now and ten years from now."

With a flatulent screed of warning, then a bovine sucking of air, bagpipe music commenced. The redheaded girl Dan had seen running from the Channel Eight crew had reappeared, recognizing her inexplicable good fortune. Rather than perform for a dying medium, for men and women bitter beneath the dust of obsolescence, she had stumbled upon TV crews whose single purpose was to obtain footage. She was a beautiful, green-eyed, freckled girl in her fillebeg and matching shoulder scarf, a shako tilted rakishly above her brow. Her face burned with the exertion of the music and the excitement of the TV lights and what they represented. The music she produced scraped and echoed around the office, putting a hammerlock on all activity and thought. Marv Urquhart, on hand for the morning news meeting, broke into a sad smile. Out of camera range he lifted his left foot in front of his right leg, crooked an arm above his head, and executed a tight spin, then another and another, until his face was scarlet and his breathing propulsive. He stopped and pressed on his chest, laughing. The girl played exuberantly. She appeared determined to play as long as the cameras were rolling. Phones rang unheard in the Highland clangor. From a sporran at her hip she drew a handful of press releases, with large, white Olde English print on tartan paper, and she dropped them on a desk as she juggled to keep her song alive. Her job done, she began to step smartly backward, pivoted, and moved, knees high, out the door. Somewhere in the hall they heard her music break off with the same belching of stray notes and shrieks that had announced its commencement.

"What was she selling?" Marv Urquhart asked.

Dan picked up a release. "A housing development," he said. "Wee Bit o' Insulation."

Urquhart laughed. "She was playing the hymn to the dead. That'll sell houses."

They took seats around the table in Muff Greene's office. She complained of a headache. Her face had the pained concentration of a hooked fish. Puncher Mudd arrived brandishing a bottle of beer, a strip of beef jerky, and a computer printout. He looked defiantly at anyone who would meet his eye. Constance Drane had arrived early. Dale Busse leafed through wire photos. She had changed blouses.

"What happened?" Danny Fain asked, touching her arm.

She plucked at the silken gray and crimson blooms above her breast. A button was missing. "We had a fight in the darkroom over the true merits of certain staff members," she said. "My other blouse took a shot of fixer in the *ba-zoom.*"

Jack Lustig, Financial Editor, arrived. He dressed like a banker, always in shades of charcoal, with pinstripes thin as a loan officer's patience, scarlet power ties, and matching suspenders. "You better not plan on living off your stock dividends," he said with cheerful pessimism. "Market's off twenty-six early." He unsnapped the gold locks on his briefcase and removed a crisp stack of printouts; listed were the stories his staff was working on that day.

"Did Mock talk to you about his meeting with Lucy?" Dan asked.

Lustig found a notebook in one of the briefcase's organizational slots. "He did," Lustig said. "I took some notes. Bottom line: Lawrence K. doesn't think it will happen. He doesn't think she can raise the downstroke and he thinks it is even less likely she will find lenders for the rest of the package." He read farther down his notes, flipped a page. "He agrees with her it was devastating for the announcement to come out before she tried to put this together. Lawrence K. informed her he won't give her any of *his* money."

The *Bugle* had two millionaires on its staff—Lawrence K. Mock and Rudy Vine—and the least part of their income derived from their newspaper salaries. Lawrence K. would appear in one less paper. Ruddy Vine would have only his TV show and movie books and syndicated review rights to fall back on.

"Lawrence K. and Rudy aren't going to part with the money you need to do this," Dan said. "They don't need us that badly."

Jack Lustig said, "And she isn't going to do it *wheedling* one or two thousand from every staffer in the building. She might raise a quarter million that way."

"Then we'll all be owners," Danny Fain said. "She can't lay off owners."

Constance Drane leaned forward. "I already saw Rudy carrying cartons out of his office," she said. "He'll be across the street or in New York by the end of the week."

"He'll never leave his house," Dale Busse said. "He can feed the syndicate, watch the movies, do the TV show. He gets prerelease cassettes from the studios. He doesn't even *bother* with screenings anymore. He's got his own TV studio in his basement. He'll only leave the house to retain the common touch and to pick up women."

Everyone laughed, in awe and envious of the man's moneymaking capabilities. Rudy Vine reviewed movies for the *Bugle*, being paid a sum reported to be nearly $500,000 a year; then he boiled the reviews down to sixty-second opinions and repeated them on Channel Four three nights a week at 10 P.M., deriving from that a grand sum of money reputed to approach $2 million a year; then he took four of these reviews and put them together with appropriate snippets of film to create twenty-two minutes of a thirty-minute show every Wednesday that ran coast to coast and possessed the power of life or death over any movie mentioned, receiving a sum of money rumored to be more than the combined sums paid for the first two endeavors; then he pared the reviews down further into little more than a cast list, plot line, and twenty-five clever words on the film's merits or idiosyncracies and packaged all these into books that sold consistently well and which were updated annually, necessitating the purchase of each new volume.

Rudy Vine's secretary was paid more than Danny Fain.

His appearances in the office were so infrequent they took on the flavor of state visits. Rudy Vine had a sporadic yet immense need to be fawned over. He was a tiny man who sat on a *Los Angeles Yellow Pages* to film his TV show, and he glided through the newsroom hubbub in his $600 sweaters, acid-washed jeans, and high-heeled diamond-backed boots, his demeanor coquettish and casually rich. His high-pitched voice, accustomed to expressing an opinion that people paid for, had a clean, cutting edge that dominated all other conversation in the room. Vine was there to be *seen,* his presence noted and appreciated by his fellow journalists, and since he was only giving them ten minutes that month he might as well make sure they knew he was there.

Jack Lustig reported, "Lucy Spriggs told Lawrence K. who told me that she called Vine and asked him point-blank to invest a million dollars to save the paper . . . and he laughed in her face."

"Or at least through the phone," Dan remarked.

"Remember Sue Batts? She used to run Features?" Dale Busse asked. "She called Vine one day a few years ago with a question about a review and *Cary Grant* answered. I can just picture Rudy doing that. He's sitting by the phone. It rings. He tells Cary Grant, 'You get that.' He talked him into taping a phone message. He collects them. 'Hello, this is Cary Grant. I'm visiting the home of world-famous movie critic Rudy Vine, who is too busy and sophisticated to have time to answer your silly call. But if you have a number, and Rudy feels like it, he might get back to you.' "

"Rudy, Rudy, Rudy," Danny mimicked, bathing in the laugh he got.

Dolly Franzen arrived. She was the current Features Editor, a smoke-gaunt woman with bleached white hair and black lipstick. No one knew what she did all day. She was required to attend two meetings, morning and afternoon, at which she reported that nothing exciting was happening in Features. She left for lunch after the A.M. confab, as she referred to it. Her husband played oboe in the Lake Forest Symphony. They had a Down's Syndrome son, institutionalized in the upper peninsula of Michigan. He was a *Bugle* subscriber. She took a seat, squinting at Puncher Mudd as he brought his beer bottle to his mouth. A shock of hair at the nape of her neck was dyed sky blue.

She asked, "Is something going on I'm not aware of? I mean, everyone is acting so *weird.* Everyone is so depressed."

Danny Fain thought he must be still asleep. He was caught in the last moments before waking, everything since he had seen the ghoul just a nightmare. He felt a thrill of hope; he was simply waiting for the alarm. Or perhaps he had been magically transported into the dream of Dolly Franzen, a woman who struck him as an utter blank, not even interesting enough to disdain, and he would be shipped back to his own consciousness when she was finished with him. Maybe because she didn't know what had happened it hadn't happened. Maybe she had the ultimate hold on reality and all the rest of them would take their cue from her.

Muff Greene set her straight. "The paper is closing, Dolly."

"Couldn't *someone* have told me?"

"You were invited to the meeting. We all heard at the same time."

She took out a cigarette and lit up, smiling cadaverously all around. "Does my staff know?"

"Everyone knows, Dolly. Now that you know, knowledge of our fate is one hundred percent."

Dan watched three men in blue coveralls come into the newsroom. They carried clipboards and silver tape measures the circumference of grapefruits—a pro's tape, the model that could be shot like a beam across the room, then retrieved with the touch of a button. They roughly divided the newsroom into thirds with a chop of hands, then each man went to measure his share.

"They've come to size us up for mourning cloaks," Dan said. Everyone turned to follow his eyes, even Muff Greene, who informed them, "I was told the owners would be sending appraisers up to calculate exactly what we are worth."

"It's kind of callous, measuring around the employees."

"We're all worth eleven eighty-nine in base elements. They need to see us working to be reminded of that," Dale Busse said.

One of the men was trying to measure Nancy Potter's desk. She was on the phone and he interrupted to ask her to move a pile of papers from a corner to clear a surface for his calculations. She refused. He persisted. She covered the mouthpiece of her headset. Danny saw her state precisely, *I am on the telephone.*

"Nancy is going to crush this guy's nuts," he predicted.

Everyone in the meeting stood to watch.

"He has that obstinate flunky's nature that compels him to forge ahead, damn the consequences," Dan said. "And they're at the perfect level."

A man, an irate official of the city, the subject of a long and vigorously detailed story of official malfeasance and illegal use of taxpayers' money, had appeared one day at Nancy Potter's desk. He was an enormous man, head like a chopping block, one hand clutching a rolled copy of the day's *Bugle* and tapping it like a bat against his opposing palm. Nancy Potter was, as always, on the phone. She politely informed the man that she was on the phone, that she would speak to him in a moment. He allowed a single moment to expire, then commenced to berate her. She quietly ended her call and in one fluid motion dialed Security. He had unrolled the paper so that the 96-point headline screaming his name and his misdeeds was clearly visible. For nearly a minute he excoriated Nancy Potter and denied all wrongdoing. She did not say a word. No one was picking up the phone in Security. He told her about his children in high school and the humiliation they would suffer, told her about his wife in tears, told her about his mother recovering from a stroke risking a relapse from seeing his name—*her* name—in letters a foot high connected to the ignominy of public scandal.

Nancy Potter typed notes into her tube. "It's a solid story," she said coolly. "I stand by it." At last Security answered her call. "*Where* the fuck have you been? Fourth floor. Newsroom. Now, *please.*" She set her headphones on the desk. "Since I have you here, let me read to you tomorrow's story. Perhaps you would care to comment."

Rolled into a club again, the paper nearly grazed the ceiling as the elected official raised it above his head. "*You*—"

Goop Traky, four desks away, was sitting closest. He had been listening in on the conversation, envious of Potter's chilled gall. But before he could intervene, before the enraged man could start the paper on its downward cudgeling arc, Nancy Potter calmly brought her left hand up like an avenging claw between his legs and clutched his testicles in her fist so efficiently that he let out a whinny of pain and went to his knees. He was on the floor and out of sight when two Security guards arrived. Nancy Potter, headphones back on, making a call, had to snap her fingers to get their attention, then point to the floor where her assailant whimpered and gurgled with his arms and his *Bugle* pressed like padding between his legs.

"Nance can take care of herself," Muff Greene announced. She shuffled story lists. "You have anything, Dolly?"

The Features Editor perked up. "Actually, I do. Eric Maas is interviewing Young Snob God today—in *this* very office."

Her contemporaries regarded her blankly.

"I don't believe it," she scolded. "And you wonder why new, young readers don't bother with us. Young Snob God is a rock band. Three men . . . *boys,* actually. Very *sexy* boys. They're at the Horizon tomorrow night. They're doing the radio stations this morning, TV this afternoon. Eric knows one of them and they agreed to an exclusive interview. The *Quill* won't have it, I guarantee you."

Muff Greene, trying to be enthusiastic, said, "Let's do a color refer on One."

"We don't have color of them," Dale Busse said without glancing up from her stack of wire photos.

"How about photographing one of their album covers?"

Muff suggested. "We could put it in the skybox."

Dale Busse cleared her throat. She said, "Their only album shows a ram's skull with an ankh burned in its forehead emerging from between a squatting woman's legs. The woman has her hands over her breasts and a snake's head is coming out of her mouth. The look on her face says she's enjoying herself."

Everyone laughed in disbelief, relieved to be adults.

"How do you know so much?"

"I've got the album," Dale said. "I actually like some of the songs. 'Booger Tea.' 'Load in My Rocket.' 'Spawn, Trout.' 'Trencherman.' "

"Which one does Eric know?" Muff Greene asked.

"I think Snob. They went to music camp in Wisconsin when they were kids."

"No refer, then," Muff Greene declared. "Anything else, Dolly?"

"Canned matter and comics," she said. She departed immediately, her blue curl springy at the base of her neck.

"We shouldn't have told her," Danny Fain said. "She'd come to work the day after we closed and wonder where everyone was."

"Don't sell her short," Muff Greene said. "She may seem dense and self-absorbed, but it's a style that works for her. Sports?"

All turned to regard Puncher Mudd, who at that moment was peering one-eyed into his beer bottle. His sweater bore a vaguely pointed star of secret sauce, like a boy's sheriff badge.

"Put the beer down, Punch. It's still a newspaper."

He stuck the beef jerky like a cigar in the corner of his mouth. "We'll have plenty of scores tonight, sister," he said. "Scores and insight and analysis."

"Can you be more specific?" Muff asked.

"Nope. A couple Bears followups. The hole will get filled, Muff. We're *pros.* " He took a determined swallow, tipping the bottle up high, but keeping his eyes on line with the people in the room.

Muff Greene sighed. "Financial?"

Jack Lustig read from a prepared statement. "A feature on merger mania. A look at the markets in the post-Crash era. Stock market down, as I already mentioned. Some odds and ends. A nice reader on a patent attorney. And—finally—a story on the imminent demise of the Chicago *Bugle.*"

"No story, Jack," Muff Greene declared.

"We'll be the only news outlet in town without one."

"No story."

"How will our readers find out?" Jack Lustig asked.

"They'll get it from TV."

"I disagree, Muff," Jack Lustig pressed. "In this situation we have to assume we are our readers' sole source of news."

"We'll work something up," Muff promised. "But it will come from Derringer." She moved on. "Since Lucy is busy saving the world as we know it, could you sell her list for her, Dan?"

Dan summarized. "VOTE and POLL can be played together. VOTE is about expectations for low turnout and an overview on general apathy. POLL is another of our interminable predictions of how everyone who bothers to vote will vote. SCAR is a potential weeper still being worked by Nan Fullwood about a girl's fight with her HMO to pay for repair of a hideous scar running across her face. She's a butcher's apprentice, the first woman in that union, I understand. A cleaver bounced off a slab of frozen meat and cut open her face."

"We have," Dale Busse said proudly, "before and after art."

"Before surgery and after?"

"No. Before the accident and after."

"She wants the HMO to guarantee up front to pay the expected eighty-thousand-dollar tab to fix her face," Dan said. "Reportedly, her husband hasn't been able to look at her—if you get my drift."

Puncher Mudd piped up: "Put a bag over her head."

Danny Fain went on. "DEV is about development of a plot

of ground west of the river that will inevitably roust from their homes three hundred families who can't afford to live in the new development. This is Potter's baby, so to speak. DANC is a nice weeper about a couple of crazy high school kids who are in love and determined to attend their school's autumn bacchanal despite the fact they're both wheelchair-bound."

Dale Busse said, "We have art of them smooching across locked wheels."

"The girl is rumoredly a babe," Dan said. "They were paralyzed in the same motorcycle accident. *She* was driving. LEFT can hold if necessary. It's a political thing about two aldermen whose views on the city have left them behind—hence the slug—in the race for funding for their pet projects. This could be packaged with VOTE and POLL, if you wish. We have mugs of the two. DEAD is kind of gruesome. Which makes it perfect for us. Seems the union that constructs or molds or whatever grave liners has been on strike for three months and local funeral homes and cemeteries have exhausted their supplies. Nobody saw this strike coming, so nobody stockpiled the liners. It's a state law that people have to be buried in these things. The homes charge seven hundred fifty bucks for one. Evidently some funeral homes have been offering cremation bargains to keep their body counts down. If a family insists on a burial, they're put on hold. The dead are piling up all over the city. The larger funeral homes have filled up *their* storage space and are now renting space at local meat lockers. No word if they're hanging them from hooks. But it's a *fun* story. Show 'em the picture, Dale."

Dale Busse turned over a color photograph of a funeral home's back room, every shadowed inch filled with corpses in tasteful kelly-green bags, a lighted jack-o'-lantern on a desk down front. "We had this yesterday," Dale reported.

"Where was this story yesterday?" Muff Greene asked.

"Dwight Spang is the reporter," Danny said. "Dwight never got a story in today that he could get in tomorrow. He *swears* he will have it ready today."

"But tomorrow isn't Halloween."

"I know, Muff. But we have the Halloween echo. Or we can kill the art," Dan said.

"And that picture looks like the same staging for the burning house picture on One this morning," Muff Greene said.

"Very observant," Dale Busse said. "It is, in fact, the very same pumpkin. Burt just moved it from one scene to the next. He even kept the candle lit when it was riding in his backseat."

"Dan?" Muff said.

"MAC is a thing about raincoat sales being up. This is a story generated almost entirely by our fearless leader who, while buying a raincoat, was informed by the salesman that raincoat sales are up a *significant* eight percent over last year. Who can say why? Bernie DeVille's on it. I haven't seen anything. My guess is Bernie will be late and long—and don't touch a word. STING is Becky Fudge on a team of scamsters reportedly working the Loop and North Michigan Avenue selling fake Visa cards for twenty dollars. They're evidently quite successful. Merchants are worried. Apparently one of the crooks once worked for Visa or still works for them—because they know how the system works and they give the bogus cards numbers that get through Visa's in-store card check. There's a move on to require a photo ID with each use of the Visa, but the boys at I. Magnin and Bloomie's and Needless Markup are leery of asking Mrs. Largesse from Glencoe to produce a driver's license with her mug on it when she wants to charge her eight-thousand-dollar tennis bracelet. The *Quill* may or may not have it. But since the retailers who are most concerned advertise more in the *Quill* than the *Bugle,* my guess is they won't be off the story for long. CTA is about an increase in bus breakdowns. Seventy-eight buses didn't start this morning—and it only got down to thirty-eight degrees. VEGAS is something out of the cop shops about a gang of car thieves who steal only Chevy Vegas. This was tipped to Stan Mansard yesterday by someone with a stake in the story. They wouldn't say who they were. They just challenged Stan to look up the reports and he did. The police say they weren't aware all these beaters were being stolen. He believes them. The police want to laugh it off because who would purposely steal Vegas? Yet this gang has vanished nearly a hundred of them. Stan says the cops are afraid because they think the tipster is a lawyer who is getting the Vega owners together for a class-action suit against the city for not energetically pursuing this rash of stolen cars because the victims are losers. XOBE is an obit on William O'Berry, who wrote a column for us in the long-long ago. He was ninety-two. We have fossilized art, and that other still-functioning fossil, Abe Skinback, is writing an appreciation, in addition to his column. God knows when either of those will arrive tonight. Deb Foster has been alerted to Abe's increased responsibilities, and she will prod him along, I'm sure. Rumor has it Abe once snaked a girl away from O'Berry nearly fifty years ago and subsequently married her—and they were mortal enemies ever after. WATER is Fred Tobin's piece about the city's water purification drive and how the water we drink today is cleaner than any water in the past ten years. PUNK came in late. Police have arrested six punks—hence the slug—on suspicion of setting at least some of the house fires last night. By punks, I don't mean little twerps in the classic sense. These are *real* punks. Needles in their cheeks. Hair shaved into arrows. Black clothes, black boots, black outlooks. Chains through their lips. And that's it, at this early juncture."

"And your thing?" Muff Greene asked. "Where does that stand?"

"My thing stands with Tim Penn in the field," Danny Fain said. "He's looking. I've made some calls to test who knows what and so far this is ours alone."

Dale Busse said, "Dunkirk can be pulled off whatever he's doing today to take a picture. He needs an hour's warning."

"I was talking to a friend at Channel Eight," Constance Drane said, "and they have heard a rumor of a rumor." She gave Dan a pooch-lipped look of satisfaction about this petite wrench she had lobbed.

"I hope you didn't confirm it," he said.

"No. She brought it up. She asked me what I had heard. I played dumb."

Muff Greene pushed back her chair. "Let's not spread this around. It'd be nice to have it to ourselves," she said. She stood, ending the meeting, then immediately sat back down, as if the next meeting was about to commence.

Muff Greene made a call, spoke in a subdued voice. A second call went to Lucy Spriggs, inviting her to join them. Derringer entered the room. His hair was damp from a fresh combing, his second tie of the day was in place; TV cameras might jump him anywhere. Muff Greene moved to give up her chair at the end of the table, but he waved her off expansively. Yet Muff kept moving and in an instant Derringer was in the vacated chair. He reportedly didn't like people sitting to his left or right; he hated having to turn his head to talk to them. He played with his wedding ring, which was a long gold fish wrapped around his finger, the fish blowing a pea-sized diamond like a bubble out of its mouth.

"You call Lucy?" he asked.

"I did."

Derringer removed a pen and a pad of paper from his inside coat pocket. He began furiously writing himself a note. These notes were cherished items, scrounged from wastebaskets primarily, but sometimes torn boldly from the pad should Derringer leave the pad on a desk somewhere. He was careless and scatterbrained and egotistical; he would never dare admit losing one of his precious note pads, and therefore he never tried to retrace his steps to find one. If he found a note missing from the pad he would doubt himself before suspecting others. The most famous of these notes was the property of Dirk Flester. He had actually removed it from the pad with Derringer in the room. Dirk had read the message upside down and just had to have it. When Derringer turned away to make a phone call Dirk reached over the desk and ripped the sheet from the pad. He folded the note away in his pocket. Back at his desk he took out the note and read it. *Tell M. shorter stories. Lunch date with T. Fuck wife. Call about copier BDs.* From the desk of W. Derringer. Derringer hated the name the W. stood for: Walter. He lamented that his parents had this great last name to work with and they botched everything with the name Walter. Why not Tad? Or Clint? Or Rex? Or even Pete? No, they went with Walter. His father's name. Dirk Flester showed the note around and was accused of forgery. He Xeroxed the original and hid it at home, lest some harm come to it. Plenty of Derringer scholars would love to get their hands on it, just as they loved to disparage the note as a hoax. Bubb Cook was selected as final arbiter of the note's authenticity. He had been on vacation when the note surfaced, but on his first morning back Dirk Flester and a couple other reporters came to Bubb's post in the smoker. He was presented the Xeroxed note. The fact that it was a copy of a Derringer note intrigued him even before he read the message. Someone thought enough of the original to take it out of circulation. He read the list of things to do. At *Fuck wife* he exploded with laughter, spitting out an unlit cigarette that caromed off the screen of his tube. He put it back in his mouth when he stopped laughing and caught his breath. "A classic," he pronounced. "Better than *Blow nose.* Better than *Have A.'s dog murdered.*" Bubb Cook's recollections caused everyone to smile warmly. These were touchstones of their common histories. These were stories that went through parties like gasoline fires.

"But is it the real thing?" a reporter asked.

Bubb Cook hefted the Xerox. "There's an underground supply of his note pads running through the newsroom," he said. "So that doesn't really prove anything. But that's his handwriting. And that's his mentality. I can hear him saying to himself in the middle of a meeting—*Oh, yeah. Better fuck the missus tonight. It's been a month.* I've gotta say this is the real thing."

Lucy Spriggs came into Muff Greene's office. She was openly chagrined at Derringer's presence. "I thought this had something to do with tomorrow's paper," she said with charmless sarcasm, which chipped frozen off Derringer's uncomprehending hide. He just didn't get it.

"It's a meeting about *tomorrow,* period," he said.

Lucy Spriggs moved to the corner farthest from Derringer. He said, "The people in this room right now—and a few working elsewhere at other tasks—have been the heart of this paper. I'm here to tell you you won't be forgotten. The severance plan is being put into place, so final numbers aren't ready just yet. But the formula they said we would follow was approximately a week's pay for every six months of service. Plus, we'll pick up your health insurance for as many weeks as you've got pay coming. So the numbers are very generous. Some of you are looking at a half year's pay."

"What about families?" Danny Fain asked. "Will the health insurance continue to cover them."

"Again, final numbers are forthcoming, Dan," Derringer said. "But I can practically guarantee that families will be covered."

Lucy Spriggs spoke up from the corner. "Would the owners be willing to put the severance money together in a loan to the staff for a down payment to buy the paper?"

"No, Luce." He pronounced it *Loose,* with a sorrowful, patronizing look. "If they were interested in keeping the paper going, they wouldn't have announced the paper was closing. That seems pretty clear to me."

"But if they have that much money to spend, why just pay people off to leave quietly?" Lucy asked.

"That's not what they're doing," Derringer said. "They're very generously easing the transition out of here for a great many people. True, they're cutting their losses, but they could cut their losses in a much more brutal fashion if they wished."

"What about the rest of the staff? What's their severance?" Puncher Mudd asked.

"Those numbers are being hammered out right this moment," Derringer said. "Obviously, their package won't be as sweet. We reward merit here."

He terminated the meeting at that moment simply by standing. A sympathetic stirring followed, like flowers bending toward the sun. When he departed, Muff Greene was just behind.

"She has her nose firmly lodged," Lucy Spriggs said sourly.

They noticed all at once that Derringer had left his note pad behind. Something was written on the top sheet, but no one was quick to read it.

"I think that's a plant," Danny Fain said. He could read the note, no problem, but he hadn't yet. He had discovered in the hours of that day that he didn't want to learn too much. He had work to do and then he would go home. *Fuck wife.* The backwater aspects of the place had begun to lose their hold on him.

"Read it, Dan," Lucy Spriggs said. She remained in the corner. The intensity of her loathing for Derringer kept her pinned there as if she wanted to allow more time to pass before she ventured through air he had fouled.

"No. He wants us to read it," Danny said. "He has spies. He's heard about the notes he's left behind."

"Sure he has spies," Lucy said, "but I don't think they relate his embarrassments to him. What good would that do? He'd just hate the spies."

Constance Drane added, "I'm sure they restrict their reports to rumors that don't directly involve him."

"Nonetheless," Dan said, "I think we should leave this room without reading that note."

"He'll *think* we've read it. Who wouldn't read it?"

"Are we all presumed to be snoops who would read someone else's notes? If he left a letter in an opened envelope, would he assume we had read it?"

"Under ordinary circumstances, no," Dan said. "But in today's climate? Perhaps. *Probably.*"

"Maybe he left the note behind to give us comfort that he can't give us on an official basis."

"Unofficial hope," Danny Fain said. "I like that. Maybe it says *Talk to J. about starting new paper.* Or *Ask company to pay off staff mortgages.*"

Everyone laughed, even Lucy Spriggs. She tore herself free from the corner and advanced on the note pad. Dan slapped his hand over it. "Don't pick it up," he said. "They'll see you. Sit down below the level of the window. Someone is always going to see whatever it is you do."

Lucy Spriggs sat across from Dan. She looked exhausted. He lifted his hand and with one finger pivoted the pad toward her. She caught it, read, winced.

"Told you," Dan said. "He's not one for giving comfort."

Lucy tore off the note. "I'm saving this one. I'll frame it and hang it in my office wherever I end up."

"Let me see."

"You didn't want to."

"I didn't want to be first," Dan said. "Now that you've seen it, I'm brave."

She gave Danny the note. Constance Drane, Puncher Mudd, and Jack Lustig looked on. *Pick up laundry. Fire L.*

"Don't jump to conclusions," Dan said. "Could be Les Burkin. He's a fuckup."

"Could be me," Jack Lustig said with a faraway glance.

"Maybe it's totally unrelated to work. Maybe L. is his maid."

"No," Lucy Spriggs said. "He left that behind for me to see. He knows exactly what he's doing. Instead of writing Lucy he writes L. Because he knows that gets in my mind more—the doubt, the question, the chance that he didn't mean me. He's the worst combination possible in a human being: innocuous *and* evil."

Dan closed the door to his office and called home.

Rita asked, "What's the latest?"

"Nothing concrete. Derringer came in after the A.M. meeting and threw around some severance numbers. He wouldn't commit to anything, but the formula they're looking at is a week's pay for each six months of service.

"So we'd get a little more than eighteen weeks' pay," she calculated. "And insurance?"

"Again, nothing firm. But he mentioned coverage equal to

the number of weeks' pay we'd receive."

"Family, too?"

"*Again*—he could practically guarantee the family would be covered."

"Shit," Rita said. "They pull the rug out from under you—with *zero* notice—and then they can't give you final figures on severance? They didn't just decide to close last night. They should've had the numbers ready to give you right after they announced the closing."

"I couldn't agree more," Dan said.

"So come home early." Her voice had softened, turned yearning. "Come home and we'll fondle each other."

"Hey, this line is tapped."

"Hey, I'm horny."

"It must be all the talk about unemployment . . . severance."

"Death," Rita said. "Like drawing up our will."

On three occasions they had visited their attorney to work out the details of their last will and testament, and each time, afterward—after all the maneuvering around the obstacles death would present—they both were so delighted to find themselves alive that they rushed to the nearest private spot to make love: the first time in a motel, then in the car in cul-de-sac darkness, then on the cool, steep stairs after the sitter was released.

"I'm lugging heavy wood."

"Braggart." Her voice had shifted again, back into her business mode. "Try to come home early. The kids wanted to trick-or-treat our immediate neighbors before they went to school. They'll be all over me when they get home. I want you with us."

"It won't be before dark," he said. "I promise you that."

"Come on, Danny. These people are *fucking* you—and you're gonna put in extra time for them?"

"Regardless, I've got work to do. The hit-and-run probably won't be nailed until five or six and it's dark by then—since the clocks went back."

He heard her stewing. "I've got to make you more of a flinty-edged bastard with the people you deal with," she said.

"You've already turned a portion of me into granite," he said.

"So it's working."

Next call went to Tim Penn, who answered on the third ring.

"Were you out of your car?"

"No. On another line."

"You have two lines?"

"Sure. Plus call waiting. It's indispensable."

"So where are you?" Danny Fain asked.

"I'm parallel to the Kennedy. Coming up on Nagle."

"Seen anything?"

"Dead kids? No."

"I'm more worried about TV crews right now," Danny said. "There's been some interest in this story. Some sniffing around."

"No TV crews. If I'd known that, I'd have gotten my hair cut."

"You don't get it cut," Danny said. "You get it professionally tousled."

"I need to get the blue in my eyes touched up, too," Tim Penn said.

"Here's what you do." Danny had his map in front of him. "Take Nagle north of the Kennedy. You'll pick up Avondale right there. Turn left on Avondale. You'll go into Norwood Park. Look there and beyond. Keep your eyes open for police, ambulances, TV trucks."

"Or bodies," Tim Penn said.

"Or a body, Tim. It may look like nothing more than a crumpled white sheet."

"Any other landmarks?"

"I should've been paying attention, but I wasn't. If I'd been paying attention I would have found a different line of work by now."

"What's the mood there?"

"Suicidal. But some work getting done. Derringer came to the A.M. meeting and told us about severance without telling us anything. They're still crunching numbers."

"Right—trying to figure out how little they can give us without looking like penurious fartbags to the people of Chicago."

"Would they close the paper if they cared about that, Tim?"

"Now *there's* a pretty girl," Tim Penn reported.

"Tim. Keep your mind on the task at hand."

"She sees me. She's *aware* of me, Danny. You know that look women get when they're aware of you?"

"No, Tim. Go back to work."

"She's tall. Black hair."

"Get out of there, Tim."

"Hispanic? Maybe. Long legs, *tight* black jeans, black fuck-me pumps, a black leather midriff jacket . . . unzipped. She's smiling at me, Dan. Oh! Oh! *Eye contact!* She's got a big smile because she knows I'm talking to someone about her. Black and red sweater. Fulsome tits, Danny."

"Leave, Tim. Depart. No circling the block. I want to be able to reach you at all times," Dan warned.

"Will she look back at me?" Tim Penn wondered, half to himself. "Will I record a look-back? It's been known to happen. There. There. Her head is turning. I have her in my mirror. She's—*sheeeee's*—looking back! Yes! That's the nine thousand nine hundred and twenty-second look-back of my life. Closing in on ten thousand. Plus the *hundreds* of thousands I wasn't aware of."

"You actually keep track of that sort of thing?" Dan asked.

"I'll be walking down the street and I'll pass a woman and we'll smile and touch eyes and go on past—then I'll turn to see if I score a look-back and I've always kept a running count. There's no better feeling. If I get a look-back smile, that means she's interested enough to smile when she doesn't have to and if I have time I'll talk to her. I met one of my wives that way."

Danny Fain asked, "How do you manage to get through the day?"

"It's a mystery, Dan. It's a life I wouldn't wish on anyone. Here's Nagle."

"Remember, you talk to me only. I'll call you again in twenty minutes."

"That's a Rog."

Danny Fain typed the DEV01 slug on his tube, found it in Nancy Potter's queue, and called it up. He could see her through his door flailing at her keyboard. She was speaking to someone on the phone. She was actually smiling; she was not famous for her smiles. Seven phone numbers with identities were typed onto the DEV01 slug, plus quick quotes taken directly, full of typos and abbreviations. She had tried a lede: *Eusebio Valdez patches potholes for the city and with his $445 a week salary rents an apartment on Wabansia for his wife, Inez, and their six children. Now he fears losing his home.*

Dan did not see Eusebio Valdez's phone number in Nancy Potter's list. She was their best reporter; he was not unduly alarmed. But the staff was required to leave all sources and their phone numbers on the stories, to be removed by the city editors. Danny periodically back-checked reporters' quotes, reading behind them in the computer and randomly trying to call people. He identified himself as a copy editor verifying the spelling of a name. The people he called seemed to appreciate the extra care. If the person's number wasn't on the story, Dan felt a burr of apprehension. He would then call directory assistance. If no number came up, he went to the reporter and asked for it. Usually they apologized and produced. This practice began after a former *Bugle* writer named Frank Huston produced a lavishly detailed and colorful story about a gang of kids—first names only for anonymity—who hijacked a Salvation Army truck and sold its contents to hotels for the indigent. The truck had indeed been hijacked and found emptied. But the suspicion was that everything else was a well-cooked fiction.

Huston was fresh from a small paper in suburban Seattle, where no one questioned what he wrote. His first mistake was to assume that *Bugle* readers would simply enjoy and believe his story. His second mistake was to give the kids wealth, to locate them, however vaguely, in "a North Shore suburb." This was like shooting a flare up over the city's TV stations. They took many of their story ideas from the papers and a colorful piece about rich kids with dark secrets was too luscious to ignore. The mystery of the kids was a challenge. When Frank Huston arrived at his desk the morning the story appeared, every TV station in town already had two calls in to him. The wire services were on the phone with Muff Greene seeking approval to pick up the story. There was a clamoring for art, for names, for *details.* Frank Huston took all the message slips and threw them away. "Let them make their own stories," he said.

His editors were skeptical, however, and he was asked to produce last names for the kids. He refused, having promised to keep a secret. The editors promised to keep the secret themselves. But they needed to know they could safely give the wire services permission to run the story; they needed to know they could stand behind what they had printed. Still Frank Huston refused. Shortly before lunch he was told to provide the names and addresses of the kids or resign. Expecting him to buckle and weep, then be fired, the editors were stunned when he informed them he would resign if that was the only alternative to breaking his word. This strategy forced the decision on management; by indicating his willingness to quit over a principle, Frank Huston challenged his editors to back him on the story. They chose not to and accepted his resignation, but he was able to depart in a righteous light. He had protected his sources. He had avoided the onus of being fired for writing fiction published as fact. Such a tag would have followed him through his career.

Danny Fain called up three more slugs; one was not yet created, the other two were empty. It was early, before noon, prelunch. Most reporters would not begin writing until later in the afternoon. There was time to kill, people to call, shit to shoot. His phone rang. Lucy Spriggs calling, though her office was dark.

"Can you come to the morgue, Dan?" she asked. "We have a minor crisis that requires your masculine touch."

The morgue was across the hall from the newsroom. Clippings, photos, and reference materials were stored there, watched over by a cadre of librarians who ranged in personality and temperament from those who were explosively helpful to those arrogantly offended at the merest request for assistance. The front desk, where slips were filled out to requisition the file needed, was the opening into a dizzying warren of card catalogs and office cubicles and desks sedimented like archeological digs with stacks menacing as termite nests of back issues waiting to be filed. Some librarians short on personal initiative but blessed with a personal friend lodged high in the *Bugle* food chain used this cluttered maze to hide with their Watchman and their headphones for a few hours at a time while clip and photo requests gathered out front like oceangoing notes in bottles. The centerpiece of the library was a huge Elecompack automated photo storage and retrieval system that consisted of eight alphabetized bookshelves that moved hydraulically like a gargantuan accordion. At a button's push, a light winked on and the shelves moved apart with a hum, opening a narrow aisle the librarian could walk down to search for the necessary photo file.

Bernie DeVille was in the morgue, as were four other reporters and Lucy Spriggs. She was on the phone when Dan arrived. Bernie DeVille affected suspenders, bright-hued straps that framed his stomach, and he used them as a barometer of his day's work. Early in the morning he kept them taut on his shoulders, clipping a ballpoint pen to one, hooking his thumbs in them when he adopted his omniscient avuncular pose, snapping them against his chest when someone had the temerity and insight to call him a master of the overwritten cliché, the patent observation, the story that died at the jump. At the end of the day, his work turned in late, he slipped the suspenders off his shoulders and took a seat in the smoker to contribute his cigar's share to the poisoned gloom and repeat stories of past triumphs: a deadline actually met, an idea truly his own, a friend who died before Bernie drove him away.

Now Bernie DeVille's suspenders were straight and hard as bands of wire. He faced a tall, thin, anguished man across the morgue's front desk. The tray of request slips lay between them like a poker pot. Lucy Spriggs hung up the phone.

"I've called Security, Grant," she said. "They're willing to send someone up here. Don't force me to make another call to them."

Grant Lopp was the head day-shift librarian. He listened stoically to Lucy Spriggs, and when she finished her benign threat he shifted his look from her without comment, as if she had not spoken. Bernie DeVille put his hand on the knob of the half-door leading into the morgue's rearward caverns. Grant Lopp froze him with a glare. The librarians had their own union and one benefit of that union was that only library union members were permitted behind the desk. Consequently, they retained the power of understanding the morgue's system and of that knowledge being required by the staff of the newspaper. Hanging like a presidential portrait in several locations around the morgue was the picture of an open-faced man with deep-set eyes and the beginnings of a smile. This was the late Thomas Pool, "St. Tommy" to the librarians, the man who before his death six years ago had had the wisdom and wherewithal to get the librarians removed from the newsroom's guild and put into the librarians' union. Their pay increased and their power increased exponentially; they became possessors of coveted knowledge. They gained a slice of the high ground, which they zealously guarded. Danny Fain had been beyond the morgue's front door because he had worked at the *Bugle* prior to St. Tommy's grand crusade. But more than half of the newsroom personnel could not remember a time when they had not waited on the morgue staff for the information they needed.

Grant Lopp had been a pallbearer at St. Tommy's funeral. He came all in black, down to the shirt and tie, and he wore a black armband to work for a year afterward, then hung the loop of thready silk over the corner of St. Tommy's picture on his desk.

"I'm working on something *major*, Lopp," Bernie shouted. "I need those clips."

"Get your fist off that doorknob," Grant Lopp responded coldly. "We may not be a paper anymore, but this is *still* the morgue."

"You're refusing to fulfill your duties," Lucy Spriggs said. "Even the librarians' union would frown on that."

Grant Lopp turned half toward her as her remark came to an end; it was not quite an acknowledgment of her, but rather like someone was blowing softly in his ear from six inches away and he was mildly curious about who was being so irritating. Lucy Spriggs was not perturbed; she *knew* Grant Lopp. It was why she had summoned Danny Fain, who came into the library like he was on business. He stood next to Bernie DeVille and filled out a request slip. "Put a rush on this, will you, Grant?"

Grant Lopp muttered tersely, "No can do."

"Lopp's refusing to do his job," Bernie summarized.

"Is that true, Grant?" Dan asked. He riffled through the stack of request slips.

Grant Lopp placed his hands on the countertop. He wore a moonstone on his left ring finger, a gold collarpin, cufflinks, a thin wristwatch. His eyes were flat and blue-ice cold, resting on the sculpted plateau of his cheekbones. He looked perfect in every way, as handsome as Tim Penn, but with an edgy, fastidious sheen that told women not to bother. Rumor had it his last three lovers had died of AIDS, St. Tommy among them, but Grant Lopp had thus far dodged that particular bullet, guiltily. Friends of friends said he almost wanted to be stricken, because the people he knew who had died of AIDS had been the wittiest, the most talented, the most gorgeous, the most creative people he knew, and he felt judged unfit for that crowd by the fact of his persistent health.

"If there is to be no more paper," Grant Lopp wondered, "what is the point of filing these back issues? And if that part of our job is extinct, by implication so is the rest of our job. *You* may choose to continue serving, but as duly elected unit representative of the International Alliance of Librarians and Data Processing Clerks, and speaking for the international body, we have decided to withhold our services from the *Bugle.*"

Danny asked of Bernie DeVille, Lucy Spriggs, the other reporters: "Could I talk to Grant in private for a minute?"

Lucy Spriggs marched everyone out, Bernie DeVille grumbling. Grant Lopp stood straight and tall at his post.

"Nobody is happy about what is happening here," Danny Fain said. "These people are just trying to do their jobs. They'll do them until the paper tells them to stop."

"They're fools."

"They're *not* fools, Grant. They're being loyal to the agreement they made with the *Bugle* to work for the pay they receive. And they're being loyal to themselves, too. They aren't happy unless they're putting out a paper. It takes their minds off their real problems."

"I can't forgive the *Bugle* its treatment of its employees," Grant Lopp said.

"Who's in this with you?"

"The considerable influence of the IALDPC stands behind me."

"This is a wildcat strike, Grant," Dan said. "Do you realize you're imperiling any severance benefits you have coming to you and your fellow librarians? They'll just fire you, Grant. They'll appreciate the opportunity. It's less money they have to pay out."

Grant Lopp sneezed suddenly, an action as effective as violently pushing Dan away. Grant took a moment to collect himself. His eyes were furtive, watery. He blew his nose into a handful of tissues plucked from under the counter. Danny Fain's photo request was speckled with suspect moisture.

"I see no point in going on," Grant Lopp finally said.

"I don't either, frankly," Dan said, "if I examine the situation too closely. But I'm feeling a little lost and desperate—and putting out the paper gives me something to hold on to."

"I can't kid myself like you can, Danny."

"Lucy will call Security and they'll haul you out of here. You'll only succeed in screwing up your chance at a smooth transition into the future."

"I'm not concerned about the future."

"Who's back there with you?" Dan asked.

"Shawna and Dwayne are filing."

"Do they agree with what you're doing?"

Grant Lopp hesitated. "Yes."

"May I speak with them?"

"Members of the IALDPC stand together—and I am their representative."

"They might like a few weeks' pay when they walk out of here," Danny said. "They might not have the courage of your convictions."

Grant Lopp gave Dan a whispery smile. "You can bet on that," he said.

Bernie DeVille's anxious, angry face popped through the library door, scowled, and withdrew.

"How about this?" Danny Fain suggested. "You step aside—let the newsroom have access to the library. Or, better yet, you call someone to work for you—tell them you're sick—and then you have a day to think through your position without doing damage to your reputation or your future in the business."

Dan waited. He never expected Grant Lopp to simply throw open the morgue for anyone's use; that would undercut everything his union and St. Tommy had fought for. But calling in sick—that had possibilities. The day off would appeal to Grant

Lopp, who had not worked one instant of overtime in all his years at the *Bugle,* who in fact was used by the rest of the newsroom as something of a timing device, so punctually did he depart the office at five o'clock each evening. Dan saw the day shaping in Grant Lopp's eyes; a walk in the crisp downtown sunshine, some Michigan Avenue shopping, a spot of lunch, maybe a movie at Water Tower, perhaps a call to a friend. Grant Lopp actually smiled. Dan saw he was practically reaching for the phone to dial up Heather White-Bucketts, who lived just two blocks away and who was known to be willing to work for anyone at the drop of a quarter, so anxious was she for the time-due that accrued to her vacation days. She would work for Grant Lopp, no questions, then pull her own shift that evening. Grant Lopp was coming to a decision, reaching for the phone, looking up Heather's number, Danny Fain congratulating himself on a crisis resolved, when Lucy Spriggs returned and shattered the moment.

"What's it gonna be, Lopp?"

"We've got work to do," Bernie DeVille said, behind her. Trailing Bernie were two Security guards. Dan saw his plan crumble as Grant Lopp's stubborn, righteous pose returned. Lucy Spriggs elbowed Dan aside to face Grant Lopp across the counter. She had no feelings for Grant aside from the irritation he had caused by fouling up the orderly functioning of the newspaper. Grant Lopp, however, *hated* Lucy Spriggs because she had challenged him; he had been about to work the problem out with Dan and then she was in his face forcing him back into his original, self-destructive position. She lacked Danny Fain's touch for allowing him room to maneuver gracefully. Worse, she had robbed him of a free day he had in fifteen seconds begun to cherish.

"Uh, Lucy," Dan intervened, "I think Grant and I were on the verge of an agreement that would make everyone happy."

Lucy Spriggs fumed, folded her arms. "What agreement?"

"Grant was going to call someone in to work for him today—we would have the use of the morgue, and Grant would have a day to consider exactly what he wanted to do."

"*No!*" Lucy Spriggs said angrily. "He gets a day off? It takes someone an hour to get in here to do *his* job? All that time, the morgue is off limits? Then tomorrow, we go through the same thing? Absolutely not. Either he opens now—or I authorize Mutt and Jeff here to remove him and he is fired."

Dan regarded the two from Security. One was not tall, the other short, as Lucy's reference had implied. But they were so bland and nondescript as to almost beg for a colorful classifying nickname. Both wore pale, wispy mustaches, hair cut to company length, blue uniforms, black Reeboks, and the dulled, give-a-shit expression of the near-minimum-wage employee. However, they were muscular enough to carry Grant Lopp as far as Lucy Spriggs instructed.

"Give me another minute here, Lucy," Dan said. "I was making progress."

"You were making progress by avoiding the cause of the problem," Lucy Spriggs said. "And the problem is Grant Lopp."

"I would've had the morgue open. Nobody would be fired. Tomorrow will take care of itself," Danny Fain said.

"No time, Dan. Grant, what's it going to be?"

"If you haul him away you still have to wait an hour to get someone in here to replace him."

"You alone back there, Grant?"

"Shawna and Dwayne," Danny said.

Lucy Spriggs murmured, "Shit."

"Let him call Heather. We can work this out," Dan said.

"Nothing is solved, the way you're handling it."

"Call Heather, Grant. Ask her to work for you."

"No," Lucy Spriggs said. She actually reached across the counter to restrain Grant Lopp, and in touching his silk sleeve she further set in ice the resolve of his decision. "What's it going to be, Grant?"

"Wait. Let's get Shawna and Dwayne up here. They should have a voice in this. Go get them, Grant."

Grant Lopp left his post. He disappeared into the labyrinth behind, his posture erect, his bearing unintimidated.

"Lucy, if you'd stayed out ten seconds more, this would be over."

"He throws a tantrum and gets a day off?" she said.

"The morgue would be open," Danny Fain said.

Grant Lopp returned, shepherding two blinking library aides from out of the rear dimness. They were Shawna and Dwayne, something of a team, working together by themselves in the quiet and privacy of the library. Today they had been putting back issues on microfiche. They ate lunch at their desks, giggling and talking in whispers. They both were forty years old.

Shawna asked, "What's this?"

"Are you members of the library union?" Lucy Spriggs asked.

They nodded. Dan noticed that Dwayne had a tattoo faded into a blue ink tracery on his right forearm. No reading the words.

Lucy continued, "Grant Lopp, as your union representative, has closed the morgue to other *Bugle* personnel. He has, in effect, gone on strike. He has done this in his role of union representative, and consequently, he has taken you on strike, too. Are you aware of what he has done?"

Shawna and Dwayne shook their heads. They looked bewildered. The word *strike,* affixed in a sentence containing references to themselves, made them nervous.

"Grant Lopp did not discuss this action with you?"

"Lopp never said *Boo!* to us," Shawna revealed. "I don't want anything to do with a strike."

"Me neither," agreed Dwayne. "We never voted on a strike, Lopp."

"They don't even know the paper is closing," Grant Lopp said with cruel disdain.

"The paper's closing?" Shawna said. They reminded Danny Fain of two people working deep in a paper-insulated cave when the world ended, and they emerged blinking in the light at the end of their shift, a trifle confused.

"Yes," Grant Lopp said. "No warning. Not even an official announcement to the employees. Just tell a few bosses, let them spread the word. But they didn't think enough of you to tell you to your face." He had turned the meeting into a campaign speech; he would by God convince these two people to support his cause, because they *were* the cause. "Don't you think that's something worth striking over?"

"Just a minute, Grant," Lucy Spriggs said. "Shawna. Dwayne. If you join Grant in this action you will be—like Grant—escorted from the building and fired. You will lose any and all severance due you under the terms of the paper's closing."

"Fired?" Shawna said. "What kinda shit are you pulling, Lopp? I'm not striking and I'm not going to get fired. Come on, Dwayne." They disappeared into the back.

"You appear to be alone in this action, Grant."

Reporters antsy for their clips had pushed into the room, Bernie DeVille in the lead. Grant Lopp was so good at his job that he could give them all what they had requested in a half hour; that was why he was there by himself with just two aides for the drone work. He had gently nudged the request tray to the far edge of the counter so that with Lucy Spriggs's final observation he gave the tray a last push and it fell off, flipping once in the air and sending request slips in a thick snow to the floor. Dan slapped his brow. Lucy ordered the Security guards to escort Grant Lopp from the building. Mutt and Jeff stepped forward, excited by the possibility of *real* action. Grant Lopp saw them coming, glanced at the locked door beside the counter, and something flickered in his eyes. He unlocked the door.

"Danny," he said. "The library is open. I withdraw my strike threat. I am . . ." He paused, racing through his options. He took a step away, two steps, down the hall where Shawna and Dwayne had disappeared. "I am open . . . but unfortunately I will be busy all day filing back issues for future reference. You have complete access to the library. But I warn you—you will be in violation of the International Alliance of Librarians and Data Processing Clerks if you come through that door."

Dan said, "Grant, don't be a prick about this."

"You can't fire me," he shouted from the darkness of the maze. "I'm performing library duties."

"Your duty is to be of service to the staff."

"I am."

Bernie DeVille and the other reporters looked at Lucy Spriggs, at each other. The Security guys were dismissed.

"A nice ploy," she muttered to Danny. "You want to break the plane?"

Dan opened the door. "Hell, it ain't radioactive," he said, and he stepped through. Others followed, but they were soon at a loss where to go. St. Tommy would have been proud; he had made something special and arcane of a procedure that was based primarily on the alphabet, and now the reporters and editors who had been denied the secret had no idea where to begin. Dan conducted a tour for a pack of them, pointing out the clip files and the microfilm machines, and explaining how the Elecompack worked. The reporters dropped out of the tour when they reached the clip files. They were anxious having one strut of their support system cut out from under them. Reporters were accustomed to getting what they wanted when they wanted it. Their job was to ask questions, hone their cynicism, be persistent, and try to put into words the gleanings from a day of that posture, preferably before the deadline passed. Hunting for old clippings silky at the folds was too much like being a file clerk. They snapped at each other, the carcass thinning out, everyone desperate for some foothold on the shivering ground.

In the privacy of old pictures, Danny Fain hunted for a photograph of William O'Berry, Abe Skinback, maybe even the woman Abe had stolen. The first folder he found was an inch thick, thumb-smudged, sign of a frequent user. It was ABE SKINBACK 1935–60 W/CELEBRITIES. Dan held the file to his chest and flipped through the pictures. Abe had not been handsome in his day; his nose was gargantuan, his mouth big-lipped and ravenous, his eyes a hair too small. But he had the light of power in his countenance, that twinkle of possessing greedily something other people could only dream about. The pics were mostly of Abe with women Dan didn't recognize. They had the hatched look of actresses, starlets, little twitches who had ridden the rails into Chicago to be seen with the legendary starmaker Abe Skinback, king of the schmoozes. Abe was willing, his knowing look shaded beneath his balcony brows. Fingers full of rings, he clutched his noxious cigar. Dan could assess the popularity of the women by where the photograph was taken. Shot at the train station, then Abe had gone to them, met them halfway in a courteous exchange of power. Pictures of Abe with Ava Gardner, Lucille Ball, Marilyn Monroe, each looking thrilled to be arm in arm with Abe Skinback, each undoubtedly on the next train out. The unknowns were snapped in Abe's office, on the edge of his desk or side by side on his sofa, Abe barely maintaining concentration long enough to look interested when the shutter opened. Women hot to be stars were willing to make a pilgrimage to be seen on Abe's arm. Dan was curious about the moments immediately following these poses. Did the women shrink away in disgust, the effect Abe had on his assistants lately? Did they shun him as a rube because he was merely from Chicago, not New York or L.A.? Did he hit on them, seduce them, misread his power as something greater than the ability to put names in newsprint in a glorifying context? And now Abe no longer came into the office. He was a rather slimy rumor to people with less than four years' time in at the paper.

Grant Lopp appeared at the end of the aisle. He pressed a button and the light went out. Irritated, Danny Fain put the Skinback file away.

"It didn't have to come to this," he said.

The librarian stepped out of sight and a moment later the two canyon walls of photographs lurched an inch in toward Dan, who yelled and jumped clear. The encroaching files squeezed his shoulders as he exited.

"Grant! Are you trying to crush me?"

Grant Lopp asked, "Is that an oblique way of asking if I have a crush on you?"

"No, it's not."

"It's exciting having strangers back here. It quickens the air."

"Are you ready to go back to work?"

"I've never stopped working," Grant said. "We're *so* far behind. I never noticed that when I spent all my time helping people like you."

"I need to find an old photo of Bill O'Berry and Abe Skinback. Can you help me?"

"For you, Danny, anything."

Returning to his office, Danny Fain discovered a man in blue coveralls at work. He was taking dimensions. He measured the width of one window, then the height. He was making a sketch of the office and as he measured something he added it to the sketch, including its dimensions. The desk was already drawn, the floor, the window facing the newsroom, the coat tree. He drew three windows in the wall.

"Where are you from?" Dan asked.

"SalvageMasters."

"What's to be salvaged?"

"Blinds. Glass. Tile. The desk. The file cabinets. The phone. The TV."

"The TV is mine," Danny said.

"Glad you told me." He took a roll of stickers from his pocket. Black block P's on signal orange. He slapped one on the TV screen. "Personal property stickers, for the movers," he said. "Anything else?"

"Hell, I don't know. I have to work here another two weeks. Ask me then."

The man shrugged. "We're just the advance team. We need to get a picture of what we're dealing with. The building is a classic of mid–nineteen fifties pretechno-era architecture. It's a white elephant. A museum piece. We should just lock it up and start the tours. Didn't you get headaches working here?"

Dan tried to remember. He had headaches in the morning, in the evening. They arrived, they departed. He rarely gave them a thought.

"You've got a fairly unantiquated computer system sitting on a thirty-year-old desk," the man said. "There's no desk-chair-console balance. The technologies are unparallel. It's like giving a cave man a typewriter, then he uses a rock for a desk. You have eyestrain, headaches, back pain, diminished sex drive. They're doing you a favor, closing this place."

He swung his tape measure around, checking the height of the room in the southeast corner.

"I don't have a diminished sex drive," Danny Fain said.

"How do you know? You get older, you think about it less often. You assume it's because you're getting older. But it's probably this office. These conditions wear you down. The light. The air. The strain of sitting all day in chairs ignorant of human physiognomy. The battering of the pulsating light from that screen. The blood vessels in your eyes contracting and expanding in time with that pulse. That's your migraine starter. That's your glaucoma inducer. You ever feel slightly off balance in this room?"

"Not noticeably."

"I ask, because either your floor or ceiling is tipped. There's a one and eleven-sixteenths inch difference in the height of the room from that corner to that corner. That's outside the parameters for ignoring the discrepancy. You've got casters on the chair, you've probably been unconsciously keeping yourself from rolling into the corner all day."

"I never noticed," Dan said.

"Your body—your *system*—noticed. Look at the black dust caked on that air vent. Do you think it comes out and just sits there? This office has *barely* minimal standards of airflow from border to border. You've got air in here that came in when they built the place. You get a lot of bronchial infections?"

"Not that I noticed."

"You're the exception, then. Staffwide, you show twenty-seven percent more throat and lung complaints that result in loss of work than the next highest corporation we've cleaned up after, which happened to manufacture typewriter ribbons. There are *factories* with cleaner air than you have here."

"The pay is good," Danny said.

The man accepted the point reluctantly. "OK. But what's money to a curved spine? To disintegrating lungs?"

"Money is everything," Dan said, "when it's about to be cut off."

"I understand. Believe me. The only offices we go into are doomed. Last year, we're doing a savings and loan. Customers are lined up at the teller windows. All the tellers are crying. We're taking our specs in the reception area. The girl on the phone has nice legs. An ankle bracelet. She's in tears. All of a sudden we hear *Ka-boom!* then another *Ka-boom!* a second later. My first thought is someone just shot himself, then the echo. But no—the president and vice-president shot themselves at practically the same time in different offices. Blood everywhere. A genuine Constable, probably worth more than all the money in the vault, has *bits* of the president all over it. Everyone rushes to see—but I watch one of the tellers and she's hanging back stuffing cash into her purse. I had to report her. But those other two? Were they better off? They'll never know. A year from today—next Halloween?—you'll look up from your new desk and you'll be hard-pressed to remember this day. This paper. The pain leaves. It wants to leave. We hold it longer than we mean to."

"Are you finished?" Danny Fain asked.

"With this office, yes. Could you step outside for a moment? I need to get a picture."

From a canvas gear bag on the floor he took a 35-mm camera

and a folder that reminded Danny Fain of a baseball scorer's book. The book had four sections, side by side, each section containing the numbers 0 through 9. He flipped the numbers until they read 0401, Dan's office number. He propped the numbers on the desk and took a picture of the room. He turned the book around and shot the office from the opposite side. He tore his sketch from his pad and put it in an envelope with others like it. "That's that," he said, shaking Dan's hand.

"What happens next?"

"We'll be here the next couple days. Very unobtrusively taking measurements," the man said. "A day or so after the paper closes, the main team will arrive and take the building down. Screw by screw. Somewhere there's a market for everything. The materials in this building are prime. You've got fifty miles of glass. Twenty-five acres of tile and carpet. Marble. Industrial diamonds. A nice computer system. A fortune in office furniture. Stationery to be recycled. Newsprint you won't get to. Pens. Pencils. Paper clips. Carbon paper. School districts lap up stuff like that. A library full of reference works. In six months, come by here. The building will be gone clean. Like organisms ate it. Like molecules dispersing."

Danny sat at his desk. For the first time he felt the pull of the lower corner. Doug Watts came to his door with a question about a story and while Dan called the story up on his tube and tried to cut through Watts's peculiarly uninteresting style, he felt his calf muscles tightening against the floor's backward tug. A small cramp grew behind his knee. Watts stood too close for Danny's taste; somewhere in his upbringing he had missed the concept of personal space.

"You need to get hold of the woman," Danny Fain suggested. "As it is, you only have the store manager's side."

"She won't answer the phone."

"Go to her house."

"She lives in Robert Taylor. On the seventh floor."

Dan pushed away from the computer. He was freshly conscious of the computer's beating light. The SalvageMaster had infected him with information. The maneuver also forced Doug Watts to retreat. He backed around Dan's desk. A warm lunchtime sun sparkled off the river. Danny said, "So go to Robert Taylor. To the seventh floor."

"I'll have to climb the stairs. And who knows what can happen on those stairs?" Genuine fear was in Doug Watts's eyes. He had taken a tip call, hoping for a story that would drop comfortably into his lap, and now he was being asked to venture into as close to a war zone as existed in the city. "I can't go there, Danny," he said. "A year ago, with my future bright, I would have. But if we're dead anyway . . . I don't see the point in physical peril."

"You've only got half a story, Doug. You need her side. From what I've read, her side is likely the best side."

But there would be no budging Doug Watts by calling to his journalistic conscience. He was what Lucy Spriggs called "a minimalist," because he brought minimal enthusiasm, effort, and ability to each day's work; it was why his wife left. Nor was he alone. A nest of them had desks in one corner. They never made the others uncomfortable with a display of initiative.

"Does she work, Doug?"

"She cleans houses in Winnetka. Her employers pay for a cab to the first bus stop inside the city limits. But I don't have any phone numbers."

"Are they working this story across the street?"

"I don't know."

"Have you been talking this up socially?"

Doug Watts squinted into the light outside Dan's windows, trying to remember what he could about his social life. He was a heavy hitter in the basement bar called Slugs, located equidistant between sewer and street, between *Bugle* and *Morning Quill,* a carved-out place frequented by reporters from both papers and flies from three summers ago. Danny Fain knew Doug Watts knew Dan knew that Doug could never keep his mouth shut about anything he was working on. Especially a tipped-in story with some fizz.

Doug Watts was honest, at least. "There's a chance I might have let something slip," he said.

"Who're you drinking with these days?"

"From the *Quill*? Teddy Neal. Ralph Blanchette. GAs."

"You find them buying you drinks?"

"No. None of that goes on. We're off duty over there."

"Those guys will take the stairs to the seventh floor of Robert Taylor," Dan said.

"They'll have a job in two weeks, too."

"You have a job now."

Doug Watts shrugged and departed, but Danny Fain called him back. He pointed to the story on the screen. "Get to the point faster, Doug. Your usual smokescreen is advertising the fact you only have half a story here." He punched a key and the story vanished. "And Doug? Your future was never bright here."

Someone came out of the TV lounge and shouted, "We're on!"

Work stopped. Everyone leaped away from their desks and crowded into a small area off the newsroom, where three TVs with ribbony color pictures were used to monitor the news. All were tuned to Channel Eight, the only station with an 11:30 A.M. newscast. A commercial for pantyhose was running. A clerk reported, "They teased us going into the commercial. We're after this."

The room was filling up, people climbing onto tables in the rear, shouting to turn up the volume. Through the glass of Derringer's office they saw him with his back to the gathering, his own TV tuned to Channel Eight.

Larry Mock was present. Lucy Spriggs stood beside him and whispered in his ear. More fiscal strategies. More doomed plans. Dan examined his own situation. The exact numbers eluded his memory; he had only to call Rita to be filled in. But he was scared all over again. It was being in that pack. He had started to forget a little in the course of the day's work. But now the air was getting warm, the words angry, and when he didn't think anyone else could fit in the TV lounge another dozen people arrived and found places. So many people stood on desks or sat on file cabinets that the room's occupants seemed to exist on two levels, like floors of a department store. This was a mistake, Danny Fain thought. He should have stayed in his office and watched it there. When this was over the staff would require an hour just to get calmed down again.

They were also about to have their futures validated. Prior to this the closing had been only a terse announcement, a passed sentence, something hardly more substantial than a rumor. In a moment it would take on the permanence of television. A half million people might hear the news with them, then that half million people would turn away to something else, the information stored, the *Bugle* staff left to deal with the consequences of that information.

A Maytag ad came to an end. The news returned. Silence fell in the packed lounge. The anchor was an Oriental woman, her beautiful features like little paint marks on porcelain, her eyes huge, luminous black almonds. She read a story about something Dan didn't catch, then a replica of the *Bugle* logo appeared over her shoulder. Someone hissed down front. A nervous laugh rippled across the room, then died. Someone with a remote control device kicked the volume up nearly to a scream. The anchor read a terse lead-in, the simple fact that the number-two paper in a two-paper town was closing, and then Derringer's big, soft head filled the screen. Hissing intensified. The TV lights made him wince, gave his skin a mashed-potato pallor. His eyes were tiny, wary, cornered. The knot in his fall-back tie was crooked. People in the lounge muttered *asshole, buttwipe, flea-condom, motherfucker.* Strangely, no one paid much attention to what Derringer was saying. They had developed the habit of not paying attention to him in the course of their work, and now that reflex held even when he was uttering banalities about the death of their jobs. The ID that flashed on the screen beneath his muttering mug misspelled his name—*WALTER DARRINGER*—and the seething crowd in the lounge heard the man himself sputter, "Goddammit!" at the mistake; or possibly at the use of Walter.

Then came footage from the newsroom: bowed heads diligently at work; Nancy Potter in her headphones, trying to type with a lens in her face; Goop Traky spitting eraser; a knot of reporters scattering at the camera's approach. Every shot contained a seedy light of failure, gave the impression that nothing of importance was being done there; all the calls were for the camera's benefit, the industrious looks just poses. If these people worked so hard, why were they losing their jobs?

Muff Greene appeared. The ID tag read *FLORENCE GREENE* and everyone laughed, but with a fond lilt. She had a good face for the camera; it conveyed her sadness, her loss. "I started at the *Bugle* twenty-one years ago as a beat reporter," Muff said. "I can remember talk of the paper closing even back then. We knew our position as the second paper in the city made us vulnerable to this. But we've put out a consistently good newspaper over the years—and I think our closing is more a reflection of the changing news habits of the population—less reading, less time to read, less willingness to look deep inside something, more TV—than of the journalistic abilities of this staff. The circulation of our final edition will be double what it was today—and that's to be expected. But if we're worthy of being a collector's item, then we're worthy of being kept in business."

Muff Greene disappeared. Bernie DeVille's face filled the screen. A groan erupted. Bernie, down front, sitting on the floor like a kid allowed to stay up for the late movie, laughed, leaned close to hear himself. *BERNARD DEVILLE, Writer,* the ID read. "I went through the closing of a paper in Philadelphia and one in St. Louis and the pain of the staff is always so much greater than the public's perception. These people have been robbed of their future. They came to work expecting to work and were told their work was no longer required. Yet they continue to work. I've never been prouder than I am of this staff."

A voice off-camera commanded Bernie DeVille to shut up

and he complied, vanishing, replaced by an old man's face, filmed at a different location, black wooden African fetish masks in the background.

"Who's that?"

The ID came up: *ABE SKINBACK, Columnist.*

"Jesus, he looks terrible."

His lips glistened as he spoke. His skin was a greyish beige, slack and pouchy. Smoke from his off-camera cigar curled into the picture. He growled, "I been doing this fifty-some years—and all of it at the *Bugle.* We're a family there. I feel for these young people with kids, houses. But personally I'm most worried about Abe Skinback. Is Abe Skinback finished in this business? I don't like to think so. I gotta lotta reporting to do. This is a terrible tragedy for all concerned."

"But especially for me," Dan finished, followed by a rolling laugh.

Rudy Vine was next. "This decision by management is a flop," Rudy said. "Box-office poison. You look at the product and you see the staff was let down. Look at the reproduction and you see we've needed new presses for twenty years. Why not make the commitment? We've kicked ass in this town with a staff that wouldn't fill the *Quill*'s lunchroom. Hire some reporters. Make the investment. You've gotta spend money to make money. No, they run things on the cheap, put money into cosmetics like painting the honor boxes, then do *that* halfway, and finally just quit. This is a disgrace."

Danny Fain appeared. He was on the phone in his office. His tag came up: *DANIEL FAIN, Associate Metro Editor.* He was talking to Dana Viola because he heard himself say, "I'm on TV." A pause followed while she made a suggestion and then his hand was rising toward the camera, his eyes betraying amusement, and there was his middle finger flying on camera. The TV lounge exploded with applause. He was pummeled on the back. Kissed on the cheek. He could not believe Dana had left that in; the story ended with that image. The room emptied, the air murmurous, people slapping Dan on the back. He remained to watch the newscast. Gretchen the copy clerk took a seat in front of the TVs and turned one to a soap opera. Danny awaited his story's appearance on the screen: a shot of the ghost, police filling the street, the hysterical mother. The anchor read through another story and then into a commercial. Gretchen stretched. Her shoes hung wobbling from the tips of her extended toes. Her breasts were squashed flat under her blouse by the long overhead reach of her arms. Did she think she was alone? Her eyes were closed, a slight smile on her lips. The news returned; Dan was relieved. The stories being run now had an unmistakable filler air, second-line features and pieces of lint that would be killed later. They would never hold a Halloween hit-and-run for such an inglorious position.

Dan left and took an elevator to the lunchroom. He bought a Butterfinger and a can of Diet Coke. Damian Drew was there, smoking a cigarette in a long black holder and reading the *Quill.* He was two years older than Dan, and he had started at the *Bugle* as a reporter under the name Dave Rockworthy. They put him on cops, then science, then general features, and in each new job an initial burst of enthusiasm and punctuality was followed by an equivalent decline in those qualities and every other quality that made a good reporter. Worse, he sulked. The *Bugle* had plenty of borderline talents who at least went through the pretense of being ashamed of their mistakes and who tried to rectify those errors in the future. Most didn't succeed, but they made the effort. Dave Rockworthy, upon being chastised for a missed deadline, a botched assignment, descended into a funk of such black impenetrability that he was volatile for the next forty-eight hours. However, this tactic worked. Nobody wanted anything to do with him; therefore his days were largely arranged on his schedule. He did what he wanted. If he turned in a usable story, fine. His supervising editor, spotting an opening in someone else's jurisdiction, was quick to push him in that direction. The other departments took him on because he had a suave, graceful appearance, he was witty, dressed nicely, and his reputation never went beyond the departments that knew about him. If word got out, no one would take him for transfer. So he was shunted into Sports for a year (the Sports Editor, Poof O'Bannon, had never forgiven the editor who lavishly recommended Drew) and then Sports managed to get him transferred to Financial. He might have died there at his Financial Department desk, or he might have finally been fired. No one had been fired from the *Bugle* editorial department in thirty years. The union grievance procedures made firing someone as drawn out and tedious a process as appealing a death sentence. It was easier to transfer the offender around in a form of rotating limbo. But Financial was the last virgin territory for Dave Rockworthy. He had worked everywhere else and nobody wanted him back. One morning, six weeks after Rockworthy had joined Financial in a vague capacity, millionaire financial adviser Lawrence K. Mock informed Financial Editor Jack Lustig that if Dave Rockworthy was staying, Lawrence K. Mock was leaving. Rockworthy had spent a week on the Financial copy desk and twice rewrote Mock's ledes, which were carefully sculpted and sacrosanct. Worse, he had changed some of Mock's figures in a column about computing tax-free bond yields and botched the final results. Mock spent a morning taking calls from angry and disappointed readers, and one from his gloating counterpart at the *Morning Quill.* He ordered his calls held and walked out of his office and directly to Lustig's desk. It was indicative of the true power in Financial that Lawrence K. Mock had the only office in the department, while Jack Lustig, his ostensible supervisor, worked at a desk out in the open like everyone else, with no view, no privacy, no personal sofa. If Lustig wanted to reprimand someone, he was forced to wait until Lawrence K. Mock was away. Mock, however, always pitched his fits in public, gesticulating like a maestro in front of Lustig's desk, his complaints filling the room. That the subject of his tirade was sitting six feet away did not diminish the intensity of Lawrence K. Mock's excoriation. Rockworthy's response was to be expected; his eyes shut down, his face clouded over. Lustig listened to Mock storm. He had to wait until Mock went to lunch before he could take Rockworthy into Mock's office and ream him. Rockworthy neither apologized nor admitted any wrongdoing. Jack Lustig made some calls from Mock's phone. He had accumulated some favors, but none so great that someone would be shamed into taking Dave Rockworthy off his hands. Lawrence K. Mock returned from lunch. He stood before Lustig's desk and asked loudly, "Is *he* still here?"

Three minutes before his deadline, Lawrence K. Mock emerged from his office to announce that he would not be writing a column that day. A little bug with his picture ran in the paper with the announcement that Lawrence K. Mock was taking the day off. It was a scramble to fill his space. Jack Lustig prayed that the situation would improve without action on his part, but when Lawrence K. Mock saw Dave Rockworthy at work the next morning he did not speak to anyone until he emerged at three minutes to deadline with word he again would not be writing a column that day. Jack Lustig took a shower with his wife that night. They shared a big snifter of cognac. He pulled at the damp roll-knot where her towel was fastened above her breasts. The phone rang beside their bed and his mood of recovery, of salvaging something from the day, was shattered. "Fuck," he muttered. It was a familiar voice, somehow, on the phone; a voice from work. The voice was distant, as if the caller were sitting across the room from the receiver. The caller made sure it was Jack Lustig on the line. He apologized for calling so late. He said he had heard the *Bugle* was planning to start an astrology column and he thought Jack Lustig might have someone who would be interested in the job. The line went dead. Jack Lustig returned to his wife with a new urgency, and a smile.

Thus was born Damian Drew. He was transferred out of Financial by lunchtime. An office was prepared for him, a closet hard to reach down twisting corridors. Damian Drew was given a tube and a handbook on astrology. He spent a week reading it, drinking coffee and smoking. One morning he was smoking with a long black cigarette holder. His left ear was pierced; a tiny gold crab dangled. He pomaded his hair to a sparkle, letting it grow until this oiled sheaf could be comfortably gathered into a ponytail and held in place with a Cancer barrette. He donned black clothes, grew a goatee, sharpened it to a point, kept his own counsel. He hung a poster—sexual positions of the zodiac—on the wall behind his head so women on their way past his office could peruse it. He bought more books, flasks and vials of spicy liquids, incense candles, charts and scrolls that he kept in a bookcase behind the door. His horoscopes began to appear in the paper. Some days they sounded awfully similar to the wire service horoscopes, but no one complained. Dave Rockworthy had been disposed of; he had vanished, become Damian Drew, and he now worked in a part of the paper where no one would be hurt or angered or offended by his forays into incompetence.

He went to the expense of having his name legally changed, then patented, and he formed a syndicate of one. When Danny Fain encountered him in the lunchroom Damian Drew had been the *Bugle*'s staff astrologer for two years and was well on his way to becoming a wealthy man. His horoscopes, it had developed, were so vague they made everyone happy with their equivocal prescience. His office walls had been corked over, the cork then papered with fan mail held up with Damian Drew Zodiac Pushpins. He was a big draw at summer fairs and horoscope confabs. His private readings commanded $100 a pop for fifteen minutes of attention. They stood in line for his view into the future.

"Pay no mind to all this talk of the paper closing," he confided to Dan, who saw only Dave Rockworthy, sulking bungler, beneath the jeweled obsidian gleam of Damian Drew.

"Why is that, Dave?"

"Because until ten o'clock tonight we're under a void-of-course moon," he said. "And we've been under it since six nineteen this morning. The moon is traveling from one sign to another—in this case from Pisces to Aries—but it's in neither one until ten. It's a rogue moon. It's free of restraints, and that attitude infects the workings of the world. Everyone is a little less inhibited. Willing to try something crazy. People start affairs. Quit their jobs in a burst of rebellion. Conceive a child they might not be able to afford. Stand up to someone who frightens them. Children born under a void-of-course moon are free-spirited, goofy, undisciplined, fun to be around, but failures. Nothing they ever do amounts to anything. It's a real curse, but they're too happy to notice. Then once the moon passes into the next sign, that sign takes over. The endeavors begun under the void-of-course moon are left behind. Men who abandoned their families realize their mistake. Affairs end in bewilderment. Why did we do this? A spur-of-the-moment marriage comes to its senses. A business that seemed so promising goes belly up. And . . . a business that was about to be closed is suddenly recognized as not being in such bad shape after all. Decisions are reassessed in a firmer light. Rules apply again. The world regains its equilibrium. So there is really nothing to worry about. Toward the end of the day the panic will subside. Events will begin to indicate the situation is not hopeless. And at ten o'clock—when the moon enters Aries—we'll be back in business."

Damian Drew smiled graciously, pleased with himself for giving a free reading. The stem of his cigarette holder was decorated with a circle of tiny gold zodiac symbols, and his name in gold cursive script ran the stem's length.

"Do you sell a lot of those, Dave?"

"The holders? Goodness, yes. About two cases a month. More if I can get a booth at a cat show somewhere," he said. "People crave glamor when they smoke. And they like to put some distance between themselves and their death. I get such letters. From all over. Everyone's afraid of the future. They want me to tell them what to expect. It's a terrible responsibility."

Danny Fain returned to the newsroom, where a fight had broken out. The combatants were Becky Fudge and Alexandra

Jones. One punch, of the two punches the fight would encompass, had been thrown. The subject was stolen stories. Alexandra Jones was nearly six feet tall, with an athlete's carriage and a stern posture that carried her above the grunting, roiling population beneath her. Her skin was glossily salon-tanned, with a dusty-pink cast where it was pulled taut over the satin-boned prominences of her face. Becky Fudge was a foot shorter, an amateur fencer, quick, slight, and aggressive. She had suspected Alexandra Jones of stealing her story ideas for about six months. Becky kept seeing stories she had been planning appear in the *Quill* and the *Bugle.* The stories were never exactly as she would have written them; they always possessed the dull undertone of an assigned piece, lacking the imagination to go to another level beneath the obvious surface, which a reporter hunting her own trail would have been excited to follow.

The thread of a story Becky Fudge planned about the boom in shopping mall valet parking ran in the *Bugle.* Nan Fullwood, still awaiting the first original thought of her reporting career, had been the writer. Becky took Nan aside, congratulated her on the story, then asked who had assigned it. Nan Fullwood smiled, blushed, inspected their immediate surroundings. She had stolen it from a *Quill* reporter who had been complaining about it at Slugs, one booth over from Nan. The story was thin because Nan Fullwood had rushed it in to beat the *Morning Quill,* which never ran the story, though there were rumors the article was written and budgeted when the *Bugle* article appeared. Becky tried to follow the tip back through the *Quill*'s hierarchy, but she did not know anyone over there well enough to make any progress. She distinctly remembered writing MALL VALET PARKING on a glue-edged memo slip. But her desk was a paper storm awaiting the proper wind and the slip was lost in a day. She expected to find it eventually, like a fresh idea hitched remoralike to the bottom of something else. It might have escaped from the building stuck to the bottom of a shoe. She believed Nan's explanation about overhearing the

Quill reporter; Nan was as incapable of brewing up a scheme to mask a stolen idea as she was of coming up with the idea.

Soon after, Becky Fudge was working late when her tube broke down. As hard as she banged on the keyboard nothing moved on the screen. A letter to her mother in Sarasota was frozen there, a testimony to company time wasted. She made a call to tech services, then moved to Alexandra Jones's desk. Becky signed on and called up her letter to her mother, but as far as the computer knew the letter was still active on the dead tube. Becky was denied entry. She yelled, "Shit!" The few people in the room, the copy desk, the night-shiftlings with their cool disinterest in daylight individuals, were not curious enough to look at her. A janitor pushing a large gray trash cart came to the end of her aisle and began emptying wastebaskets. He emptied CooCoo Tweeble's, then Les Burkin's, then her own, then Alexandra Jones's. He was an older man who spoke no English but he tipped Becky Fudge his imaginary cap. She smiled at him and he slid Alexandra's wastebasket under her desk so recklessly it clonked Becky in the shin. She winced, waved him off. She glanced down and there was her mall valet parking memo at the bottom of Alexandra Jones's wastebasket. It was stuck, idea up, by the strip of glue on the back. She peeled it off and held it close to her eyes. Nothing else had been written on it. Bits of dirt and hair adhered to the glue. But did being in Alexandra Jones's wastebasket mean Alexandra had put it there? A young guy with a magnetic screwdriver arrived from tech services. He worked at the back of her tube and whistled. His hair was shaved down at the sides of his head and beauty marks like ovals of walnut ink were visible through his burred hair. The letter to her mother disappeared; gone out into the world like electricity. She hadn't stored the letter; it never existed. The kid touched keys. Nothing happened.

"It's locked," he said. He unplugged the keyboard and took it away.

She wrote a bogus story idea on a gummed memo: TV DAY CARE. Vague enough to mean almost anything. The slip remained stuck to her tube for two weeks before the *Morning Quill* ran a story about mothers' increasing willingness to use television to occupy their children. The story was skimpy, one-sourced, and written with the bored, condescending outrage of someone who did not share the passion.

So she was dealing not only with a story thief, but also a spy. They were known to exist. A network of rumors had attended the hiring of two prominent *Morning Quill* writers—a reporter, Duke Bowman, and a high-gloss gossip columnist, Trish MacKerrel—by the *Bugle.* The move was for money, it was explained. They gave the *Bugle* an alleged implied prestige. They arrived together, had adjoining offices, unpacked from the same boxes. They spent a lot of time on the phone with each other. In two years at the *Bugle* they produced such a mudslide of trivial stories, inaccurate stories, just plain damn stupid stories, and stories so libelous they engendered four separate lawsuits against the paper, that the staff came to suspect they were *Quill* plants sent to undermine the *Bugle.* Reportedly they continued to draw their salaries from the *Quill,* like combat pay, even as the *Bugle* paid them more than anyone on the staff except Rudy Vine and Lawrence K. Mock.

After two years, on the same day, they resigned. Trish MacKerrel stayed at home to have a baby. Duke Bowman went to New York for six months to work on a book that was reportedly two good drafts away from having a hope of being published, and then he returned to the *Quill* in an editor's capacity; nobody knew exactly his duties, only that he was highly regarded as a man who had come safely through a dangerous mission. The *Bugle* settled two of the lawsuits his slipshod work had engendered for a little less than a million dollars. The other two refused to settle and were out for blood, so randomly and viciously had Bowman defiled them. Now the *Bugle* was closing; in some way, Duke Bowman and Trish MacKerrel seemed to have succeeded.

The second punch of the fight was thrown a moment after Danny Fain arrived. Becky Fudge threw it, aiming for Alexandra Jones's high, arrogant face, but she was fast and ready and drew her head back like a boxer. Becky's fist whistled under her chin.

"Who did you give stories to over there?" Becky Fudge asked. A dark spot was rising on her neck. "Did they pay you in money or promises?"

Alexandra Jones did not respond. She sat at her desk and picked up the phone. Becky Fudge displayed that morning's *Quill.*

"Look at this," she said to Dan. The headline, below the fold on Page One, read HOOK FACES TAX INVESTIGATION. "This is *my* story. Look. Here." She typed furiously on her keyboard. She called up HOOK00. A story appeared.

"See? My notes. My calls. My numbers. My dates. I've been working this on the sly for six months. I know a guy at the U.S. attorney's office. I kept in touch. I made him trust me."

Alexandra Jones, on the phone, put a hand over the receiver. "You mean you blew him full of gratitude."

"Fuck you," hissed Becky Fudge. An eager gathering of reporters laughed, reveling in this sordid crumbling of their world. "This guy told me Hook was in trouble," Becky Fudge continued. "Hook hadn't filed a tax return since 1980. He owed nearly two million in back taxes and interest. A grand jury was expected to be called. When they were called, he would give me the story. He calls yesterday at lunchtime, I'm out, he leaves a message. The girl who took the call swears she put the message on my tube. I never got it. Then this story runs. I called my guy this morning, pissed as hell. I want to know why my story showed up in the *Quill. He's* as surprised as me. He said he talked to me yesterday, gave me all the particulars on the Hook grand jury. I told him I never called. He told me I had returned his call—and I said, 'What call?'—and he said he left a message for me to call him. Now lightbulbs are going off above my head. Someone called him, said she was me, what did he have for me? He gave that person the news, then he said he was surprised because he had to run down a lot of the little details of the story—he thought I understood it better—and the caller said she was sorry, she had a million things going on. My guess is Jones here tipped her link at the *Quill,* who in turn had someone there call pretending to be me. I called Diana Pocketta, whose byline is on the story and who also is a friend, and she said she simply rewrote from a phantom, but very comprehensive, file of notes that was sent to her without any explanation, only an order to write the story."

Danny turned to Alexandra Jones. She was chewing a painted nail, unperturbed, on hold. "Any truth to this, Alexandra?" he asked.

She blinked once, heavy-lidded with disdain. "I'm on the phone here, Dan." Her legs stretched under her desk and out the other side, long-muscled, her insteps pale where they arched up above the rim of her shoes.

"I need to get an answer, Alexandra."

She tucked the mouthpiece under her chin. "If there was any truth to it—and I'm admitting nothing—would it make any difference now?"

"It will always make a difference. It's aiding the enemy."

"It's treason," Becky Fudge interjected.

"If I were going to steal stories, would I steal from Fudge? She hasn't had a decent story in months."

"Because you keep ripping me off and selling my ideas across the street," Becky Fudge shrieked. "If I have a good idea, in three days it's in the *Quill*—poorly done."

"You're crazy, Fudgepack. I can't read your mind . . . although it wouldn't take long if I could."

"You can read notes. I take a lot of notes," Becky Fudge said. She shrugged. "My memory isn't the greatest so I take a lot of notes. You hang around my desk long enough, you see my password. You might be logged on as me right now."

Dan watched Alexandra Jones's eyes glance at her screen. Becky Fudge smiled wanly. Her points made, her job gone, she was content to let Alexandra Jones off as merely defective, someone to avoid in the future. Becky Fudge was a good reporter with solid, major metro experience, and she was female. She would be employed elsewhere within a month of seeking a new job.

Alexandra Jones's call went through. "It's me. I'm done here," she said. "I can't talk, but I'm done." She closed her eyes, listening. She exhaled a breath around the finger she was nibbling. The quiet surrounding her had radiated through the room, down the hall, out the windows. Everyone was listening. She nodded, smiling, hearing what she wanted to hear. "That sounds good. I know. I can't talk. But I was worried, yes. That's good news. Believe me. I really can't talk. I'm right here. I'm done. Good-bye." She put down the phone. She smiled at Danny Fain. "Anything else?"

"Just an answer."

"I've given you an answer."

She ducked under her desk, pulled out a canvas tote bag with worn leather handles. She scraped personal belongings off her desk and into the bag: dictionary, Rolodex, pictures, a thesaurus, a cactus, a paperweight, a coffee mug.

"We've got a paper to put out," Dan said.

"I resign."

"You just got a new job over there, didn't you?" Becky Fudge demanded.

"Fuck off," Alexandra Jones snarled.

"Shit, you've been feeding stories to them—and now you're done, so you're leaving?"

Alexandra Jones did not respond. She went through her drawers, rifling supplies, leaving her notes behind. The knot of witnesses had grown. Their air was now dangerous, aggressive, Becky Fudge's charges making sense to them. Bad news, scandal, hints of deceit, they traveled through a newsroom like electricity through bathwater: unimpeded and joyous. The people in that room loved bad news; someone else's preferably, their own if necessary, and here they had a spy in their midst gathering up her code books and her magnifying glass to catch the last train back before the border closed. Alexandra Jones had to reach between Goop Traky and Les Burkin to retrieve her coat from the tree. It was a burgundy, down-filled coat, calf-length, very warm; the coat hissed when she put it on.

"Are you going to the *Quill*, Alexandra?" Dan asked, trying to keep his voice from carrying to the back edge of the gathering.

Like a fist tightening, the staff pressed in for an answer. Danny saw latecomers from Sports, from Financial, up on their toes to get a look at the carnage. Dan realized he would have to escort Alexandra Jones out of the building.

"I'm leaving now," she said.

"Let me walk you." He turned toward the door. He saw it way over there beyond some thirty confused and angry people. He felt Alexandra Jones tuck in behind him like a car following a snowplow. "Coming through now," Danny said.

Bernie DeVille was in his face, then he wasn't. He leaned out to the side and spat once, a thin string that arched over Danny Fain's shoulder and into Alexandra Jones's hair. It hung there like a bauble, the tail end adhering to Dan's shoulder, tethering him to Alexandra in a shameful way. "*Bernie!*" Dan cried. He pushed him aside. Alexandra Jones clawed at the mess in her hair. Another wet glob came from somewhere, landed, and she screamed. Next fell a shower of pencil shavings, a filthy cloud of powdered graphite that made Alexandra Jones cough. Another disembodied hand poked through the knot of people to pour cold coffee on Alexandra Jones. A pattern, an etiquette, was established. Women threw things. From men came projectiles of spit—some clear, some phlegmy, some with tobacco bits—raining on Alexandra Jones, who was screaming as if she believed the pain she would inflict on her tormentors' ears would drive them back. Danny realized she had hold of his hand, squeezing him with such fervor he tried to run. He saw friends, colleagues, women he had loved from afar, come before him and spit or slap or throw something convenient at Alexandra Jones and then fall away to the side as he battled through them. Lucy Spriggs waited by the door. Her face was stricken. She alone seemed aware of him; everyone else had eyes only for Alexandra Jones, whose hair and face and back were filthy with expectorant, coffee, ashes, waste. She continued to scream. Some of her attackers were pushing through the door ahead of her, seeking the space provided by the empty hallway to re-form the gauntlet, to get punching room, to really let go on her. Danny Fain had seen the doorway as a goal, beyond which was safety, but once they had burst through he saw fresh faces drawn to the slaughter. It was a mile to the elevator.

Puncher Mudd, immense, drunk, the eyes of a sad boy lost in his fat face, blocked the way down the hall. The mob bunched up behind Dan and Alexandra, who were stalled by Mudd's bulked plug and surprising agility. He danced into their path each time they tried to go around. Dan estimated Puncher's weight at three hundred pounds, a weight made volatile with beer and the day's spirit of anarchy.

"Come on, Punch," he said. "Let us through."

"You gonna fire me?"

"No, Punch. Let us through, please."

"She fed 'em stories. She helped kill us," he declared.

"Maybe. But it's only a newspaper. She's got twenty pounds of spit and crap in her hair. She's been punished enough."

"No, she hasn't."

"You can't hang her. Let her go."

Alexandra Jones was whimpering, her wet face pushed into the hollow between Danny's shoulder blades. The mob had settled down; like true newspapermen and women they had stopped their yelling and pushing to eavesdrop on the debate, to listen for the telling quote. Dan realized Puncher Mudd was showing off for the News staff, which treated the Sports side with contempt. Puncher brought a hand up from behind him, something held in it flashing dark. Dan moved to protect Alexandra, but Mudd's quickness of hand pushed a beer bottle past Danny's shoulder and poured a quantity of foaming Budweiser over Alexandra Jones's spit-slippery hair. "Put a little head on that head," Puncher Mudd guffawed.

Then he leaped aside like a ballerina and the path was clear.

Danny Fain hurried with Alexandra Jones down the long hallway toward the elevator. The mob, his coworkers, stayed behind. They had extracted what they needed from Alexandra Jones. She was wet, disheveled, disgraced, whimpering. She would not be able to walk immediately over to the *Morning Quill* and begin work. Perhaps they hadn't instilled shame in her soul, but at least they had forced her to go home and change her clothes. At the end of the hall, by the doors out to the elevator foyer, Dan stopped and looked back. The hall was empty. He could hear Puncher Mudd's drunken chuckle, then the plastic rattle of someone typing on a tube.

"Let me go in here," Alexandra Jones said. She veered into a women's restroom. Dan glimpsed a sofa, a pot of coffee, a full-length mirror. People came off the elevator. He was given strange looks, there was dampness at his shoulders and errant diamonds of spit in his hair. Wet ash and pencil lead had left dark dots across his shoulders. He went into the men's room, soaked paper towels, and wiped them over his hair and his shoulders. He washed his face and hands, retied his tie, tucked in his shirt, combed his hair. Derringer came out from one of the stalls. He blinked in the light, looking sleepy, the *Quill*'s sports section folded under his arm.

"What was all that yelling?" he asked.

"Alexandra Jones leaving. She quit."

"What's the rush?"

"We'll see more and more of that in the next few days."

Derringer shrugged. "Let 'em all leave." He began the long, fondling process of tucking in his shirt. Danny Fain said, "Later," and departed.

A group of people were coming down the hall on their way to lunch. Another knot, six or eight strong, followed a half-dozen yards behind, and Alexandra Jones emerged from the washroom into this cluster, this sudden mob, squeezed all over again by people who regarded her with disgust. Dan was nervous seeing her isolated in that crowd of his associates, her eyes abjectly searching for his protection. The group came toward him as if bearing Alexandra Jones along and when they passed an alcove leading to a door off the hall the people at the head of the group looked into the alcove and laughed, startled. Alexandra Jones did not notice; she had her head down, counting steps until her release. The witch doctor lurked. Danny Fain saw him, yelled a warning to Alexandra Jones, but she was stupefied. The masked figure with his baby rattle tucked in his waistband leaped toward her from the alcove, people giving him room. His X-acto sparkled. He reached with his free hand toward the freshly brushed and bundled hair hanging against Alexandra's back, about a foot of blond wire that reflected gleaming in the falling blade, and he clutched this hair and pulled it taut, yanking back Alexandra's head so that she screamed again, her eyes ripped wide open, her throat long and clean and beautifully veined. Danny Fain expected to see the petite triangular knife pass across this exposed target, leaving a thread of blood behind. But the witch doctor sliced only once, twice at the hair and it was free in his hand. He ran the blade once more lightly down Alexandra Jones's back, goring the coat so that it spilled its fluffy innards in a torrent, then he was pushing through the crowd with his trophy, making no sound.

The witch doctor wanted to leave now. Danny feinted, reached for him, and the blade came up in a reflex of protection, the tip passing into his forearm, through a half inch of flesh, then out again. Danny Fain cried, "Gah!" Blood rolled from his arm and into the carpet. He hoped to leave a stain. Derringer came out of the bathroom.

"*You!*" he shouted at the witch doctor. And though he put a hand over his chest, the knife was quicker, and Derringer's fallback tie was sliced off as the witch doctor passed, a wiping of Dan's blood left on Derringer's shirt. The witch doctor burst through the doors, then down the fire stairs.

A butterfly bandage closed up Danny Fain's arm. He was given small red pills for the sting. When he returned from the nurse he shut himself in his office. Derringer wandered around without a tie; he had no second fallback. Under what circumstances would he possibly need three ties in one day? He couldn't think of one, none existed, and now he was tieless on the one day the media would be interested in him. Regrettably, both cuts had been made too close to the knots. A little more tail and he could have worn the remains as long as they were within the dimensions of the TV camera frame.

Danny Fain had no fallback shirt. His sleeve was stiff, meat-brown, where the blood had touched. His forearm was wrapped thick with chalky gauze, like a new muscle. He rolled his sleeves up over his biceps. He felt like a punk, but the bloodstain was hidden under successive foldings of the shirt. He sat with his back to the newsroom and tears in his eyes. Though work went on behind him he felt the paper had officially died when the staff defiled Alexandra Jones.

He called his wife. He said hello, looking forward to telling the story with witty embellishments, to having a fuss made over him. But Rita easily contained her enthusiasm about hearing from him.

"I saw you on TV. Did you have to make that disgusting gesture?"

"I didn't think they would use it."

"You shouldn't have done it regardless. It was crude and embarrassing. What if my mother had been watching? What if one of the kids saw you?"

"I'm sorry. I was on the phone with Dana Viola, it was her cameraman, she told me to do it."

"*The* Dana Viola?"

"Yes."

"You do everything she tells you to do?"

"I wanted to get rid of the guy. She said to give him the finger, he would leave. Then she used it."

"Jesus, you're so naive," Rita said. "She just wanted something to put on TV. She doesn't care about you."

"They won't use it at ten. The audience is too big."

"For your sake, they better not. I don't sleep with crude men."

Danny laughed, feeling the situation come around, hearing his wife warm to him.

"Why were you talking to Dana Viola?"

"I called her about the kid getting hit. To see if they had it."

"Did they?"

"No. But my call tipped her to the existence of it, and she'll get it if she has enough time."

"Are you having lunch with her?"

Dan laughed. "No. It was a business call."

"It had better be, Buster. I've seen you with her. You're all dick, no brains. Your groin glows."

Danny Fain said, "Rita!"

"Why are you still at work? Why aren't you home tending to someone who really wants you?"

"I got stabbed today."

"*What?*"

"We caught a reporter who was passing stories to the *Quill*. Evidently she had been doing this for quite some time. She'll probably be working there tomorrow while the rest of us scramble for jobs."

"Forget that. Tell me about the stabbing."

"Well, they caught her, or Becky Fudge accused her, and the evidence was conclusive enough to convict her in the eyes of the staff. They started to spit on her, throw things on her—and on me. It was horrible. I was trying to get her out of there. Out in the hall we ran into this fat ass from Sports and *he* poured beer on her head. That seemed to satisfy everyone. Alexandra—the reporter—went into the washroom to dry off. I went into the men's room to dry off."

"When did you get *stabbed*?"

"I'm getting to that. Don't you want the context?"

"Jesus. It's like you said, 'Honey, I got shot today.' Then you start with, 'Well, they manufactured this gun in nineteen eighty-four and since then this person and that person have owned it. . . .' Just tell me about the stabbing."

"OK. I come out of the washroom. A bunch of people are

coming down the hall. Alexandra Jones is with them. This guy in a witch doctor's mask with an X-acto knife jumps out of a doorway and slices off a bunch of her hair. So he's got this clump of hair. He wants to escape. He runs down the hall toward me. I make a move toward him and he just brings the blade up. It goes into my arm. I don't think it was intentional. So I'm OK."

"Did you get a tetanus shot?"

"No. It wasn't a rusty blade."

"You come home *right* now. That's an order."

The prospect was appealing. His arm ached. He had ample excuse to check out early. But he also had Tim Penn loose in the field and no one to guide him or call him back. Tim Penn wasn't the type to stay out all night until told otherwise, but he had a reporter's lechery for a good story, and he would expect Dan to work with him. Also, the ghost was out there somewhere. Maybe he was expected home from school for lunch, and was late, and now his mother was at the window watching the street for him. The first filaments of dread would be affixing themselves to her heart. Her first worried call would go out to the police. "I can't come home just yet, Rita," Danny said. "The arm doesn't hurt too much. I've got work to do."

"What a sap," she declared, and hung up.

Lucy Spriggs, watching from a distance for him to get off the phone, came to his door. "You want lunch? I'm ordering. Gretchen's fetching."

Danny Fain smiled. "You can say that again. I'll have a cup of chicken noodle soup, a roast beef sandwich, a bag of Fritos, and a Diet Coke." He threw her a ten.

"You know what Derringer asked me when I went in to get his lunch order?" Lucy Spriggs said. "He asked me to buy him a tie. Something that went with his shirt."

"Something that goes with the food stains on his shirt," Danny said.

"Do I look like his mother? He wouldn't ask you to buy him a tie."

"He knows I have no taste."

"I should get him something a foot wide. In plaid," she vowed.

After she left he called Tim Penn, who answered after one ring. "Tim, I'm proud of you. You're still in the game."

"Just barely. This is getting boring."

"Where are you?"

"At Avondale and Harlem. Up beyond here is all industrial and then it's Park Ridge."

"Have you gone into Park Ridge?"

"Just a nudge," Tim Penn said.

"How about police or ambulances? TV crews?"

"Nothing. You're the only one who sees a story here, Dan."

"That's why it'll be great when you find the kid."

"And say I do find him. What then? Do I leave him there until we can get a shooter here? Do I call the police? Once I do, it's not our story anymore."

"You call me first."

"You're such a ghoul, Fain. Do I bring the mother by the hand to show her the body?"

"Don't be a pain in the butt, Tim."

"Philosophical questions aren't pertinent?"

"You're just trying to shame me into bringing you in. It won't work," Dan said. "I saw a kid get hit by a car. He's out there somewhere."

"I've got to get gas, Dan. And something to eat. I'll be out of the car for a while."

"What about schools? The kid would go to school around there. Look for a school."

"With an anguished mom outside?"

"This is the best assignment going. You have permission to drive around and solve a mystery. If you complain any more, I'll haul your ass in here and send Goop Traky out."

"Hah!" Tim Penn scoffed. "He'd walk to a pay phone a block from the office and call in bogus reports until it was time to come back."

"So don't complain," Danny Fain said.

"Heard about you and Jones. Are you OK?"

"Who told you?"

"I keep in touch. How's the arm?"

"I'm OK. She's better."

"You know who was the witch doctor?" Tim Penn asked.

"Do you?"

"*Everyone* does. Didn't you notice his shoes? He's worn the same shoes for the past ten years. They're a perpetual joke in the office."

Dan tried to remember; he saw only the mask, the knife. Again, he hadn't been paying attention. "Who?" he asked.

"Can't say, Dan."

"Don't talk about this story, understand?"

"Hey, I understand. Jones wasn't alone in there. Probably two or three other night *Quill* spies were flinging hockers at her in feigned outrage."

"Do you know them?" Dan asked.

"Sure I know them. I just don't know if they're spies. My guess is they're second-line reporters, because if they were really hot stuff the *Quill* would just hire them over there. At the *Bugle*, they're just feeding ideas. They're stringers. I bet Jones is treated with contempt over there, if they hire her at all."

"She'll be hired. She practically told us she was going across the street," Dan said. "That's what started the riot."

"She might have called her contact, true, and her contact might have hinted at a promise just to get her out of there and save her picturesque butt. But that doesn't mean she has a job. My guess is the *Quill* is feeling pretty smug. It's their town now. They kicked us—and I think they're cold-grained assholes enough to rub it in. So they're willing to let us know they had a spy at the *Bugle*. They pull her out with a lot of fanfare just to twist the shiv a little more. Jones was a no-talent. You know it, I know it, and the *Quill* knows it."

"Who was in the mask?" Dan said.

"I'll call you."

A young *Bugle* reporter named Kirk Oketo, on a dare, once entered the *Morning Quill*'s offices. He wandered among the *Quill*'s hushed, intense, cubicled nests and stole a variety of personalized stationery and inter-office mail envelopes as proof he had been there. A security guard followed him out of the building and over to the *Bugle*, and in that sense the visit was a success. His presence was reported, as was his destination upon leaving. The *Quill* was aware he had been in their offices, but they could find nothing amiss. They would worry for a long time that his mission had been so subtle and sophisticated that they could not figure it out. He had planted a virus in their imagination. Kirk Oketo commenced to harass them from afar, using the stolen stationery to set up so many false appointments that the *Quill* ultimately had to issue new memo pads. Nothing written on the old pads could be trusted. Too many staffers had waited outside the offices of editors who had received a memo summoning them elsewhere at that moment. Kirk Oketo enjoyed the idea of this immensely, of *Quill* staffers hovering, waiting, their summons in writing like the final proof of their reason for existing in that spot at that moment.

Dirk Flester came to Danny's office. He carried a small box and a handful of money. "You want in on the job pool, Dan? A buck a chance. You draw a slip, each slip has someone's name on it. If that person is the first to land a legitimate, verifiable job before the paper closes, you win the pot. If we close and no one has a job . . . you get your dollar back."

"Who has Alexandra Jones?" Dan asked.

"She's not included."

Dan took out a dollar. "It's up to eighteen bucks," Dirk said.

"Anybody pick me?"

Dirk Flester consulted a paper in his pocket. "No. You haven't been picked yet."

"How about Lucy Spriggs?"

"Debra Foster has Lucy. Dwight Spang has my favorite—Potter."

"Is Potter in?"

"Are you kidding? She hasn't invested a shred of personality in this place that wasn't part of her job. She didn't even bother to verbally refuse. She just *looked* away."

Dan relinquished his dollar. Dirk Flester made a note. "What if I pick myself?" Danny Fain asked.

"Then you'll have even more incentive to go out and look for a job."

Dan selected a slip. *Bernie DeVille.*

Both men laughed. Danny said, " 'Wanted: no-talent prima donna to fill gaping hole in paper with excessively windy stories.' "

Dirk shrugged. "Bernie might surprise you. He knows a lot of people and he's pushy. It doesn't have to be a newspaper job, you know. But it can't be a 7-Eleven."

"Well, whoever picks me won't be too excited about it, either," Dan said.

Dirk Flester departed and Danny watched him stopping at people's desks, explaining the pool, taking the money. Gretchen returned from the lunch run. Dan ate at his desk. Tommy Boyd, the wire editor, the day's first member of the night shift, arrived at half past noon. He had a punctuality (Tommy Boyd was *exactly* a half hour late every day) that Danny Fain relied on to signal the approach of the back half of the day.

Tommy was a short, cheerful man who carried a flammable odor with him, a lingering residue of the thousands of drinks he had downed, one per day, just before coming to work. He rode the L in from the north, reading the papers in the bouncing car, then walked six blocks to Slugs. This brisk walk, he believed, was the exercise that kept him alive. He arrived at Slugs with twenty minutes to spare, time enough for a throw of darts and one long boilermaker. He tipped thirty percent on his monthly tab for the privilege of having his drink on the deck when he came through the door. He urinated once before sitting down at his double-screened tube, and then was famous in his small way for never rising again except for the 4 P.M.

news meeting and when he got up to go home. He was called, respectfully, the man with no bodily functions: he didn't eat, didn't drink, didn't use the restroom, didn't waver from his assigned task.

Danny Fain took the seat beside him. "Did you hear the news, Tommy?"

"Hard to miss."

"The night side will have to be told, officially."

"That's not my job."

"I know."

"They'll know, though. They probably had an inkling last night before they went home." He wiped a handkerchief over his face where perspiration bubbled, the byproduct of his system burning off the boilermaker. Tommy had been within a day of being fired for alcoholism, but was saved by his wife leaving him. Derringer still wanted to pull the trigger, but Muff Greene bought Tommy Boyd a month's reprieve, and later a sixty-day extension of that, and during that time Tommy Boyd, who was then an assistant to Bruce McCall, had cleaned himself up and cut back on the drinking, and then watched in horror as Bruce McCall died of a heart attack on deadline. Bruce was putting together the day's line story when he looked at Tommy and said, "Take over." He fell cold to the floor. Being in charge focused life for Tommy Boyd. He still had that painful burned look to his skin, but he did the work required and often a little more, and eventually the prospect of being fired never came up again.

"Any talk of severance?" he asked.

"They're still working up the final formula. Rumor has it they'll be generous."

"They'll pay us as little as they can get away with."

Danny Fain smiled sadly. "That's what I said."

He returned to his office. A call came in. "Can I meet you for lunch?"

"I've eaten."

"Meet me anyway. I've got to talk to you."

"Who is this?" He had thought it was his wife talking in the fake-sexy voice she adopted in moments of privacy and want; he thought it was her ruse to get him home. But then a note at the end of her words, the way she said *talk to you* struck him as alien and exciting in a half-remembered way.

"It's Dana. I want to discuss a matter that is both personal and professional."

"I can't leave the office."

"I heard you got stabbed," Dana said.

"Jesus. Who told *you*?"

"I've got people all over."

"Who?"

"What difference does it make?"

"Can't anything go on around here without everyone passing it along?"

"A stabbing at a paper that's about to fold? That's news. News gets passed along."

"Why did you show me giving the finger?"

Dana Viola laughed, satisfied. "Our little joke," she said.

"My wife hit the roof."

"Nobody watches that lunchtime news."

"Other news people do—people I may want to go to for a job."

"Have you ever thought about TV?"

"I think about it when I tell my kids to turn it off."

"I mean working in TV news."

"Not seriously," Danny said. "What would I do?"

"Write copy. Work on the assignment desk. People in TV are intimidated by newspaper people. They think you're the real thing, not just thirty seconds of good visual. You'd command a lot of respect over here," she said.

"That's seductive talk, Dana. I can't believe you want my story so badly you'd offer me a job for it."

"Now would I do that?" Dana Viola purred.

"Well . . . would you?"

"In fact, we have a nice opening in tonight's cast for a good feature. We've about exhausted our backlog of filler tape and unless something breaks nobody is expecting anything. If we could get a really good story like a kidnapping we could give it a very *lavish* two minutes."

"I don't have any kidnappings for you, Dana."

"We've got a crew idling in the garage, loaded and focused."

"My guy hasn't even dug anything up. My instinct is there won't be a story tonight, Dana."

"Just an address. A street."

"I don't even have that," Danny Fain said.

"All right." He heard her voice pull back, that cooling calculated to make him fear she was disappointed.

Dan asked, sweetly, "Does this mean I don't get the job?"

"It *wasn't* a job offer, Danny. I just thought in your position you might want to examine the future a little bit. I thought if you wanted to help us out a little we might be able to do the same for you."

Dan said, "We just ran a reporter out of here covered with spit for doing exactly what you're asking me to do."

"I heard about that. What was that name again?"

"Why, Dana?"

"Curious."

"You going to film her for react?"

"It's part of the story. Without a good story we might have to really blow up the *Bugle* folding—make it our leader."

"And leave me and my finger in?"

"No. That's out. I ordered the trim myself."

"I'm not going to give you her name," Danny said.

Dana Viola sighed. "Why are you making this so difficult?"

"We're competitors. Why would I want this woman on TV making the staff here sound like animals?"

"We'd include your side, too. She'd probably refuse to talk. It wouldn't make her look very good, either."

"Can't help you," Dan said.

"Just a second." He was put on hold. Derringer, looking vexed, swooped into Muff Greene's office. He slammed the door. Dan sat up straight for a better look. Derringer was jawing agitatedly to someone—Muff Greene, presumably—out of Dan's sight.

Dana Viola returned. "This is odd, Danny," she said. "We're getting reports over here about a riot in your pressroom."

"Gotta go." He broke in on Derringer and Muff Greene. "Is there a riot in our pressroom?"

Derringer was startled. "Where did *you* hear that?"

"Someone at Channel Eight."

"Shit," Derringer said. "They must've called."

"A riot?"

"Not a riot," Muff Greene said.

"An act of terrorism," Derringer sputtered.

"Some machinists have taken the presses hostage," Muff Greene said. Derringer picked nervously at the skin on his Adam's apple, at that point where on a better day his necktie knot would have crisply hung, reassuring as a surreptitious tug on his nuts.

"What do they want?"

"To cause trouble, what else?" Derringer said. "To get on TV. To be famous."

The presses were three ancient dark castles in a vaulted basement room two stories deep. In their heyday they had run round the clock with special orders from out of town and the insatiable demands of a booming circulation. Danny Fain had brought his sons to the pressroom. They liked the little packets of earplugs offered like candy in a tray next to the time clock. They wadded the cylinders of sponge into their ears and began to yell even when the presses weren't running. The men who worked there in inked clothes watched the visitors warily, but with a cocked pride in their walk. They worked with an air of negotiating danger. They sported no jewelry, nothing dangling to be snagged by the swift roll of machinery. A little man with a squashed hand pushed a broom past Danny and his boys. He appeared to play the role of symbol, a reminder of what carelessness could bring. A stranger and two children made everyone down there nervous, but because they worked in their own world at the pleasure of men who dressed like Danny, they didn't dare complain; against all odds, he might be someone important. When the presses kicked on, a shiver went through the building. His sons grabbed his arms. Their eyes were nervous with delight. Dan felt like he was vibrating on a thin coating of ink and dust slippery as ball bearings. The noise intensified, all whir and whang, an insistence of commerce moving the air. Wide sheets of newsprint flew through a precise riddle of rollers and plates and somewhere in that roaring eminence ink was applied. Decisions he had made took shape in the printed word. The work he had done became tangible, something of value.

"Three machinists have locked themselves in an office with the override switch," Derringer said. "They control all three presses."

"Have they made any demands?" Muff Greene asked.

"They want the paper to stay open."

"Is anyone negotiating with them?"

"Negotiate? Their demand is absurd."

"We've got to talk to them," Muff Greene said. "*Someone* has to. We've got a big paper tomorrow. The food section has to be printed this afternoon. Jewel and Dominick's and Cub want to see the ads they bought."

"Harry Moss is talking to them," Derringer said.

"Nobody respects Harry," Muff Greene pointed out. "Where's O'Hara?"

"He retired Friday. They hate *him* because they think he knew up front and jumped off early," Derringer said.

"If the worst happens—" Muff Greene said.

"What's the worst?"

"We can't get back control of the presses," Muff Greene said. "Or they damage them in some way. Can we print at the *Quill*?"

"They'd hold us up," Derringer predicted. "They'd charge us by the letter."

"Call someone over there," Muff Greene urged. "We should find out if it's a possibility."

"Call whom?"

"Go to the top."

"Barton?"

"He's going to approve it eventually—if it gets approved."

Derringer departed. "I'd like to listen in on that conversation," Danny said.

"Well, you won't. And you didn't hear this one, either. OK?" Muff Greene said.

He wanted to go to the pressroom gallery, a long carpeted hallway with windows looking in on the dark tops of the presses. The men in there with their plugged ears and headgear cupping the plugs could look out and see people talking soundlessly, as if all their precautions against deafness had been futile. Dan wanted to see the pressroom under siege; he wanted to see the men who were refusing to acquiesce to the final plans of management, a plan he had embraced for the lure of its familiarity.

Dwight Spang came to his office. "I heard they're flooding the pressroom. A pressman has a fire hose and they can't get it away from him."

"Good story, Dwight. Who's your source?"

"No source. It's a teaser. I was hoping you'd set me straight."

"What's new on the grave-liner strike?"

Dwight Spang leaned forward. "They've covered the gallery windows with newsprint. Why the blackout? Are they torturing guys in there?"

"I don't know anything."

"You were in there with Muff and Fluff. You have *access.*"

"What have you got?" Dan asked impatiently.

Dwight sighed. "Back to business," he sang. "Something interesting *has* developed. But it turns it into a two-day story. This new thing . . . I won't be able to get it firm today."

"It's still early," Dan said. He looked at his watch, then at his phone, wondering where Tim Penn was.

"I can give you a story on the strike and the pileup of bodies waiting to be buried," Dwight Spang said. "I've *got* that story. But I turned something else up. I was calling around to some of the bereaved to get their reaction to having their loved ones in cold storage. I was hung up on twice, the third time the woman called me a fiend from hell, and so I was all set to take a hint. But I tried one more family. Their mom is in Wolf Funeral Home in Evanston. They don't know what I'm talking about. Mom was buried just fine last week. I thought maybe they had liners then—so I called another family from Wolf—their grandma died Thursday. According to the other funeral-home directors I've talked to, someone who died Thursday would be about three hundredth on any waiting list for liners. But no—Grandma is planted snug as a bug. Four others—all from Wolf—who died Thursday or Friday have been buried without delay."

"Maybe he had liners stockpiled," Dan said.

"The story is there isn't one in the state."

"Have you confronted Wolf?"

"Sure. I think they're working a switch. They go through the ceremony, drive Grandma to the cemetery, say prayers around the site. Then everyone goes home and Grandma goes back into cold storage. They peel a layer of sod off the top to make the grave look fresh. The family has paid their money, he has that money to pay for storage, etc. Does it matter precisely *when* they're buried as long as the family believes they are? He's concerned about the emotional comfort of his customers. This way, the grieving process can begin. They don't have to think of Grandma with frost on her brow. What does he tell the customers who call angered by claims made by a nosy reporter? Namely, that Grandma *has* found eternal rest, that Wolf Funeral Home is so large and influential and *expensive* because they have connections that give them access to grave liners unavailable to less successful funeral homes. However, and this is the beauty, if these people still are unsatisfied, well, they are free to *exhume* Grandma to make certain her grave is properly lined. That ends the discussion."

"That's a good story," Dan said.

"I think so."

"It sounds like you have enough to go for it all today," Dan said. "Spreading it over two days doesn't make sense to me. You'd have a news story today, which TV and the *Quill* will have. Then you come in with some interesting impact tomorrow. Put them together today and you've got strike, impact, and possible illegal—at the very least distasteful—consequences. The way the news is shaping up, that kind of story might find itself out front."

"We'd need to have a family willing to dig up Grandma's grave," Dwight Spang said. "Without that, Wolf will just say, 'Hey, prove it.' "

"What about another home saying it's impossible for Wolf to have grave liners?"

"Nobody will cross Wolf. These funerary types are like doctors. They watch out for each other."

"What if someone visits the grave?"

"Who can say what's under there?"

"Can you get a family?" Danny Fain asked. "Maybe someone who wasn't too fond of the deceased?"

Dwight Spang got a funny look in his eye. "Can you suggest a line of questioning that would lead inevitably to someone offering to dig up their relative?"

Both men laughed. Dwight Spang had made his reputation as a young reporter with his eagerness to call up the families of the recently deceased. These dead calls were the most difficult in the profession, the winnowing ground that produced the hard-nut reporters or steered those unable to make the calls to another department, another line of work. Dwight Spang, however, found a certain fascination in the duty and soon developed a reputation as someone who, for a twenty-dollar bill or a case of Grolsch or a bequeathed vacation day, would take another reporter's notes and ask patient, insistent questions of the mother whose son had been shot through the head or the husband whose wife had been found strangled and raped. Such calls were a responsibility that led Danny Fain to actively seek editing work. He had never paid Dwight Spang, but many times he'd been relieved to have someone hang up on him. And though he told every new reporter always to call back if they were hung up on, he never—as a reporter—had followed that rule. His understanding of this fear led him to feel slightly unworthy in the presence of Dwight Spang, so he said, meaning to pay tribute, "If anyone can come up with that line, Dwight, it's you."

Dwight Spang shrugged modestly and departed. Dan immediately dialed Tim Penn. While it rang he noticed more night staffers floating in, their expressions alternately anguished and befuddled. They had been out in the real world when the closing was announced and Danny imagined that would be worse than being at work. In the office he felt part of the picture, of the charged air and rumormongering that would be distilled into fifteen-second news bits on the radio to tantalize absent staff members with bulletins of their doom.

Dirk Flester approached Melvin Devlin and Bobby Parquet, copy editors with a combined seventy years in at the paper, to join the job pool. The two copy editors watched him suspiciously. They were pretty much representative of the best of their ilk: patient, cynical, precise, disinterested in fashion, happy to stay indoors the entire shift to tinker with the fine points of the language and write headlines. Halfway through Dirk's presentation, Melvin Devlin had to sit down. Both men, however, put up their dollar and drew a name. Upon opening his slip of paper, Bobby Parquet looked into Danny's office and gave him the thumbs up, wishing him well in his search for future employment.

Tim Penn did not answer his phone. Dan hung up and tried again in fifteen minutes and again got no answer. It was going on three o'clock. In an hour the four o'clock news meeting would begin. It was different from the morning meeting only in that the stories on each department's budget would be presented as actually existing. The news editors, the men who dummied the paper, would be at the four o'clock and they would plan and shape the pages according to what stories were presented to them.

Lucy Spriggs appeared in his doorway. "Have you got anything?"

"I can't reach Tim."

"It's three o'clock."

"I know what time it is."

Lucy Spriggs didn't budge. "Can I push this story at four?"

"I won't know until I reach Tim."

"If he found something—he'd have called you, right?"

"Those were his instructions."

Lucy Spriggs took a seat on his couch. "Convince me of what you saw."

"I can't. Until Tim finds something . . . *I* won't be convinced."

"I'm going to type up the story list at three forty-five," she said. "I need to know by then—or I can't take your story to the meeting. It hasn't firmed up any more than it was this morning."

"I'm aware of that, thank you," Dan said acidly. He stared at her for several moments. Her eyes, locked on his, were nevertheless engaged in other contemplations.

"Did you know my office is tilted from one corner to the other?" he asked.

She came out of her spell smiling. "The air in mine has more particles of dust per cubic foot than the pressroom."

"It's lucky we're still alive," Danny said.

"I got a strange call from Derringer," she revealed. "He wanted me to call Barton to see if we could print over there."

"You know Barton?"

"We've done lunch a couple times," she said demurely. "No postsundown contact, however."

"What did he say?"

"I haven't called him," she said. "If Wally is afraid to call him, that's a bargaining chip for me—for the staff."

"But if you wait, we lose the time we need to get set up on their presses," Dan said.

"Who feels that squeeze, Danny? Do you? I certainly don't."

"I just don't see much value in waiting, personally. Either Barton OKs it or he doesn't," Danny Fain said. "Making Derringer sweat isn't going to keep the paper alive."

"It might sweeten severance."

"No. If you refuse, he'll just order Muff to call."

Lucy Spriggs grimaced, shrugged. "That's true. But it was something."

"And if you make the call," Dan continued, "you might be able to buy a little good will for yourself."

She was offended. "I would *never* do that."

"I know. I would, but I don't have your outraged mettle."

She leaned a taut hip against the rim of his desk and from memory punched an outside number on his phone. Danny Fain was distressed to be so close to her (where he could see the lace pattern of her slip pressing through her skirt like a coin-rubbing), and to have his access to Tim Penn removed even for an instant.

"Bret?" she said in a jungle voice, with a roll of her eyes for Dan. "Luce. How are you? I know. It's a shame. Worse, it's an outrage. You guys better not get any more bloated than you are—without us to compete with." She laughed, absently twirling a necklace of blue glass Buddha beads. She was listening. Bret Barton, *Morning Quill* publisher, had her attention. A faint rose tint was sweeping across her face. She raised up from Dan's desk, turned away from him, smoothed her skirt over her skinny haunches. "Is that a standing offer or a contingent offer?" she asked warily, sinking deeper into the corner of Dan's little tilted space. She paid attention to Barton's response, then laughed again, almost with relief, for she turned back toward Danny Fain and theatrically gave

Barton the finger through the phone. "Uh-huh. I understand completely. Actually I'm calling on behalf of Wally. We're having a little trouble with our pressmen—and Wally wanted to know if the *Quill* could print our paper tonight, should we be unable to resolve this minor labor dispute." She listened again. "What sort of time would be required? . . . Right. We could set up a shuttle system if it came to that. How about cost? What would you charge?" His answer made her wince, get angry. "Why bother, Bret? We might as well not come out tomorrow. Can't you come down from there?" She was on the phone a moment longer, then said, "We'll get back to you," before hanging up.

She slumped back into his couch. "What a prick. They'll be glad to do us *after* their first two editions are out. On their auxiliary press. And they'll only charge us thirty cents a copy." She stood up again. "I'd better tell Derringer. He'll want a SWAT team to clear out those machinists."

He tried Tim Penn again and got no answer. This was not unexpected, but irksome nevertheless in light of Dan's warnings. Of course Tim might be out of his car aggressively reporting the story and getting so much good stuff that he didn't want to break to call in, but it was just as likely that he had met someone, the uncanny sexual instinct that was the envy of every other man in the office drawing that woman to him.

Into the newsroom hubbub came two fantastical people bearing a press release. Clomping across the tile floor in boots spray-painted the color of sweet peas, their genders and identities mysterious under loose-fitting camouflage garb and ski masks augmented with dry flaps of moss, they posed wide-stanced before Goop Traky and presented a sheet of paper. "Read and heed," they said.

Goop Traky considered their demand. "Who are you? The plant people?"

"We are The Green Years."

Goop Traky skimmed the contents of the press release. "Okay, you're mad because you can't afford a car, so no one else should be allowed to drive."

"The Green Years are poised to bring the city to a halt."

"No," Goop said condescendingly, "The Green Years *is* poised to bring the city to a halt."

"Your lack of introspection will be your ruin," they predicted. "Failure to pay attention to our gesture will deny you the best story of the day."

Goop Traky shook the release. "This?"

"That is the flame held to the fuse."

"What do you want from us?"

"Documentation. We are offering to each of the city's major media outlets an opportunity to provide a representative to accompany The Green Years as we bring Chicago to a halt."

"Print and TV?"

"And radio."

"When?"

"Immediately. We begin at once."

"We've got better things to do with our staff," Goop Traky said.

"Do you have the power—sitting out here in the open as you are and not in an enclosed office where the true power resides in most media conglomerates—to decide that your paper is not interested in the best story of the day?"

"He doesn't," the other judged.

"Who else is going?"

"Each outlet is receiving its invitation from The Green Years at this moment. Synchronization is our calling card."

"Let me talk to a couple people," Goop Traky said.

"Departure is imminent," they warned.

"I've got to see who's available," Goop said.

"*You* are available. Accompany us."

"I've got duties here."

"Perhaps a more flexible attitude toward breaking news would have allowed your particular media outlet to compete successfully in Chicago," they said.

"You're right. We're dead. Why bother with us?"

"Because you're coming out tomorrow—and as such have value as a publicity mill for The Green Years."

Goop Traky stood. "A moment of your time," he said.

"Time is slipping away," they warned.

"Cool your jets. Chew on a blade of grass." He went into Danny Fain's office. Goop looked back and The Green Years were speaking to Dirk Flester. Goop Traky felt that old panic at the prospect of losing a story with some juice, that sweet jealousy of wanting to do well and fearing that the opportunity was evaporating for lack of his personal initiative.

"I need your attention out here a minute, Dan," Goop said.

Danny Fain did not look up from his tube. "Can't it wait, Goop?"

A Nikon motor drive began to whir. Puffs of light went off around The Green Years' heads. They posed in this storm light, stiffened their bearings, curled fists on hips. A disrespectfully curious crowd of journalists had gathered.

"I've been offered the story of the day," Goop said.

Dan looked up from his work. "How could you have the story of the day? I have the story of the day."

"My story has been so advertised," Goop Traky said. He handed over the press release. Dan was half through when The Green Years filled his office door like a wall of untended ivy.

"You have run out of time to decide," they said to Goop. "The smooth execution of our gesture requires that we leave within the half-minute."

"They asked me to go," Goop said to Dan. "I want to go."

"Exclusive?" Danny Fain asked.

"His view of the events will be his own—and thus exclusive," they said. "But other media outlets will be represented."

"We need an exclusive," Dan said, fudging, staring into the green-shadow eyesockets of the masks, through the hanging tendrils of moss. He imagined he saw hard, young, calculating eyes in there: terrorists' eyes.

"I think that's out of the question, Dan," Goop Traky said.

"They could kidnap you," Danny Fain said. "They've already taken pains to hide their identity."

The Green Years addressed each other: "I *told* him that would be a problem."

"I'm willing to take that chance," Goop said.

"Let me make one call," Dan said, "to see if anyone else is biting."

"No time," The Green Years said.

Goop Traky grabbed his coat and a notebook. "Gimme a pen," he pleaded. Dan tossed him a Bic.

"Keep in touch," Danny Fain said.

"We have car phones," The Green Years said. "TV will supply pictures, undoubtedly."

Danny immediately called Dana Viola. "Have they left?" he asked.

She was breathless, laughing. "Just now," she said. "With a reporter and crew. They knew exactly what they wanted."

"Have you read the release?" Dan asked.

"I skimmed it. I made sure that bringing the city to a halt did not mean any destruction of property or endangering of my personnel," Dana said. "They assured me, so what else was I to do? Let another station have a team along and not us?"

Bobby Parquet, outside Dan's office, flattened a slip of paper against the glass so Danny Fain could read his own name. Dan raised a finger.

"When will you start airing pictures?" he asked.

"We're going to see what's involved first," Dana Viola said. "We're going to see if anything happens worth televising. Until then, you guys over on print are going to have to wait, aren't you?"

"I never questioned your power on this kind of story," Dan said. He hung up.

Bobby Parquet was a dapper little man who dressed in pastel shirts and clashing bowties. A bachelor in his sixties, liver spots in profusion across his untroubled brow, Bobby Parquet was reliable in that he trimmed stories to the desired length, wrote adequate headlines, and came to work on time and sober. But he wanted to learn nothing else about the paper, no extra responsibilities were desired, and if an unfamiliar or slightly complicated task was given to him he began to balk and sputter like an overburdened lawn-mower engine until the task was removed and passed to someone who would perform it without an attendant fit. His passion was travel, his vacations spent on the hoof through the Valle Longitudinal in Chile or the back streets of Antwerp or at a boat launch on the Hooghly. He was passing through the world unfettered by responsibility or accomplishment, and he had his admirers on the staff.

"Any job prospects, Danny?"

"Why do you ask?"

"Why do you think?" Bobby Parquet had a wintergreen smell and little liquid brown eyes that gleamed out of the web of wrinkles ironed into his face by a lifetime of squinting into exotic suns. "I drew you in the pool." He dropped the slip on Dan's desk. His name looked strange, printed there by someone else, being on the mind of another for even the briefest moment. It gave Dan comfort that he existed outside the personal anguish of his circumstances.

"I like my chances," Bobby Parquet said, retrieving the paper, putting it in the pocket of his cranberry shirt. "You're the type who gets picked up right away."

Danny Fain smiled, liking the sound of that prediction, but sensing in Bobby Parquet's wizened little face some contemptuous irony or disrespect. "You don't just toe the line," he continued unbidden. "You do more than you're asked to. Corporations like people like you."

"Who'd Melvin draw?"

"Bubb Cook." Bobby Parquet laughed cruelly. "Hose him down with lye. Hang air fresheners on him. Somebody *might* hire him then."

"Bubb has a skill," Danny said. "He'll get a job."

"Skill, yes. Image, no. You need a sheen now to get anywhere. A *look.* Bubb's like me—history."

"If someone picked you, how would you assess their chances?"

"Nil," Bobby Parquet chuckled, shrugged. "I'm going to take the money and go. I'll be sixty-two next month. I can't see trying to train another slot man to my way of doing things. I'd have to fake all that enthusiasm for the work just to get hired—then they have to go through the sequence of being angry at me, then at themselves for hiring me, then disappointed in me. It takes a good two years before they're comfortable with the situation. It's easier if I just disappear. But *you*—I'm counting on you."

"Well, don't spend the pot yet." His phone rang.

"That's your destiny now," Bobby Parquet predicted, leaving.

It was Dale Busse. "Dunkirk's back," she said. "He has an hour before he has to shoot a prep football kid. Do you need him?"

"Wait." He put her on hold, dialed Tim Penn's car, listened to it ring twenty times, then went back to Dale Busse. "I don't have anywhere to send him. My man in the field is out of touch. Until I hear from him there's no story."

"He'll be here for a half hour," Dale Busse said.

Danny tried Tim Penn's home number on a hunch. He lived with his third wife above a beauty parlor at Wilson and Damen, he could be there and in her arms and back on the case in forty-five minutes if he was hard, reckless, and caught every light. But on the first ring a phone machine answered and a woman with a husky, inviting voice announced they were unable to take the call but were eager for messages. At the tone, Danny said, "Are you there, Tim? It's after three. I need you to call me. I'm getting desperate."

If Tim Penn was home pounding away at his wife, would he pause to call? Probably not; that would be an admission he was off the job, disobeying orders. But in the present situation, what weight did orders carry? The system of punishments had broken down.

Danny Fain stood and scanned the reporters at their desks. As they moved into the deep end of the afternoon the pace began to intensify. Serious typing was being done, at least by some reporters. The knots of gossiping staffers had broken up as the awareness of deadlines sent reporters to their desks.

Dan was looking for someone who might be a confidant of Tim Penn, someone who might have been granted the name of a girl whom Tim Penn was apt to steal away to if given the irresistible opportunity. But Tim Penn was without friends on the paper; women were all potential to him, something to be won over in the future; men didn't want to hear his stories. He went to Tim Penn's desk, which butted up against the back of Bernie DeVille's desk. Bernie was on the phone, doing the listening. Dan sat at Tim Penn's desk and tried the drawers; files, bits of notes, strips of used white-out paper that revealed only the errors in the clues. But there were no phone numbers Danny could use. The top of the desk was cool, almost dusty, as though no one had worked there in weeks.

"You should've sent me," Bernie DeVille said, getting off the phone. He faced Danny Fain. He looked exhausted, his hair caught in the wind of the future, his mouth drooping at the corners, his suspenders lax. For ten years Abe Skinback had promised to anoint Bernie DeVille his successor when he retired. Now both men were up in years and looking for new jobs.

"I've got you in the pool, Bernie."

"I know. I'm doing my best to help you win."

"Do you talk to Tim Penn much?"

Bernie DeVille shook his head. "Four years ago I tried to tell him a story about my divorce and he shushed me. He says to me, 'Every moment of life does not require your verbal commentary.' Our friendship is over from that point," Bernie said. "I will still talk to him—but only of unimportant matters. It gets under his skin."

"Does he confide in anybody?"

"He doesn't confide," Bernie said. "But this I'll tell you—you should've sent me on your wild goose chase. Maybe I wouldn't find the kid, but you could at least find *me.*"

Goop Traky reported from the field. His cellular signal was pure: "I'm in the front seat of a hand-painted green Chevrolet Vega. I'm at the far right-hand side of a line of—I count six hand-painted green Vegas—each with a masked driver and masked shotgun rider. I am the media representative for my particular group of cars. I must say I'm proud. We're on the Ontario feeder heading for the Kennedy-Ryan fork. The Vegas are . . . just a sec—" He was gone for an instant. "I've been told to refer to them as The Green Years at all times. So . . . The Green Years and I are traveling six cars abreast at the pace of a brisk walk up the Ontario feeder. Traffic, as you might expect, is packing behind us. Looking behind me . . . behind me looking from the crest of the feeder I can see an unbroken river of traffic. We'll be going under Milwaukee Avenue in a minute. More Vegas waiting on the shoulder at the fork. I see a minicam overhead on Halsted. Any of this on TV yet?"

Danny Fain burned through the channels. "Nothing yet," he told Goop Traky.

"Can you hear the horns?" Goop asked. "It sounds like every car behind us is honking. The wind from the curses ought to propel us forward faster than we're traveling. The Green Years are bottling rage behind us. The Vegas on the shoulder have divided—two going with us, the other five going three and two around the ramp to the Ryan. Can you picture this? We're now four and four abreast down the ramp to the Kennedy northbound. The driver of my car could tap a cigarette into the ashtray of the car to our left. Traffic on the Kennedy is heavy but moving well and about to stop. Here we go here we go here we go. Picking up speed for the merge."

His report cut out. "Goop?" Dan said. "Goop?"

Dirk Flester ran to Dan's office. He still carried the job-pool box, his hand spread over it to hold down the booty. "The Green Years are a household word already. Green Vegas in and outbound on the Edens, the Ryan, the Ike, the Stevenson, the Tri-State, LSD, the Kennedy. Traffic reporters going apeshit. It's dissolution of the social fabric, to be denied the power of the public byways and your automobile. You watch . . . someone's going to get shot before this is over."

Dan pleaded into the phone: "Goop, where are you?" He

paused a moment, then said, "Shit, I can't reach anyone when I need them."

A procession of six men and six women filed like a jury through the newsroom. Dan saw Eric Maas at the rear, a paragon of after-closing-hours journalistic restraint in Porsche shades, midnight-black Gucci T-shirt, and black leather pants. The blue-curled Dolly Franzen, Features Editor, was at the head of the line. Behind her came two very frail-looking young men with spotted complexions and wet-cat bearings; they seemed to be walking in their sleep, for they kept accelerating up Dolly's spiked heels, causing her to stumble, and eliciting apologies from a man in a gold satin record-company jacket whose purpose seemed to be to follow these two young men and clean up after them. Behind the record company flack walked five strikingly beautiful women, all exposed skin, feathers, fringe, piled hair, perfect makeup, and choreographed garment rips. Another guy in a satin record jacket tailed them. Then came a third very pale young man in a blue sequined tuxedo who kept turning to pass asides to Eric Maas, so hip, so *there,* so chilled behind his shades and jaded smile. This conga line bunched up at the door to Dolly's office. She had a beautiful view of the river, so she solved her seating dilemma by arranging the five gorgeous hood ornaments along the ledge where they could listen to the interview or check their makeup in the window.

Dolly came out alone after a moment and screamed for a clerk, although all the clerks had been canned the year before in a budget slaughter that followed a ninety-thousand-reader circulation drop. She looked around for someone to follow her orders, even clutching at Dick Cahan's sleeve as he went past, pleading, "Can you make a deli run for me?"

Dick, a caption writer, a voluble fellow, said, "Nope."

She came deeper into the newsroom, her manner shading toward apoplexy. "Will *someone* make a deli run for Young Snob God?" Reporters, editors, rewrite men, hard-bitten types, looked up from their work, bemused, but nothing more.

"I'll pay extra. I've got their order right here. Please?"

Someone called out, "What did God order?"

She consulted a list. "Two packs of Luckies and two diet root beers. Young wants a watercress sandwich, a pound bag of regular M&Ms, and tea straight. Snob wants a cheeseburger and three cold Heinekens. The backup singers want hot tea with honey and ten bags of Fritos. The record guys want coffee black and change back from their hundred." She displayed the bill, as if in final proof of the seriousness of her offer.

Lucy Spriggs, to everyone's surprise, stepped forward. "I'll go. I've got to buy some champagne anyway." She took the hundred and the list. "But I keep the change." She winked at Danny Fain. "If I'm not back for the four o'clock, you take it. The slug list is on my tube."

Her office was thick with the smell of her, the signature perfume a little too strong after years of surreptitious applications in that small space. Her screen had gone blank, but he hit a key and the slug list came up. At the top was typed STORIES FOR TUESDAY, NOV. 1. First on the list was HITRUN, with nothing after it but DF'S THING????? It was 3:30. He tried Tim Penn's car again and got no answer. Sitting in the warm, fragrant shadows of Lucy's office, in a place where no one would look for him, he felt his day coming to an end. His story would not make the paper. The kid would not be found. Dan would be free to leave early to go home to his wife and children. Maybe he *had* seen nothing; maybe the car had not stopped because there was nothing to stop for, no thud of impact or crack of headlight or airborne child. He had only a picture, an instant of the day burned into his mind: a running ghost, a speeding car, a point of impact. Then the outbound train. It was all left to his imagination.

Danny turned on the TV in Lucy's office. Channel Eight was first to go on the air with Green Years pictures, a jumpy image framed by a windshield in a car puttering west at negligible speed out the Eisenhower Expressway. An eerie scene: the multiple lanes ahead empty but for cars swooping down the entrance ramps, drivers doing double-takes back at their good fortune. The camera swung to the right, went out of focus, then sharpened down a line of precise green-hooded heads. No waves for the camera, no hints of smiles or divergence from the mission. The background roar of the detained, the inconvenienced, the frenzied—the *slowed*—poured through the line of green cars like drool from a sewer pipe.

Channel Four weighed in with a camera in a truck pointed south on Lake Shore Drive. The imposing, pillared Field Museum was visible down at the end of the long, empty avenue. Five Vegas going south had stopped in line with five Vegas going north and a fat-linked silver chain passed through them all like a string through beads and locked around the doorposts of the outside cars. Cars caught heading north cut out of line to try their luck on another route. A helicopter dropped to within five feet of the empty southbound lanes. The black nub end of a TV camera was aimed out the side door. Danny went through the stations until he came upon the elevated perspective. A white capital letter had been painted on the roof of each Vega so that GREEN YEARS was spelled out. People were getting out of their cars, climbing on their fenders and hoods to seek out the source of their anguish. The more impatient danced sideways down the lines of cars toward the front, where they might have hoped to lay a hand on their tormentors. The copter twirled over the scene, rose, shot out over the lake and returned. They caught sight of a cop on horseback galloping at a hard angle across a strip of park land, the horse's drumbeat hooves chopping through the leaves. The cop's butt went up and down in a crunching rhythm against the saddle. The camera's line soared and turned again, picking out three squad cars coming with angry intent the wrong way down Lake Shore Drive. They fanned out when they reached the Vegas, turning dramatically sideways to add a layer of redundancy to the blockage in the road.

Danny Fain started to pull stories up from the computer.

Many were far from completion, with only a half-hearted lede and a scattering of notes and phone numbers to indicate any work being done. Several of the shorter, more innocuous stories—nothing more than PR retypings, notices of blood drives, announced appointments to anonymous bureaus of the city government—these were finished and ready for shipping. He gave them a final tinkering, digging twice into the computer reference files to check the spelling of a name, and sent them on to the news desk; first to arrive, they would be the last bits of stray fill to get in the paper.

He dialed the wire desk, where he could see Tommy Boyd at work with a slashing proficiency going through the mountain of news beamed from around the world into the wire queues. "Yo," Tommy said casually into the phone.

"This is Danny. How big's the paper?"

"Eighty-eight. A mother."

"You got anything?"

"Maybe a line. Three hijack bulletins have come in on Reuters and two on AFP. AP just sent one, too."

"Americans?"

"KLM—Amsterdam to New York. I'd say positively. It's sketchy, but too many sketches for it to be a false alarm. They've already diverted the plane toward Beirut."

"Thanks."

A big paper: 88 columns. He remembered papers from barely five years back that routinely clocked in at 120 columns, a news hole with some suck to it, news vanishing down the hole in their efforts to fill all that space. Big pictures, long meaty stories, good reading. But fewer and fewer people bought those papers because the ads that shaped the news hole were for cut-rate meat wholesalers and impotence clinics and used-car dealers and department stores where people went in search of bargains and finance companies and betting tip shops and auto salvage yards and schools that taught the science of asbestos removal. As circulation fell, a few thousand a month, economies were exacted in the form of smaller news holes, shorter stories, reduced staff. Ownership changed three times in Dan's nine years, after being solidly under the control of one family for sixty years. Each new owner put his particular obnoxious stamp on the product, one mogul puffing up the size and inky weight of the headline fonts, always on the lookout for a moist crime, then selling to a sucker for a $70 million profit. The new owner took a staid, aristocratic approach to the news, the gray-matter coverage augmented by splashy contests for simpletons. Reporters sent to cover a story were instructed to take down random license numbers to run in the paper, where the owner of that license would see the number and win a cash prize. The news hole was clogged with long dispatches from civil wars at the ends of the earth, and stories about famine where famine was as common as the sun, while legitimate concerns of the city were given only a cursory glance. This new owner loved to see his name and picture in the paper, so money was spent purchasing for him a series of Man of the Year awards from charitable organizations. A shooter was sent to each of these events to photograph the owner in his tux and jug ears, the wife on his arm like a platinum handbag, displaying that evening's cut-glass vase or walnut plaque. But circulation continued to fall and advertisers stayed away when it became apparent that the ponderous coverage of obscure world events was not attracting any readers even remotely upscale. Furthermore, after the paper cut city coverage, the blue-collar readers who were the backbone of *Bugle* circulation had stopped buying the paper. Strapped with a crippling debt service after paying too much for the paper, the owner soon had no choice but to sell. He entertained offers, none of which were high enough to allow him to back out a millionaire, which had been his goal all along. The current owners, out-of-town number mumblers, their past record littered with folded tents, finally came forward with an offer to take over the debt load and pay the man of the year a half million dollars to leave quietly.

Which he did. That had been two years ago. The new owners set about gutting the contracts of unions that had no power, representing as they did men and women in dying trades, trades on the frontier of computerization and subsequent obsolescence. These doomed men had to accept the pay cuts and increased working hours because to strike would give the owners exactly what they wanted: the opportunity to fire them all and replace them with near-minimum-wage employees. The only union that didn't buckle was editorial, and only because they possessed several high-profile individuals such as Rudy Vine and Lawrence K. Mock and Abe Skinback, who understood how the media could be used to transmit their desired message to the ever-absorbent public. Management finally came across with an acceptable package scant minutes before a strike began, but three months of being called worthless by their employer did not sit well with many people and a staff talent drain commenced that paralleled the steady dwindling of circulation.

The most recent resignation had been three weeks ago, when Emily Wheems, a reporter of adequate ability and industriousness, had jumped to some Sun Belt rag in Arizona, from which she had sent back one postcard showing bare-assed beauties sunbathing at an oasis while a leviathan Gila monster licked its chops just beyond the nearest dune. She claimed to be happy; certainly she was relieved.

Dan came blinking out of the dimness of Lucy Spriggs's office. He tried Tim Penn from the nearest phone. He would fire him regardless, he decided. That stigma would be attached to his personal record, denying him the tribal honor of being shipped out with the rest of them, although Danny had no doubt Tim Penn would effortlessly talk his way around such a blot with any future employer.

He watched over Tommy Boyd's shoulder; on one screen the wire editor was putting together his budget of stories to be offered at the four o'clock, on the other screen he was scrolling for updates on his big story, the KLM hijacking, which had coalesced into an unknown number of heavily armed Arabs in control of a jumbo jet carrying 243 passengers and a crew of 11. No demands had been made, at least that the world's news outlets had been apprised of. The jet was presently in West German air space.

"It's a line," Tommy said without looking up.

His assistant, Ben Cardan, had arrived. Ben was heavy through the jowls, sad-eyed, keeping a lightly spiked thermos of coffee always at hand. His aura turned more jovially argumentative through the shift until he was a disruptive chatterbox of minutiae whom Tommy Boyd sent home an hour early to get him out of everyone's hair.

More copy editors straggled in, their eyes terrified, their ears pricked for the slimmest hopeful clue. Because they were the final people to have any influence on each morning's finished product, they secretly feared they might have been the ultimate reason the paper was closing, while outwardly maintaining the remove from disaster that their innate arrogance and sense of superiority gave them.

"What do you hear, Dan?" one asked, a veteran named Phil McKoosh, who had occupied the same chair for seventeen years, bequeathed by the legendary Sunny Underwood, because it provided excellent back support and also was positioned to observe before anyone else each person who entered the newsroom.

"I've heard what you've heard," Danny Fain said. "Hard facts aren't exactly flying around this place."

"Shit," another muttered.

Melvin Devlin, fresh from the smoker, reported, "A buy is imminent. We'll be sold, but not closed. Retirement will be sweetened. Nobody replaced."

"Maybe Dink will buy us," Bobby Parquet said, and the small group chuckled nervously. And, as if cued by mention of Dink, slot man Reg Swain came around the corner wearing his usual haunted look.

Reg Swain was owner of the $27 million bottle of scotch. Nobody from his staff had ever been invited to his house, but others who had visited reported the liter bottle was displayed like an icon on a pedestal behind his wet bar, a subdued light filtering through the amber liquid. The brand was McDonough, a quality scotch, twelve years old, with a smoothness and bite that made it Reg Swain's personal drink of choice. The McDonough had been the big prize when Abe Skinback instructed his assistant at the time, a beautiful, fed-up girl named Alicia Butterknob, to lug out to the copy desk a box containing all the gratis booze that Abe received for the holidays from various press agents and lackeys attempting to buy some Skinback good will in the coming year. Abe didn't drink, and he didn't want people to think he could be bribed, so he donated everything to the copy desk in tribute to a year of catching bad spellings and incorrect addresses and birthday wishes sent out to people cold in their graves. There was a suspicion that Abe held back the good stuff, or that his bribers didn't feel compelled to woo him with quality hooch, because the dozen or so bottles he donated each year ran to black Israeli wines, thick-lipped yellowish liqueurs, and very green champagne.

A drawing was held by the copy editors to determine the order of selection. The liter of McDonough increased the pool from the usual eight or so committed drinkers, who would put away anything with a buzz potential, to nearly twenty men and women, including slot man Reg Swain, who previously had always conducted the lottery but never entered, his palate having been refined by the subtleties of good scotch. With Swain entered, Danny Fain was enlisted to draw names from a hat. The first name picked was Dink Otto, who had called in sick that day. The other names drawn had to wait until Dink made his choice, but there was no enthusiasm for anything but the bottle of McDonough. When Dink Otto returned to work the next day, his boss, Reg Swain, had prepared a trade offer to gain possession of the first pick. He had gone to the deli and purchased one lottery ticket for that Saturday's drawing. The pot had rolled over three times and currently stood at $25 million, and was expected to go higher by the end of the week. Reg Swain offered Dink Otto this lottery ticket, with all its potential for unimagined wealth and a life free of financial worry, in exchange for the very tangible liter of McDonough scotch. As it happened, Dink Otto had missed the previous day's work because he had passed out *under* his bed and when he awoke at two in the afternoon thought the dust-brown darkness beneath the mattress was actual night, and he had plenty of time to sleep off the impact of ten Manhattans and eight warm Bud Lights. His wife made the call to work. But when Dink came out from under the bed at seven the next morning (after crawling back in once to retrieve a piece of his skull that he thought had fallen off), his wife was waiting with coffee, four Excedrin, and a promise that next time she would be gone for good.

Reg Swain's trade offer caught Dink Otto at the perfect moment. The sight of the McDonough made his stomach twitch, made the room start to come unpinioned. He was determined to quit drinking once and for all, so turning down a bottle of scotch that he could not stand to look at made him feel proud and self-righteous. He phoned his wife to report the rigidity of his spine. He put the ticket in his wallet. By Saturday, the pot had grown to $27 million, and Reg Swain had set the McDonough on the shelf in his bar for a special occasion.

The lottery did not roll over again; one winning ticket was out there somewhere, although by the Wednesday after the drawing no one had come forward. Dink Otto was firm in his resolve for two days, then he downed a couple longnecks Monday before getting the train home, where his wife had already gone to bed and freed him to put together a nice cool string of G&Ts.

By Friday, the fact that no winner had come forward had developed into the kind of "what-if" seminews story that the

Bugle loved. The location where the ticket had been purchased was well documented; the deli owner had already cashed a $270,000 check, his one-percent bonus for selling the winning ticket. The paper liked that he was nearby; they didn't have to send a shooter far to photograph him. But the deli sold thousands of lottery tickets per week and the owner had no specific memory of any individual buyer. His smiling mug ran with a story about the procedures for reporting a win of that magnitude, advice from financial planners about how to invest the money while reducing the tax burden, and reports of past lottery bonanzas that had gone unclaimed in the allotted year. Finally, the six winning numbers were repeated.

Dink Otto, editing the story Friday night for the early Sunday paper, read all the way through to the six numbers before he remembered the ticket in his wallet. He was operating at the moment in a haze of hangover pain, his brain and senses dialed down to a quasi-conscious level that reduced his agony and kept him alert only for the most egregious typographical errors. But as he repeatedly told the media that would subsequently descend on him, "I just felt a lightning bolt of certainty pass through me as I reached for my wallet to check my ticket."

The numbers on the ticket matched the numbers on his tube. Dink Otto did not say a word. His head was clear for the first time in a week. He walked to the bathroom to splash water on his face; then he returned to the newsroom to verify that the numbers in the followup story were the actual numbers drawn Saturday. He looked in the previous Sunday's paper, found the lottery numbers, and they matched those on his ticket. Next, he called the lottery's hotline, where all the numbers for the week were recorded, and he quickly took down the numbers from Saturday's drawing and they matched. As it happened, Dink Otto never worked another moment at the *Bugle.* He stood up at his desk and began to shout, "It's me! It's *me*! *It's me!*"

Reg Swain had plans to tap the McDonough later that weekend. He assumed Dink Otto had checked his ticket and thrown it away like all the other losers, and Swain felt pretty smug about swinging a heavy bottle of fine scotch his way for a dollar chance at pie in the sky. But late Friday night he was awakened by the first of the calls, this one from Rex Hatton, working the slot for the early Sunday editions.

"Dink Otto just quit," Rex reported. "He won the lottery with that ticket you bought for him."

Reg Swain struggled to keep from falling out of bed. His wife had her hand against his back. He maintained a professional tone. "You have enough staff to finish?" he asked.

"Sure. Dink was off in an hour anyway," Rex Hatton said.

"OK. Anything else?" Reg Swain was a master of the intimidating tone, the you're-bothering-me air.

"Just thought you'd want to know."

The next call came in ten minutes, when Reg Swain was seated at his bar in his pajamas staring up at the $27 million bottle of scotch. It was a reporter from the *Morning Quill*, someone Swain had met once or twice, calling to confirm a report that Reg Swain had swapped a lottery ticket for a bottle of scotch, and then the ticket came up a winner.

"It was McDonough," Swain pointed out.

"I'd do the same myself," the *Quill* reporter said.

"I'd make the trade every day of my life," Swain said forthrightly.

"But you must be kicking yourself now," the reporter ventured.

"I don't entertain self-doubt."

Reg Swain was asked to appear with Dink Otto at the winner's press conference, but declined. He politely took calls from the media for one long weekend, until all the major outlets had been satisfied, and then he unplugged his phone. He was back at work Monday, nothing more to say. Dink Otto spent his leisure time and his random fortune at a saloon near the paper, buying killer rounds for everyone, then wandering out to catch the last train home.

Tim Penn had disappeared, but Goop Traky was on the

Green Years story like a manhole cover: "We picked up five more Vegas at Addison and now we're nearing the Edens junction. Cops and spectators are on the overpasses. A paper bag of something resembling fecal matter was dropped on us at Hamlin. Bottles have been thrown. The shotgun riders have passed a long chain from car to car so that all the cars—except the outside one I'm in—are linked together. They tell me my car is being kept loose because they want the print reps to be able to return to file reports. It does them no good to have us locked in traffic. You might be interested to know that the inbound lanes are completely stopped up, too."

"Can you see Vegas inbound?" Danny Fain asked.

"No. Traffic is just stopped. We've stopped, too, right at the Kennedy-Edens split. I see half a dozen state police cars, three city paddy wagons and three IDOT tow trucks."

"Let us know if you get arrested," Dan said.

"Will do. I think I'm going to exit here and become a reporter who happened on the scene."

A belligerent query cut through the newsroom. "Where's my fucking snack?" It was one of the spotted boys leaning out from Dolly Franzen's office.

Muff Greene came to Dan's office.

"You going to the four o'clock?"

"If Lucy isn't back."

"Where did she go?"

"To buy champagne."

"Champagne," Muff Greene repeated with a frown.

"What's new in the pressroom?"

"No change."

"Did he call Barton?"

"He won't call Barton. They loathe each other. And at thirty cents a copy—why bother?"

"Product continuity?" Dan said. "If we don't publish tomorrow, we won't publish again."

"We'll publish—maybe late, maybe not many copies—but we'll publish."

Danny read one last time through the story list; it was basically the morning list hardened up. He had seen better lists. If Tim Penn could come home now with the hit-and-run he would stand a good chance of landing on Page One, with the hijacking and The Green Years. But he could top the page if the KLM situation resolved itself without bloodshed, which was possible. The Green Years would wind up on One only because it was so odd and because it had been anointed by TV. But it would not get to the top of the page; by morning it would be old news, another rush hour already begun. If they could scramble on the dead kid, get a picture, then they would be in business. Derringer was a sucker for big-eyed dead kids on his cover, believing with some justification that weepers pulled coins into the honor-box slots. But they were late and lame on the story, as with so many stories, and there was every possibility that the dead kid could run deep inside, short as an afterthought.

The four o'clock meeting was held in the room where the death of the paper had been announced. Muff Greene occupied Derringer's spot at the head of the table. To her left was Dale Busse with an agglomeration of the day's photos, wire and staff. On down and around the table were Danny Fain; Jack Lustig from Financial; Kelly Lauren, Dolly Franzen's assistant in Features; Duke Taffy, the night Sports Editor; Tommy Boyd, smug as a wolverine with his sure-thing hijacking; then Sledge Martin and Ozzie Todd, the news editors who would actually dummy the paper.

Muff Greene was stirring a mug of tea with her finger.

"Isn't that hot?" Dale Busse asked.

Muff cast a startled look Dale's way, then withdrew her finger. "Now that you mention it, yes," she said. "Who wants to start? Kelly?"

Kelly Lauren said, "Eric is going to write up his encounter with Young Snob God. Dolly may do a sidebar, if she is so moved . . . and we have the funnies. Sounds like a section to me."

"Eric will write for tonight?" Dan asked.

"Of course."

"He hasn't made a same-day deadline in six years. Why start now?"

"He will retire to his office to listen to his Walkman and try to make art out of his experience."

"Forget art," Danny said. "Tell him to shoot for coherent."

"Don't jump on me because your local side has no one with Eric's talent," Kelly snarled.

"Send him over. He'd learn to write in English."

"Stop it, you two," Muff Greene scolded mildly.

"And you give that piece of frippery an office?" Danny said.

"Stop it, Dan. Jack?"

Jack Lustig passed copies of his budget to the people at the table.

"Stock market up eleven when I left. Larry Mock has a very prescient column that he's been tooling with for the past two weeks about how to survive the first month after you lose your job. His advice—don't panic, pay your mortgage and utilities, let everyone else go scratch."

"Easy for Lawrence K. to say," Dale Busse remarked dismally.

"No. Larry's actually tried to imagine this from the perspective of people who aren't independently wealthy," Jack Lustig said. "We also had a merger announced today. SynDataPro has absorbed a small but aggressive frozen food company in Atlanta called Mealtech. Nobody cares, I know, but that will tie nicely with our merger-mania piece. Then Wanda Tanner was on hand for the announcement that Pedro's Nuts on Washington is closing. Pedro actually called a press conference. We've also got the patent attorney reader. And, finally, a last plea to have something about the demise of the *Bugle.*"

"No story," Muff Greene said. "Mock doesn't mention it in his column, does he?"

"Not directly."

"Send me a copy when he's done. I want to read it."

"He'll refuse. His contract stipulates he doesn't have to."

"Ask him. Duke?"

Duke Taffy wore a thin line of beard like a string of animal fur glued to his jawline. He scratched at it with his pencil.

"Bulls play tonight. Bears followups. Hagen Manley sat in with them when they watched films. He's got a story about that. Prep football playoff picture. A soccer player for the Bees was stopped for drunken driving last night in Oak Lawn and still had his cleats on when ordered to get out of the car. He allegedly kicked the arresting officer—soccer-style, I assume—in the nuts, hopped back in his car, and led them a merry chase through the city, thirty-one separate suburbs, and portions of southern Wisconsin. A helluva driver, evidently, with too much car for the police to run down. They lost him and found him and lost him again on three different occasions and finally just sent a couple cars to his house in Naperville—they arrested him when he came home at six A.M., a hot takeout breakfast from McDonald's on the front seat."

"Let's start that on One," Sledge Martin said.

"One is spoken for," Muff Greene said. "Tommy?"

Tommy Boyd said, "The KLM jet is somewhere over Yugoslavia. Heading toward Greece. Beirut has told them they won't be allowed to land. The airline says it would be touch-and-go to make it to Tehran, if Iran'll take them, which is questionable. Athens offered to let the jet land, but the hijackers said no dice. Nancy Potter knows someone at United who looked in their computer and found the names of four people from Chicago who have connections on United for O'Hare out of Kennedy who are on KLM 404. We've got the usual ton o' wire copy on this. The international community in an uproar. Violated airspace and all. West Germany scrambled two fighters to escort 404 through their airspace and now everyone is showing off. Yugoslavia sent up four jets. This story could be growing when it's time for us to go home. Or it could end before this meeting. It feels long to me. Something that could go on for days. Then I've got rioting chefs in Paris because some godless souls are using the wrong kind of eggs in their soufflés. The pope named twenty-four new cardinals today.

One a native American Indian from Seattle now named Ignatius Cardinal Limping Dog. We learn after the fact that a meteorite the size of Jacksonville, Florida—bigger than the one that is rumored to have extincted the dinosaurs, but which missed Abe Skinback—passed within the intergalactic equivalent of a split hair from Earth last month. NASA knew it was coming two weeks before the fact, but decided nothing would be solved by alerting the populace. I personally applaud their decision. I've got a gold miners' strike in the Transvaal, with violence and cracking of heads. Their demands include light in their huts after dark. Not electricity, just candles. A good reader on the most successful counterfeiter in Japan. He happens to be an American who did federal time for counterfeiting here and went to Japan because he was too well known to the G after he got out of prison. Couldn't get work in his chosen trade. Japan can't catch the guy and they're accusing the U.S. of helping him avoid detection because we want his counterfeiting to bring the Japanese economy to its knees. A very paranoid scenario. Next on the list is a family from upstate New York—a mom and her three kids—who are raising money to go to Peru to search for their husband and/or father who—from all indications—has simply abandoned the family to pursue his dream of being a soldier of fortune. She's held a cable TV telethon and rented billboard space to raise funds to pay for her crusade to Peru because a psychic has told her her husband is working in the foothills of the Andes with a cadre of Shining Path guerrillas as a military adviser . . . like they need one. Then I've got record prices paid for a portfolio of erotic Picasso sketches. Well-thumbed and damp wire art has been promised. Dale?"

"They sent one print over but it was too light for us to reproduce," Dale Busse said. "It didn't turn me on."

"Breasts on the side of the head? Nose and eyes all in one corner of the face?" Tommy Boyd asked.

"Hardly more than a doodle," Dale opined. "The good stuff is all in museums."

"I've got campaign stuff," Tommy Boyd said. "Nothing

great. Candidates reacting to the hijacking as expected. It's a terrible thing. The perpetrators will be caught and brought to justice. No mention of how. A half dozen other things. I can give you as many as ten hijack stories or as few as two. Will city side handle the story of the Chicagoans on board?"

Muff Greene looked at Danny Fain. "Do you have someone to do that?" she asked.

"Nancy Potter could write the story," Dan said. "But if we call these four people on the flight, who's going to be home to answer the phone?"

"Relatives. A spouse. A mom," Muff Greene surmised.

"Let's pray it isn't four single people who went to Europe to find the romance that's eluded them in the Windy City," Danny Fain said.

"Don't be so callous," Muff Greene scolded. "What are the odds of that?"

"We'll do the story," Dan said.

"What else have you got?"

"Our top local story was the kid hit-and-run thing until these Green Years nuts showed up. Goop Traky is on the scene. He's been in touch since he left. At last report he had exited his vehicle at the Kennedy-Edens split, where about a dozen green Vegas were chained together across the outbound lanes."

"Their strategy is reminiscent of the French truck drivers in 1984," Tommy Boyd said. "After the customs strike on the France-Italy border?"

"How well I remember," Danny said. "There is no new news. Regardless, the cops are going to have to saw the chains apart, arrest The Green Years, and tow the cars away. Rush hour is terminally bolixed. Do we run their press release?"

"I don't see why we should," Muff Greene said.

"It explains what they were trying to accomplish."

"What do you mean *trying*?" Sledge Martin asked. "They accomplished it."

"I think printing the release will encourage like-minded

groups to attempt other such stunts . . . possibly more dangerous stunts," Muff Greene decided. "No. We don't print it."

Danny Fain shrugged and moved on. "My kid story is at the mercy of Tim Penn, who's dropped out of sight. I know what I saw . . . but you couldn't prove it by me. Most of the rest of the morning list can go or hold."

"Wait," Muff Greene interrupted. "Are you worried about Tim?"

"I'd like to strangle him," Dan said, "so I must not be."

"Shouldn't you send someone to fill in behind him?"

"Send them where, though? That's been the problem all along," Danny Fain said. "I'm still at the mercy of Tim. He could surface with the story, reported, written, and ready to run. I don't think he will, but he could. Until I hear otherwise I have to hate him from afar. OK. Nan Fullwood's SCAR story should run because the woman in question is eager to talk to anyone with a notebook or camera. We were promised before and after art, Dale?"

Dale Busse extracted two glossies from her pile. The first, a photograph of a photograph, was of a young, plain-faced girl with long, lank hair parted in the middle, a slight underbite, a little crop of blackheads on her chin, her arm around a boy with bangs to his eyes and a tie knot the size of a baseball. The second photo was of the same girl some years later, a close-up of her face unattractively aged by pain and fate, a scar that was a quarter-inch wide in some places extending from just outside her left eye, down over her cheek, cutting her lips into four segments, and ending just above the bend in her chin.

Danny showed the picture around to the quiet room. "Can you imagine?" he said. "This guy in the first picture is her husband now. He's claiming alienation of affection because he can't stand to look at her. Nan got a great quote from the HMO. This case drone said the work the woman wanted authorized was extravagant in nature, that she quote 'had not been a beautiful woman before the accident and shouldn't expect the HMO to foot the bill to make her beautiful now.' She cried when Nan read that quote to her. She said she'd be happy to be merely homely again."

"There's your headline," Ozzie Todd chimed in.

Danny said, "Dwight Spang is getting the DEAD story together. He's got a nice grisly twist. Wolf in Evanston may be staging fake burials. STING is the bogus credit cards. It should go tonight just because the *Quill* will get it soon enough—if not already. It's Becky Fudge's, and we have no way of knowing if Alexandra Jones shipped the story tip to the *Quill* before she was run out of here. We've got CTA. Holdable. Bernie's raincoat story isn't something that everyone will be trying to beat us on. VEGAS obviously was tipped to Stan by The Green Years. Their little attempt at media irony. We can fold whatever Stan has into Goop's story. Abe the Skin is writing his appreciation of William O'Berry. I put Grant Lopp on the case looking for a shot of them together."

Again, Dale Busse descended into her stack of photos, removing a brownish print cracked at the edges. She passed it along. Abe Skinback looked hardly a boy in the picture, a round, chubby face, cheeks rouged with the cold night air, his legendary nose merely enormous and pluggish in the center of his face, dominating all other features, giving the awe that seemed to light his eyes at being in the company of William O'Berry a sardonic quality, as if he already understood that the thin man standing before him, wearing a checked sport coat, open-collar sport shirt, and straw fedora was a man in Abe's way, a man on the way out, someone to be crushed. The third person in the photo, which bore a NOV. 11, 1941, time stamp on the back, was a slim blond in a cozy dress whose print was so similar to O'Berry's sport coat that she looked stitched to his side.

"Is that the woman Abe snaked?" Danny Fain asked.

"No one knows. She isn't named on the back," Dale Busse said. "Abe's not around to ID her. She doesn't look like his wife now."

"I think this is wife three he's working on."

"We can run this piece of prehistory or we can pull O'Berry's mug," Dan said. "Abe's already called asking for a refer from the appreciation to his column." He went back to his budget. "DEV can hold. WATER can hold. PUNK should run. We've got mugs?"

"They're being printed," Dale Busse said.

"Studly guys?"

"If you like 'em violent and unwashed," Dale said.

"OK," Muff Greene said. "Your best is the GREEN story?"

"I don't want to give up on Tim," Dan said.

"But your best *concrete* story is GREEN," she insisted.

"Sure."

"With art?"

"We've got all the backed-up traffic you could ever want," Dale Busse said. "Getting a picture of all the cars stopped and chained together and spelling GREEN YEARS is another story. We're working on it."

"We need something for the front," Ozzie Todd said. "It's the one story that has affected just about everyone in the city today."

"You can't play this above the hijacking," Tommy Boyd complained.

"Maybe twin them?" Ozzie suggested. "Hijacked jet. Hijacked city."

"You'd better hope that jet comes down in one piece, Oz," Tommy Boyd warned. "We'd look like real assholes if someone dies after the paper goes to bed—comparing that to a bunch of people getting home late from work."

"Let's see what happens," Sledge Martin said.

"If we don't have a picture that says it, we can't do anything anyway," Ozzie Todd said. "We need more than a standard rush-hour shot."

"Don't give up on Tim Penn for One," Danny Fain said.

"You seem to have," Muff Greene said. "Why shouldn't we?"

"No. I'm a Tim Penn fan until I have intelligence that indicates otherwise."

Lucy Spriggs returned to the newsroom, a delivery boy in tow balancing three fat sacks of deli takeout in his arms. Lucy carried two magnums of Tott's. The kid with the bags waited eagerly while she put the champagne in her office. Seventeen years old, tops, he wore the dilated look of the sexually humming, of the locked-in lover.

Danny Fain returned to his office just as his phone rang. A woman said, "Scroll Metro News," then hung up. He hit a key on his tube. Metro News was a service of young, underpaid journalists hoping to move up to the papers or the wire services, but who until then performed the invaluable service of keeping an eye on those smaller civic dramas the *Bugle* and the *Morning Quill* didn't staff on a regular basis, primarily cops, fires, and lesser courts. They were little more than a tip service, alerting the media to situations that deserved their closer attention.

The slug jumped out at him: BOYFOUND. It had come across at 16:21, while they were in their meeting, but since that initial bulletin three other BOYFOUND entries had come into the queue, each a minute apart, the hallmark of a heating story.

He called up the first item.

The body of an unidentified boy believed to be the victim of a hit-and-run driver was found on the city's far northwest side early Monday afternoon.

MORE TO COME.

The 16:22 item added:

Police are seeking clues to an apparent hit-and-run accident on the city's far northwest side that took the life of an unidentified boy. Police were alerted to the body, found at 117 N. Avondale, near the Chicago and Northwestern railroad tracks, by an anonymous informant who called the Jefferson Park District. Police from the suburb of Park Ridge have been asked to join the investigation.

MORE TO COME

Danny Fain, feeling viciously betrayed but undeniably alive, jumped out of his office. Young Snob God had the bags of food torn open on the floor in front of Dolly Franzen's office, the orders being passed down the line of the hungry. The delivery boy was a fan; he butted in on the feeding frenzy for autographs, happy even to possess one of the backup singers' signatures, but they only glanced beyond him for their drinks.

"DeVille!" roared Danny Fain.

City and suburban Park Ridge police are seeking the driver of a car that fatally struck an unidentified boy in a Halloween costume Monday. The boy—described as approximately ten years of age, five feet tall, one hundred pounds, black hair and green eyes, dressed in a sheet—was discovered by police at 1171 N. Avondale alongside the Chicago and Northwestern tracks after receiving an anonymous tip.

Police canvassing near where the body was discovered northwest of Monument Park found no witnesses to the accident nor anyone who could identify the boy. Park Ridge police were summoned because the boy may be a resident of that suburb, whose boundary is near the scene of the accident.

Jefferson Park District commander Ross Bulwark said, "We've got a little kid dead and not much else. This case is very fresh."

MORE TO COME

Bernie DeVille arrived. "You should've sent me," he sang.

"Shut up, Bernie. Look at the map." Dan spun it around, his finger in place. He dialed Dale Busse. "Dunkirk still available?"

"Barely."

"He's mine for the rest of the day. He's going with Bernie DeVille. They found my kid."

"Your kid?"

"My story."

Was Dana Viola the anonymous one? The driver himself? He would find Tim Penn and roll his testicles through a typewriter carriage, then type his dismissal notice on them.

Lucy Spriggs came running out of her office. "You see Metro News?" she asked, her eyes stricken.

Bernie DeVille went in a hurry across the newsroom, hooked up with Dunkirk in the hall. Dan yelled after him, "Stay away from the Kennedy."

His phone rang. Dana Viola asked smugly, "Is that your story?"

"Are you the anonymous tipster?"

"I see it for the first time before me."

"I'm busy," Dan said.

"You should've played with me." She cut off their call.

"Can you put it on your list?" Lucy Spriggs asked.

Danny nodded. "A weeper, anyway."

"Somewhere there's a mom," Lucy Spriggs said. "If you could find the mom you could make up some of the ground you lost."

Dan said bitterly, "The story's in the open now. Nobody is going to have an exclusive piece of any of it."

"Don't be such an obnoxious prick," Lucy said, catching Dan with the heat of her words.

"Journalistically speaking," he said.

"In *any* shape or form. Some poor mother and father are about to go through the worst experience imaginable," she said.

"And to me—it's just a story I lost."

"Asshole," she condemned him.

"Newsman. Why the champagne?"

She left without answering and he thought: Why is it *my* list now?

Bernie DeVille, as ordered, called the instant he reached his car. "We need a name," Dan said. "And after you get a name we need a family history. If you see Tim Penn . . . not a word to him. He no longer exists."

His phone rang the moment he hung up.

"Turn me on," the caller, a female, possibly Dana Viola, said, and hung up.

He snapped on his TV set, found Channel Eight. The picture was slow to come in, with a scraping of electricity across the inside of the tube, the sound an annoyance of static out of which gradually emerged a nervous, familiar voice that was just tagging out. The picture came clear on a commercial. He ran to the TV lounge. All three sets were on but no one was watching.

"Anybody see Channel Eight just now?" he asked of the newsroom. No one had. He called home. "Did you have the TV on just now?"

"No," Rita said. "Your car's ready."

"How much?"

"High double figures. But less than the VCR."

He was startled to notice it had begun to get dark outside. His big story was blown and Bernie DeVille had been thrown into the hole. Dunkirk would come back with a photo of police cars in the dark, cops' eyes glowing in the flash.

"They found the kid I saw," Dan said.

"Who is he?"

"We don't know yet."

"That poor family."

"Yeah."

"Is it yours alone?"

"No. There was never a chance of that, really. I'd been hoping to get enough of a head start on it, maybe corral the mom before she went into hiding."

In fact, he could not remember what his strategy had been; his intent was to find the kid, for his own proof of what he had seen, and also for the news goose it would give the paper. He wanted to be out in front again, if only for a day.

"Any word on severance?" Rita asked.

"Nothing spendable."

"My mom called," she said. "She opened her bank book to us. She told me exactly what's in the account—and said it's all ours if we just ask."

Dan laughed. Rita's mother—a widow—was relentlessly chipper, but squeezed her money as ardently as a lover. "How much?" he asked.

"I'm not saying—because you'll count on it," Rita said. "And actually getting the money from her is something else entirely."

"I turned down a job in TV news today."

"With Dana?"

"Yeah."

"A *legitimate* job offer?"

"More an offer to exchange items of value. A hint at a job."

Rita hesitated. "I could go to work," she said.

"You'd hate it."

"You can watch the kids. Do the housework."

Pondering that arrangement freshened the anguish of his predicament. He loved his children but he could not stay home with them. His job had stretches of pressure, of grinding routine and psychic bombardment, but it was a treat to come to work after spending a day while Rita was away and the kids were in his care, their demands, their fights, their ferocious, insatiable energy pushing him rather quickly past exhaustion and into a state of jittery rage.

"I'll find work," he said. Rita laughed.

"When are you coming home?" she asked.

"It'll be a while yet."

"The kids have already done our block. They're making threats."

"What kind of threats?"

"They're high on sugar. They want to visit every house they see," Rita said, her voice going up in artificial desperation. "They want people to put treats directly into their mouths. Bypass the bag."

"I'll be home as soon as I can."

"By six?"

"Not likely."

"Seven?"

"I'll try for seven. I'll call you from the station to tell you which train to meet," he said.

Lucy Spriggs emerged from her office with the two big bottles of Tott's champagne, then made her way down the center aisle of the office cooing, "Party. Party. Party in Wally's office." She poked her head into Danny Fain's office to sweetly proclaim, "Party, asshole. I need witnesses." She carried the chubby green champagne bottles like Indian clubs at her side.

Deadlines be damned, the *Bugle* staff followed Lucy Spriggs to Derringer's office, then hung back while she went in alone. He was leaning back in his chair, his gaze elevated, tossing a baseball autographed by the 1984 Cubs up toward the ceiling, trying to see how close he could come without touching.

"Who has Luce in the pool?" a voice asked.

She unpeeled the foil from the champagne, removed the wire cap cage, and began to work at the cork with a knowing coax of thumbs and fingers, the bottle braced against her haunch. "Got any glasses, Wally?" she asked.

He kept a sleeve of plastic glasses on a counter behind his desk. He got one out and assembled—stem into base—just in time to catch the golden spew that rocketed from the bottle when Lucy Spriggs shot the cork. It left a dent in the ceiling.

"What's the occasion?" Derringer asked blithely, assembling glasses and pouring.

Lucy Spriggs had gone to work on the second bottle.

"I'm leaving," Lucy Spriggs said.

"Today?"

"In a moment," she said.

Derringer stood motionless over his spread of golden glasses. "I thought I could count on you to see the job done," he scolded.

"I thought I could count on you, too."

People came in and hoisted glasses. The moment had been spoiled by Lucy's announcement; she was no longer one of them, evidently, and they were no longer interested in her. Some toasted her silently and meandered back out the door, killing their champagne with one swallow, irritated at being drawn from their work on deadline for such an undeserving occasion as a staffer leaving before it was proper to do so.

Danny Fain picked up a glass. The base fell off and he didn't bother to reassemble it. "Where?" he asked.

"PR for the American Dairy Association," she said, shamefaced, smiling with relief at having it out and having the job.

"Milk?" Derringer said.

She aimed toward him with the second bottle. Danny wondered afterward if it had been her plan all along or if the opportunity was just too irresistible. But she pointed the cork at Derringer's head with the precision of an assassin and it went off like a cannon against the side of his head. The cork reported sharply off the thick bone of Derringer's skull, then champagne shot through the void left when he fell to the floor. He did not go all the way down, only to one knee, so that his pose was vaguely abject and romantic; a proposal might be forthcoming. His shoulders and across the top of his back were splashed with champagne.

"Get out," he commanded. A red crescent wound gleamed meanly a quarter inch from his temple. "You haven't officially tendered your resignation . . . so I'm firing you."

"No. I quit."

"Too late. Your timing was lousy." He got to his feet. He pushed gently, wincing, at the wound on the side of his head. "You should've planned better, Lucy. Now I'm going to dog the rest of your career with a firing."

"No one cares about that stuff, Derringer." She left with the second bottle.

"Milk?" Dan said, following her to his office.

"They called just after lunch," she said. "I'd interviewed with them four years ago when I was fed up here. They even offered me a job then. But between the interview and the job offer I got involved in the Betterman scandal stories and I loved my job again." She fell onto his couch with her bottle of champagne and took a swallow; elongated neck tendons working, pulling the liquid in, gave Dan disquieting visions. She said, "So I told them no *then.* They heard we were closing and called just to see if I would change my mind under the circumstances."

"It's nice to be wanted, I'll bet," Dan said.

"A company car. A three-year contract. Corner office on the fifty-first floor facing east and north. More money," she said.

"Hell. Money, period."

"Hell yes."

"How much more?" Danny asked. He *had* to ask.

"Thousands."

"Ten thousand?"

She held her champagne bottle up to the fading window light to check the level. "Don't do this to yourself, Fain. You'll get another job."

"PR for the Apple Pie Association?"

"Don't be bitter. The Motherhood Foundation?" she cracked, and he laughed. His phone rang. He wanted her to stay and help him run Bernie DeVille and Dunkirk in the field, but she was on her feet and out the door with her hand raking through the nest of her hair, her walk all hips, challenge and insinuation.

Danny picked up the phone. "See me," Derringer said.

He was back in his chair tossing his Cubs ball at the ceiling. The cork hole in his head had begun to cool.

"You're the new Lucy," Derringer said. "Starting now. Get to work."

"Pay?"

"You made about the same."

"She made ninety more a week than me," Dan said.

"OK. You get ninety more. Go do what she did, whatever that was, only better."

"One more thing," Danny Fain said. "My severance, when the figures come out . . . mine gets computed at my new rate, correct?"

"That's not up to me," Derringer answered.

"Sure it is. Everything is up to you," Dan stroked.

"You have my backing then. If you can wrangle the paperwork out of whoever, I'll sign it," Derringer said.

"Thanks."

"Go to work."

Bernie DeVille reported in. "We're still twenty minutes to a half hour from the scene. My scanner is picking up all kinds of action on this. Every TV station's dispatcher is going nuts. Traffic is fucking incredible. Everyone is heading where we're heading, except Eight. They have a truck going to some other location. They had the driver call the station by telephone to keep the location a secret. I tried to call 'em and pretend I was their driver but they have a *password* and that caught me."

"I bet they found the mother," Dan said.

"My guess. Somebody. You got the kid's name?"

He scrolled through the incoming wire. "Nothing," he said. "The police are mum."

"Metro got us on the scent. That's all they claim to do. You know the *Quill*'s on it."

"How could Eight have found the mom if no one knows the kid's name?" Dan asked.

"TV does things to people. Opens doors. Loosens mouths."

"Where are you now?"

"We're on Milwaukee. Just passing Addison."

"Turn left at Higgins. Take Higgins to Canfield. Go right. Jesus, you'll never get there."

"We're running into all kinds of traffic, Fain. We're seven hours late on this story, you realize."

"Get as close as you can, then walk. Call me as soon as you get a name. I can work it from this end, too."

He hung up the phone. Quickly he snapped through every TV station; after-school pap, *Barney Miller* rerun, animals eating animals on the public station. Only Channel Eight was carrying news, their 4:30 broadcast running; a light-skinned black reporter was interviewing a darker-skinned black man about a liquor store robbery on the West Side. Behind the two men jumped a hundred little black kids, mugging for the camera, pulling grins, waving, sticking their faces one in front of the other like a dance line. It seemed to Dan a small story. Then the reporter cued a piece of film with a warning that what was to follow should not be witnessed by children. Somehow Eight had come into possession of a strip of security film; the angle was from the ceiling, the picture grainy, grayish. Two men in ski masks came into the liquor store, a brief set of demands were uttered. The man behind the counter was quick to do as he was told. He jammed cash into a paper bag. The robbers asked for a pint of rum. The cashier complied. One robber took the loot and walked out of camera range. The other raised a gun and fired into the cashier's face, then Channel Eight was back on the street.

Dan's phone rang.

"Did you see that?" Muff Greene asked.

"On Eight? Yeah."

"Call over there. See if we can get a freeze-frame of the guy with the gun aimed at the cashier," she said.

"Why should they help us?" Danny asked. "We can't repay them in the future."

"Just call." She hung up on him.

He phoned Dana Viola.

"Hey, I was just about to call you," she said. "Where did I put my notes?"

"Notes on what?"

"On you," she said. "I was calling to interview you."

Dan replied, edgy, "For a job?"

"No. A story. News."

"Do you have the kid's name?" he asked.

"Name. Age. Address. School. Best friend," Dana said. "Why didn't you contact the police as soon as you saw the boy struck by the car?"

"Who told *you* about that?"

"Hey, I'm a reporter. Why didn't you go to the cops?"

"I wasn't sure what to tell them," Dan said.

"Wouldn't it have made more sense to get the resources of the Chicago Police Department on the case immediately?"

"That sounds like it's written down in front you, Dana."

"In shorthand, it is. Let me get this straight in my mind: Rather than notify the police, you sent a reporter out to look for the body?"

"Is this being recorded?"

"I have to tell you beforehand if it is," Dana Viola said. "What were your motives for sending out a reporter rather than calling the police?"

"Do the police know the kid's name?" Dan asked.

"Of course."

"Why isn't it on the wire?"

"Do your own leg work, Dan. Don't count on the wires. The *Quill* doesn't. We don't. Would you admit that you saw the boy as a possible scoop for your paper?"

He tried to deflect her. "Everyone likes a scoop," he said. "Gotta go."

"Let me ask—"

"Got work to do."

Once more through the incoming wires; no names, nothing new about the story. From the coverage it was getting after the opening burst it might never have happened; a mistake by the wire service, a stutter, a practical joke. He looked in the *Bugle*'s computerized reference files for a phone number to the Jefferson Park District station. He reached a lieutenant and identified himself.

"We're too busy to talk to the press," the lieutenant said. "When we have something to tell you we'll call you."

"Can you give me the kid's name?" Dan asked.

"When we get it, the parents will be told. Then *you'll* get it. OK? I know you're just doing your job, but shit, it's a creepy job."

"We have reports you know the boy's name," Dan said.

"Are you calling me a liar?"

"No. I'm trying to get the kid's name. I'm trying to make some sense out—"

"Is that my job?"

"Don't tell me the kid's name. Just tell me: Do you even *know* the kid's name?"

"As far as I know—and that isn't far—and off the record, the body remains unidentified."

Melvin Devlin wandered over from the copy desk. He had a little white mustache and suspenders. "You've got a name spelled three different ways in this Nat LaRue story," he said. "Whitsell. Witsell. Whitesell."

"Talk to Nat, Melvin," Danny said.

"She quit."

"She did?"

"That's the story I was told. LaRue quit and I'm supposed to see you. You're the new Lucy."

Danny went out to the city desk.

"Nat LaRue quit?" Danny Fain said.

Muff Greene was in the City Desk slot. Frazzled, she looked up from her tube. "Nat and Constance Drane," she said. "All gone. They gave the traditional two minutes' notice."

"They have jobs?"

Muff Greene said, "Connie is, and I quote, 'Going home to have a baby and let my husband support me. I don't need this shit.' Unquote. Nat just quit and walked out. I wasn't interested in her when she worked here; I'm not interested in what she'll be doing now that she doesn't work here."

"Can you help me with this spelling?" Melvin Devlin pressed.

Danny sat at Goop Traky's tube, its keys stiff, blue, and crusted with nubs of eraser glued to the high-tech landscape with dried spit. Goop's notes from the last year were stacked in an empty printout paper carton; everything in it was old, yellowed, slick with a powder like cremation ash. He signed on to Goop's tube and called up the notes from the story that presently bedeviled Melvin Devlin. In the notes the name Whitsell was spelled three different ways. "Fuck," Dan muttered. He wrote down phone numbers. "Here's four different phone numbers, Melvin," Danny Fain said. "One of them might belong to Whitsell."

"How does slipshod work like this get through?" Melvin Devlin asked rhetorically, drifting off.

"A story at a time," Dan said.

"Did you talk to Eight about that frame?" Muff Greene asked.

Dan lied. "Yeah. They won't do business with us. It doesn't, and I quote, 'Behoove us to provide art elements for you when you will not be in business to provide future quid pro quo for us,' unquote."

"Flaming dickmongers," Muff Greene cursed.

"It was just gore," Dan said. "We don't need gore. Let's take the high road in these last days."

Muff Greene gave him a scornful smile. "You who've wasted a day and two staffers chasing a boy hit by a car say let's take the high road?"

"We're guaranteed an audience of mourners and vultures for our last editions," Dan said. "Let's be the next two weeks' paper of record, what do you say?"

"Go back to work."

"It isn't wasted yet," Dan said.

Satin-clad and smoking, a record company guy emerged from Dolly Franzen's office and cut a line toward Danny Fain and Muff Greene.

"I've just heard disquieting intelligence," he said, drawing his glasses down out of his hair and settling them on his nose.

"You can't smoke here," Nancy Potter said. She had come up behind Dan; she was tall, her hair sapped of texture by the creature within her, the knob of her pregnancy bundled under the humorless blue and white stripes of her shift. "We've got a lounge for smokers. Please use it."

"She's right," Dan said.

"You're closing?" the record guy asked. "Ceasing publication?"

"Yes."

"Please extinguish all smoking materials," Nancy Potter stated like a brochure. "Secondary smoke is more harmful than direct smoke, and research has shown a correlation between cigarette smoke and diminished birth weight in infants."

"The boys can't be wasting time talking to a moribund pub," the record guy declared.

"We thought you knew," Dan said.

"*I* didn't know. It was a favor. We broke pattern to fit this in because Snob knew this Moss asshole. Never would have happened if we knew you were belly up."

"We aren't yet," Muff Greene said.

"We don't need you." He made a signal over his head with a finger that got his party to their feet in Dolly Franzen's office, the singers slinking down off the windowsills, everyone standing and looking for pockets or free hands to stash the remnants of their snacks. The second record guy led them out in the order they had entered, Eric Maas in step beseeching his friend Snob to remain.

Nub of butt pinched between thumb and finger, the head record guy scanned the terrain for a receptacle to deposit his waste. Nancy Potter advanced from her desk with a cup of something. It was coffee—a cool, creamy brown—that she poured over the guy's hand, dousing the smoke with a hiss, then flinging the last eighth-inch of liquid against his chest.

"No wonder you're dying," he said equably, dabbing at the spotted satin with a handkerchief passed immediately by his assistant. "This rathole. A staff of psychopaths. It ain't my fault, Lips, that you're history . . . but it *pleases* me."

Young Snob God had paused in their retreat to witness this exchange. The record guy jumped on them: "What're *you* looking at? Did I tell you to stop? You should be in the car by now. Sell one less record next year and you'll be looking for a new way of life like these chumps. Go! Get 'em out of here, Mur!"

Eric Maas trailed them some distance out of sight, then returned.

"I got enough to pencil something into the ether," he announced. "You want it?"

"Dolly has your length," said Muff Greene.

"She's sobbing in her blotter."

"Wait until she stops. *Then* ask her."

Goop Traky called from a pay phone at the Albany Park police station on Pulaski. "Can you send someone down to bail me out?" he asked.

"Is this your one phone call?" Danny Fain asked.

"More or less."

"Are there green people waiting in line to use the phone?"

"No. This bunch has its own lawyers," Goop said. "I may be the last to get out of jail."

"They're seriously going to arrest you?"

Dan heard Goop Traky sigh. "I can't tell. I haven't been printed or booked, but they won't give me permission to leave."

"Can you dictate?"

"I could. I've got some good stuff. But I'd like to keep at this until the last minute."

"Did they arrest any TV types?"

"That's what I hear. But all the TV guys I've seen have been working."

"Is the story over?" Danny asked.

"The obvious parts of it, yes," Goop said. "The IDOT trucks had bolt cutters and snipped the chains. That freed the cops to get the Vegas open and haul our green friends off to jail. Then they started pulling green Vegas off the road. By the time we were carted off all but one lane of the Kennedy was open. It'll be slow going until all evidence of The Green Years is removed from the shoulder and people don't have anything to slow down and look at. We got here about twenty-five minutes ago. The expressways are the state police's jurisdiction, but their lockup at Des Plaines isn't big enough to handle this many people. So they sent some here. The Green Years had a lawyer waiting. Presumably he carries sufficient cash to spring them. There are about a dozen here now. About the same number at Des Plaines. They've also shipped some to Crestwood, Blue Island, Elgin. Most of the green people off the Stevenson are at Brighton Park. Ryan blockers are at Wentworth. From where I'm standing I can see a small pile of moss masks on a table."

"Any IDs yet?" Dan asked.

"No. They're kids. Some females, maybe four or five out of the bunch here. They've got auto theft charges to deal with besides whatever they give them for fucking with the rush hour."

"Do you really need us to send a lawyer?" Danny Fain asked.

"I don't know. Let me nose around here. I've got a little time," Goop said.

Five to five and nearly dark. Traffic of the normal and at peace streamed up and down the bi-levels of Wacker Drive across the river, everyone in a hurry to get home, as he was. He sat down to watch the news. His phone rang.

Dana Viola calling: "Do you have any response to the fact three *Bugle* pressmen were injured during their arrest and removal from your pressroom?"

"*What?*"

"Where do you work, Chile?"

He confronted Muff Greene. She told him to talk to Derringer. Derringer was on the phone, his back to the room, feet up, head back, baseball going up to graze the ceiling. Dwight Spang in the TV lounge shouted, "Hey! Look at this!"

Danny Fain stepped in. Tim Penn had been found, onscreen, sitting in a Channel Eight blazer, interviewing a weeping woman.

"Tell us about Ralph, your son," Tim Penn said.

The woman sat up straight. She was in her early thirties, rather pretty beneath the haggard fatigue of her grief. She had presence enough to hook the dark strands of her hair behind her ears. Her name came on the screen: *LAUREN MUSTAIN.* "Ralph was just a sweet boy. He loved Halloween. He loved all the holidays. I'm the first to admit he had a little mischief in him. He spent an hour last night cutting the eyes and mouth out of one of my good sheets without asking me. He went as a ghost."

Tim Penn turned. His killer looks were made electric by the camera, a layer of enhancing light buttered over the perfection of his features.

"Are those his real eyes?" asked a girl in the TV lounge.

"Yes, he went as a ghost," Tim Penn said into the camera

with a sleazy polish Danny Fain had to credit, "and now police are seeking a witness to the hit-and-run accident that killed Ralph Mustain."

They cut to a nondescript brick building that had the institutional look of a school. An address was flashed beneath this image. Tim Penn, in voice-over, continued: "Ralph did not appear at his fifth-grade class here at the Edgar Allan Poe School in Park Ridge. . . ."

Danny Fain shouted, "Is someone getting this down?"

Dwight Spang was sitting in front of the three sets with a pad of paper and a pencil. "I'm monitoring," he said. But nothing was written on his pad.

"We need an address," Dan said.

Neither of the five o'clock news programs on the other sets had mentioned the hit-and-run. Quite possibly they were waiting until their crews, frozen in the Green Years jam, reached the site. There was nothing to report if there were no pictures.

"Ralph's teacher filed an absent child report, assuming that Ralph's mother had called to say her son would not be at school today," Tim Penn went on. "It was not until almost noon that Poe School officials determined that Ralph Mustain had an unexcused absence."

A second woman, her eyes nervous and distraught behind thick stop-sign lenses, her mouth pinched around every word, appeared on screen behind the name *ELISE DONOVAN, Teacher.* Tim Penn was right there with her, the afternoon breeze snapping playfully at his sky-blue lapels.

"Ralph was a good boy," the teacher said. "But an indifferent student. He had a history of cutting classes, taking the easy way out, not shouldering his share of responsibilities. Only because it was Halloween and Ralph had been genuinely excited about our class party was I troubled that he hadn't come to school today."

They cut to the site where the body was found. The scene had been shot earlier in the afternoon; the light was inclining faintly toward dusk. Dan did not recognize the location from the angle it was shot, low to the ground, looking up at the track berm, as Ralph Mustain might have viewed the scene if he had been afforded a last glimpse back before he died. An inbound commuter train hurtled through the picture.

Tim Penn's voice said, "Police believe Ralph Mustain came on a secret errand to this neighborhood near the border between Chicago and Park Ridge prior to going to school. It is several blocks out of his way and police are speculating that drugs might have been involved."

A police officer appeared onscreen. His name: *LT. CARL SCANLON, Park Ridge Police:* "We have reason to believe the victim had begun a flirtation with drugs and met someone here or possibly at Monument Park to purchase those drugs."

"Were drugs found in Ralph Mustain's possession?" Tim Penn asked.

"Yes."

"What kind of drugs?"

"We don't want to reveal that at this time."

"Cocaine?"

"Not cocaine."

The cop disappeared. Tim Penn was back in the Mustain house, seated on an ottoman in front of the weeping mother.

He said, "Police sources report three marijuana cigarettes, or joints, were found in Ralph Mustain's pocket."

Tim Penn continued, "Poe School officials notified Lauren Mustain at approximately one o'clock that her son had not come to school today. She first made a tour of the neighborhood, visiting places she knew her son might go when he was hiding out with his friends. She could not find her son and at one-thirty she notified Park Ridge police that he was missing."

Lt. Carl Scanlon reappeared: "We spoke to officials at Poe School and determined that the victim had a history of truancy and unexcused absenteeism. Our officers made a canvass of the immediate area and found nothing."

"Did you discount Lauren Mustain's report because of what the school told you about Ralph?" Tim Penn asked.

"Not at all. But we had every confidence the boy would return home safely and hopefully get a good licking for causing so much trouble," Lt. Carl Scanlon replied.

"Did you, in fact, not look very hard for the boy?"

"We *looked* for the boy," the cop said irritably.

"Can you respond to reports that from where the boy was found and the location of his injury, the car that hit him had to be going the wrong way down a one-way street?" Tim Penn asked.

Lieutenant Scanlon stuck out his jaw, squinted at the reporter. "You'll have to talk to Chicago about that."

The camera returned to where the body was found. This was a different angle, still daylight, looking down a narrow lane, the railroad on the left, a line of garages on the right, in the distance the police department's yellow scene-freeze tape fluttering in a loose square around a group of cops crouching to sift the grit for clues. Tim Penn stepped into the picture.

"Chicago police received an anonymous call at three twenty-eight this afternoon alerting them to where they could find the body of Ralph Mustain. He was found precisely where the tip said he would be. Ralph had sustained injuries to the legs, hips, and head consistent with being struck by a car, but police sources reported being perplexed because the positioning of the body on the left-hand side of the road indicated the car that hit the boy was traveling the wrong way down this one-way street. Police also are reportedly puzzled about why the body was not discovered sooner. It was found clearly visible along the side of the road."

Dwight Spang noted idly, "Tim's reporting the hell out of this story. Didn't I see him in here this morning?"

"Fain!" It was Derringer calling. He was in his office with his face pressed close to the TV screen. Tim Penn was talking to him; he was back in the mother's house, still plunked down on the ottoman.

"Isn't that Tim Penn?" Derringer asked.

"Yes it is."

"Isn't that your guy on this story?"

"He was."

"I didn't realize he was such a good reporter," Derringer said admiringly. "He's kicking some butt here for a pretty boy."

"He should be kicking butt for us," Dan said.

"This is unprecedented," Derringer said. "Who'd you follow him with?"

"Bernie DeVille."

"We're safe there. Bernie doesn't have the face for TV," Derringer said.

"I'm hearing rumors about the pressroom," Danny Fain said.

"Ignore them. We print on our own presses tonight as always," Derringer said.

"I heard three men were injured."

Derringer looked one-eyed at Dan across the horizon of his baseball, as if aiming. "It's over, Danny."

"It's news."

"This dead kid is news. KLM is news. The Green thing is news. Our pressroom *isn't* news," Derringer said. "Anything Bernie turns up on this story is already old because your guy in the field didn't respect you enough to stay on the team. These guys are going to go in living color at ten o'clock."

"If he had a paper to work for he'd still be with us," Danny Fain said.

"Oh, sure. Blame the closing. Everybody's blaming everything on the closing," Derringer said.

Dan returned to the TV lounge. "What do the others have?" he asked.

"Four has film at the site. The bones," Dwight Spang said. "Nothing more. Penn is all alone on this story."

"Where are they playing us?"

"Nothing yet."

"Come with me," Dan said.

Dwight Spang followed him to his office. "I want you to go downstairs and find out what happened in the pressroom," Danny Fain said. "Somebody will talk. Discretion is everything. No clue you're doing a story. Write up what you get and send it to me."

"I don't want my name on it," Dwight Spang said.

"It won't be."

"Will you get it in?"

"I just want to find out what happened."

His phone rang. Lucy Spriggs was calling from a crowded locale, a festive place, music and laughter like a ceiling she had to crouch beneath to be heard. She had to yell, "This is Luce! Did you see Channel Eight?"

"Yeah. Needless to say this will effect his severance benefits," Dan said.

Lucy Spriggs laughed, but perhaps at someone else.

"Are you drinking milk?" Dan asked.

"On the rocks. What has Bernie found?" she asked.

"Nothing. He's not even there yet."

"Prick that he is, Tim's all over this story," she shouted. "You've got to give him that."

"No I don't. I've got to go, Luce."

Bernie DeVille reported in. "We've been here ten minutes," he said. "We got the kid's name. We've got verbal lameness from Park Ridge and city police. Dunkirk has some night shots," Bernie summarized. "We went to his house to talk to his mom but she's wrapped up tight. No media."

"Tim Penn talked to her at length," Dan said.

"Penn's still on this?"

"He's working for Channel Eight. He's their lead man on this."

"Holy mother—" Bernie DeVille shouted.

"He's got a drug angle," Dan said. "He's got the chronology. He's got the car going the wrong way down a one-way street."

"Drug angle?" Bernie DeVille said meekly.

"Three joints were found on the kid. Did you talk to cops or meter maids?"

"I'm blind on this, Dan. Don't give me that sarcastic shit. If you'd have sent me first thing I'd be right with Penn on this story," Bernie said.

"What about the kid's father?"

"Stepfather. Real father unknown, except probably to Penn. All indications at the house are the stepfather was functioning as the mom's filter. Some said more like an agent."

"How about school? His teacher? Principal?"

"We're still fuzzy on where he went to school," Bernie DeVille admitted.

"He goes to Poe. Go talk to *somebody* who knows what the fuck's going on," Danny Fain ordered, and slammed down the phone.

Tim Penn was next to call. "Timothy Penn, Channel Eight news," he said, so serious Dan thought he was kidding. "We wanted to get your version of what you witnessed of the Ralph Mustain hit-and-run this morning. Do I have your permission to record your comments?"

"Tim!"

"Timothy Penn, Channel Eight. Do I have your permission?"

"No, you don't. Now talk to me as Tim Penn, *Bugle* defector and treasonous slimepod."

"Business, babe. Nothing more. Can I get your comments? I've got a million calls to make."

"When did they give you the job?" Danny Fain asked.

"This afternoon. Now, tell me what you saw from the train," Tim Penn said.

"Were you the anonymous tipster?" Dan asked.

"I can neither deny nor confirm that. As I recall, you said it was a red car that hit the kid," Tim Penn ventured.

"Did I say that?"

"We'll leave that line of questioning to the police," Tim Penn said. "The more interesting side of the story is why you did not notify the police immediately of what you saw."

"No comment."

"As I recall, you wanted to find the boy yourself so you could make a better story out of the tragedy for your paper."

"No, I wanted *you* to find the kid," Danny Fain said.

"What were your plans after you found the boy?"

"What time did you find him?" Dan asked.

"I can't go into that."

"Did you plant the joints on him?"

"Come *on.* This story didn't need grass on the kid to be a beauty. That was just gravy. Did you see the mama?"

"Now that's the Tim Penn I know talking," Danny Fain said.

"Timothy. Bigger salary, longer name."

"How did Dana find you?"

"I've been flirting with her for years. We'd see each other at parties or at functions and I'd ask her when she was going to hire me and she'd say I was too handsome to be taken seriously and bullshit like that," Tim Penn said. "Today I called with something to trade and we cut a deal on my car phone. They had a crew out in twenty minutes with my very own blazer and I've been smoking you ever since."

"Such a prick you are," Dan said.

"Get your story together, Danny Fain. The media isn't through with you yet," Tim Penn threatened.

"Did you move the body?"

"Hey, I'm a reporter."

Danny Fain hung up and called directory assistance, asked for the number of Lauren Mustain in Park Ridge. No such number. He called Bernie DeVille.

"Where are you?"

"We're outside the kid's house. I've gotta start typing and Dunkirk has to print if we're going to make the first edition," Bernie DeVille said.

"Head in, then. Who's there?"

"TV trucks. A couple police cars. Lots of civilians willing to talk. The hit-and-run hasn't curbed the trick-or-treating. But the mom is locked inside."

"Is Tim still with her?"

"I can't confirm that, Danny. There's a Channel Eight truck here but they've got a million trucks."

"Do you have a phone number for the house?"

"No. Try four-one-one."

"I did. Nothing for Lauren Mustain."

"Her first name's Karen. And she's taken the stepfather's name. Brickland. Spelled like the land of bricks. Chuck Brickland. Unemployed. Neighbors report he yells morning to night. The houses here are very close together and you can hear him up and down the block."

"That's good color, Bernie. What does it have to do with this story?" Dan asked.

"The police have, off the record, a passing interest in Chuck Brickland. He negotiated with TV for an exclusivity fee to talk to the grieving mom," Bernie DeVille said, his voice dripping with happiness over this telling bit of dirt.

"How much?"

"Ten thousand is the figure we heard."

"Did it get paid?"

"Who can say? She would only talk to Eight, though. You'd think she'd want her story to go wide so more people would be aware of it, better chance of catching the driver. You'd *think* that."

"Is the stepdad a suspect?"

"He doesn't own a car. But the police aren't ruling him out. And, really, why run the kid over if you wanted to kill him? It's awfully inefficient, if killing him was your goal," Bernie DeVille speculated.

"What about the kid's friends?"

"All in school," Bernie DeVille said. "The moms are out thick getting their kids' alibis perfected. *Everyone* was in school. The three joints in the kid's possession have changed it from a neighborhood tragedy into a kid they didn't really know that awfully well and whom their children didn't really spend all that much time with getting mowed down. But we have seen the odd kid crying. Dunkirk got some good neighborhood grief."

Directory assistance had no number for Karen Brickland. They did have a number for Charles Brickland. It was busy. Danny Fain's phone rang.

"Todd Sowell, Dan, from AP. How you doing? We met at a party on Nancy Stone's roof outside Wrigley? The Pirates were in town? I hit on you for a job and you blew me off, remember?"

"No, Todd. But I believe you."

Todd Sowell cleared his throat. Danny Fain could almost hear his notebook cover flip open. "You're news, Dan. How does that make you feel?"

"Well, I hate to blow you off again, but I'm in the busiest part of my day and I don't have time to talk. Here's a quick one that I'll try to retinker for everyone who calls so they won't all sound alike: I'm damned disappointed the *Bugle* is closing. It's a dark day for journalism and the city of Chicago. When UPI calls I'll say it's a black day. When Reuters calls, gloomy."

Todd Sowell laughed drily. "Funny, Dan. But that's old news. You're *new* news. Is it true you witnessed this Mustang kid getting hit by a car and then didn't report it?"

"Yes, that is true," Danny Fain said.

"Jesus, Dan. That makes us all look like bloodsuckers."

"Gotta run, Todd."

"Will you be holding a press conference?"

"No."

"It would be a service to your colleagues."

"Let them dig," Dan said.

He had missed the six o'clock train. He walked down the hall to Financial. The room was empty and dark but for Lawrence K. Mock at work in his office, one goose-neck light bent above his head as he tapped at a calculator with the eraser end of a pencil. Dan moved in a whisper to the tray on the desk where the Financial dummy duplicates were stacked. He secreted the dupes in his hip pocket and returned to his office. Down in the corner of the section's third page was the perfect spot; inconspicuous, a small hole, for Dan did not expect Dwight Spang to have much to write about.

He tried Charles Brickland; busy. He called his house.

"I missed the six o'clock," Danny Fain said. "Seven is iffy."

"So the earliest you can be here is eight-thirty," Rita said.

"It's looking that way."

"I'm going to take them out, then," she said. "Tracy's already crabby. If we wait for you we might miss the whole night and they'd be crushed."

"Sure," Dan said.

"If you get home . . . maybe you can take them on a late run," she said.

"They're starting to nip at my heels on this kid thing," Dan said. "I got a call from AP suggesting I hold a press conference."

"Tell them to call me. I'll be your alibi," she teased.

"The actual dead kid story is getting cold," Dan said. "But a member of the media who withheld information about a fatal accident in order to enhance his paper's coverage of the event . . . *that's* news. That's something the man on the street can get inflamed about."

"I had doubts myself," Rita admitted.

"I didn't know what I'd seen."

"You saw *something.* You didn't know exactly *where.* But I agree with them, you should have gone with that to the police."

Danny Fain winced. "Maybe I won't have them call you," he said.

She didn't bite on the joke. "I'm just telling you what I think. I don't think I'll be alone in thinking that, either. For instance, you didn't know whether the kid was dead or not. They might have found him in time to save him."

"What should I do?"

"Tell them what happened. Take your lumps."

His next call was from the police, or a man claiming to be the police; he had a cool, refined manner of speaking that somehow soothed Dan's anxiety and made him want to talk.

The cop said, "You're in a pickle, Dan, and I think it would be best if you just told us what you saw and what you were thinking when the boy was hit and we can get this resolved. No one suspects you of being *guilty* of anything beyond perhaps a case of questionable professional judgment."

"What did you say your name was again?"

"Lieutenant ter Horst. Jefferson Park District. We'd sure appreciate it if we could handle this over the phone," he said. "Our manpower is stretched pretty thin between this, those environmental nutballs, and Halloween pranksters. Crooks are just kids at heart and they seem to get all excited and *active* on Halloween. We're going crazy out here since the sun went down. It would be a big help if we didn't have to send a man downtown just to take a few facts from you."

"I've got to insist on a face-to-face, Lieutenant," Dan said. "I'm getting calls from the media already."

"They wouldn't pretend to be cops, though."

"If I won't talk to them as reporters, they'll pretend to be cops."

"Leaking scrotal sacs, all of em," Lieutenant ter Horst opined. "Present company excepted, of course."

"Sure."

"What color car did you see hit Ralphie?"

"I've got to insist."

"Jesus, Dan. Can I give you a number at the district you can call to check me out?"

"The press room?"

"A little trust, Dan? Can I have a little trust? This would be a huge help to me."

"You've got a dead kid on your hands. It's worth it to spare the man to come downtown to talk to me. I saw something. I couldn't place the location at the time, but now that's beside the point because the kid has been found."

"Why didn't you call and tell us you saw *something*?"

"Lieutenant . . ."

"You weren't hoping to capitalize on what you saw, were you?"

"I've got to see your badge before I go into that."

"OK. If you can't help me."

"I'm not going to hang around here all night, either."

"Hey, drop the prick act. You've made your point."

"I just didn't want you coming down here and finding me gone."

"You live in the city or the sticks?"

"Sticks."

"Can you hang around an hour?"

"It's a chance you'll take."

"I can't promise I'll be there in an hour. What if I gave you my badge number and a number to call for verification? Would that convince you?"

"Not tonight."

"Christ."

Next came a call from one George Proctor, *Morning Quill* reporter: "I hate to do this to a fellow pro, Dan, but I drew short straw on ringing you for your version of what happened today. Pencil poised, I listen."

Danny Fain laughed and hung up.

The phone rang immediately and it was Goop Traky.

"Did they arrest you?"

"Nah," Goop said. "They had enough paperwork without dragging me into it. Here's the deal," he said. "Twenty-one in toto shipped to Des Plaines, and still there. The oldest a male, twenty-four, the youngest an eighteen-year-old female from Winnetka. Citywide, it could be as many as a hundred green people arrested. The lawyer I met is named Howe, he knows nothing about the organization, only that they paid his fee up front and promised him an additional percentage of whatever the total bond was. He knows of other lawyer types who were hired and dispatched to any lockup in the city that held a member of The Green Years. Howe says his only instructions were to make sure none of them stayed in jail overnight and to reiterate to the media to print or broadcast the press release in its entirety. Even in chains they remain committed to having their message heard."

"Muff says it doesn't run," Danny Fain said.

"Maybe I can quote from it?" Goop said. "It doesn't make sense not to explain what these people were trying to accomplish."

"You won't get an argument from me," Dan said.

"You got a copy of it?"

"The only one I saw was the one they gave you."

"I thought I left it on your desk."

"I don't have it," Dan said.

"It's around," Goop said. "I talked to an IDOT spokesman who told me something neat. At the height of the Green Years initiative—well, first, see, IDOT has sensors in the roadways to gauge traffic speed and flow, to monitor trouble spots. On a normal day a car traveling at sixty miles per hour will hit the sensors with its front tires and then its back tires like this—boom boom, almost no time between at all. As traffic slows, the time between the front and back tires hitting the sensors increases, until it gets to a point where if there is a five to eight second gap, that's considered a traffic jam. Classic bumper to bumper, he called it. Well, at the height of the Green Years initiative, one of the sensors on the inbound Ike recorded eight *minutes* between contacts and one on the outbound Stevenson recorded eleven minutes between touches. This IDOT guy says that is equivalent to parking."

"Does that fit the definition of a city brought to a halt?" Dan asked.

"I'll write it that way," Goop Traky said.

George Proctor, *Morning Quill* reporter, called back as he was trained to do: "Dan. George Proctor. *Morning Quill.* I know you guys are closing, but have they already started to unwire the phones? We got cut off. Give me your side of all this

I've been hearing. Wild stuff. You saw the kid get hit by a car and sent a reporter out to find the body rather than call the police?"

Danny Fain hung up.

The phone rang immediately. "Dan. George Proctor again. We've got that new instantaneous redial feature. Amazing invention. Program it to redial a number you expect to have to call back fast like a radio contest or someone like you who doesn't want to talk on the record and before the busy signal has sounded or—in your case—before the disconnect has registered at the main computer, the number is being dialed again. We've got the money to invest in high-tech toys like that and I've got the persistence to keep bugging you until you talk to me."

"You win a lot of radio contests, George?" Dan asked.

"I do all right. I won my honeymoon."

"That means your wife lost?"

"Fill me in, Dan," George Proctor said with a laugh. "What did you see?"

"I'll comment on the closing of the paper. Nothing more."

"Did you think finding the kid first would give your circulation enough of a stroke to save the product?" George Proctor asked.

Danny Fain hung up. The phone rang immediately, but it was not George Proctor.

"This is Mabel Grass in Promotions," a squeaky-voiced woman announced. "I understand you're the new Lucy."

"Yes, Mabel."

"Because it's your first day on the job I will forgive you for being late with tomorrow's ad card copy. But you'll have to dictate."

"Ad card copy?"

"Teasers for the fronts of the honor boxes," Mabel Grass explained. "Lucy called every afternoon at four o'clock. She had good and bad days, but she was always on time. When she didn't call today I could spare an hour because I understood how she might be down about losing her job. But when she still hadn't called at six I was coming up on *my* deadline . . . and I've never missed one of those. Here I'm told she's quit and you're the new Lucy. So dictate."

"Couldn't you write it just for today, Mabel?" Dan pleaded.

"Sure I could, but I won't," Mabel huffed. "I asked for the job two years ago but they said I wasn't qualified. I didn't have enough schooling. To write three or four words in big letters? How much schooling does that require? I never would've teased an article that wasn't in the paper, and Lucy did that a couple times. So *dictate.*"

Dwight Spang was at his office door. Up and down his sleeves were worm trails of black printer's ink like avant-garde design elements. He drummed his pencil in a tick-tock beat against the pages of his notebook. "I got something," he whispered, leaning in.

"Mabel. I'm putting you in charge," Danny Fain said.

"Hey now, Lucy," Mabel scolded. "I wanted the money that came with the job two years ago and I didn't get it and you're not going to dump on me now because your time is precious."

"OK. What do I tease?"

"How should I know? What's in tomorrow's paper?"

"That's being decided," Dan said.

"Pick something."

"SAYONARA! WE'RE GONE! SO LONG, CHICAGO! Something like that?"

"I wouldn't tease the fact the paper's dead," Mabel advised.

Muff Greene approached nearly running, a round, anxious mass skating across the scuffed tiles toward Danny's office. Dwight Spang turned his back to her, folded his arms, made a show of examining his notes.

"They blew the jet up just south of Crete," she shouted at Dan. "We've got to make calls. Who're you talking to?"

"Mabel Grass in Promotions," Dan replied.

"That's me and I'm waiting."

"I know Mabel. Tell her hi," Muff Greene said.

"Muff says hi."

"Three or four words. It can't be that difficult. I'd do it if you were going to pay me the two-hundred-dollar bonus Lucy was paid every week."

"Two hundred dollars?"

"Obscene, isn't? Now let's have it."

"HIJACK HORROR."

"The KLM thing? That will be on One, so it's redundant to tease it when it will be right above the card. Anything in Sports? Features? Business?"

"MOCK colon JOB hyphen LOSS TIPS."

"That's serviceable."

He hung up. Dwight Spang dropped onto the couch, furiously flipping through his notes. "We work for a Gestapo house organ," he proclaimed. "I hope you know that."

"They pay well, though," Danny Fain said.

Dwight Spang intoned from his notes with the authority of a man who was happy with his lede. "Three pressroom mechanics with a combined seventy-four years of vaunted service to the Chicago *Bugle* had to be transported by ambulance to Northwestern Memorial after being *subdued* not by Chicago police but by members of the building security force acting on orders of Fluff himself. I've got the names of the three anarchists. The rent-a-cops Maced them in the eyes, beat them on the arms and shoulders with truncheons, and dislocated one guy's shoulder by twisting his arm up behind him removing him from the pressroom. The *Quill* had a reporter down at the front security desk asking a bunch of questions. He offered to buy into the building but I had to turn him down. Security herded all the pressroom personnel into the lunchroom before they went into action but my source was hiding up on the catwalk and they missed him in the roundup. He's gonna be all over TV tonight. He talked like a madman he was so fired up. He clutched my sleeves with his hands, got fucking print ink all over one of my good shirts."

"Write what you've got," Dan said.

"Is there a chance this will run?"

Muff Greene called. Dan saw her sitting in the city desk slot. Her mouth moved. "Take down this number," she ordered. He did. "That's the K. Jamison residence. We don't know any names, only that K. Jamison . . . not Kay like the girl's name, but just the initial K., was on KLM 404 bound for New York with connections to O'Hare."

"I'll get someone on it," Dan said.

"*You* call it, Danny. It needs your touch."

"I don't have a touch on this sort of thing. I'll put Dwight Spang on it," he said, their eyes locked through his office glass, watching each other's mouths move.

"He's a butcher," she declared. "He *likes* to make those calls because he likes the pain they cause. This needs sensitivity. The Danny Fain touch."

"I can't, Muff."

"Jesus, Dan. We've all got work to do and I need you to do this."

"I can't make the call."

"Be a pro." She fired the phone into its resting place, letting her eyes hold their angry connection with him for a long moment after.

"I've got a call for you to make, Dwight," Dan said.

"No can do, chief," Dwight Spang responded, standing up from the couch. "I'm out of the business of bearing grief."

"What'll it take to buy you?"

"Your severance check," he said with a smug grin, departing.

Trying not to think too much (K. Jamison could very likely live alone and probably did if he or she was flying alone from Amsterdam to New York and then on to Chicago), he tapped in the numbers and someone snapped it up on the first ring.

"Yes?" a man's voice, wary; not really fearful, just impatient.

"Mr. Jamison?"

"Yes?"

"My name is Danny Fain."

"Are you with United?"

"No."

"I'm waiting for a call from United."

"Are you K. Jamison's father?"

"Husband. Who are you?"

"Danny Fain, sir. I'm a rep—. . . I'm an editor with the Chicago *Bugle.*"

"*What* is going on?"

"Your wife is flying United?"

"She's on KLM into New York. Then United to O'Hare. Why are you calling? Has she crashed?"

"Sir, I . . . I think you should get in touch with the airline."

"She's crashed!" he stated, pitching toward hysteria.

"Hijacked, sir."

Mr. Jamison took a moment to reflect on this. "Hijacking is better than crashing," he finally decided.

"Call KLM." Danny Fain hung up.

Muff Greene was waiting at his door. "Now, was that so bad?" she asked like a mother.

"He didn't know *anything.* He thought I was calling to tell him his wife had crashed."

"Can he give us a picture of her?" Muff Greene asked.

Danny Fain stared.

"Call him back. Tell him we'll send a cab to pick it up. He can leave it in an envelope on the front porch. We won't bother him anymore."

"No," Dan said.

"Get a picture."

"Hey, fire me. I'm not going to be the one to tell that man his wife is part of the Mediterranean now," Dan said.

"Lucy would call," Muff Greene murmured.

"Maybe. But she's a milk flack now, so that's a moot point," Dan said. She didn't smile at his joke.

Bernie DeVille returned, puffed up with the evening's excitement and his own natural self-importance. He draped his coat over the back of his chair and logged on.

"You reach the mom?" he asked when Dan approached.

"Her line's busy."

"Stepdad's got it off the hook. Dunkirk called someone he knows at the phone company who ran a check. It's a clear line. The phone guy said he could hear a TV."

"With the news on?"

"No. *Addams Family.*"

"Does anyone care about this kid besides me?" Dan asked.

Bernie DeVille sneered, "Your bad breath is all over this story. There were creeps from fucking *suburban* papers making fun of you by name out there tonight."

"They don't know any more than you do," Dan said.

"Penn is everyone's source for everything on this. I think he's the anonymous call."

"I agree. I think he found the kid where I pointed him, then he went and called Dana Viola at Eight," Danny Fain said. "When the deal was done and the camera in place, he made his anonymous call."

A sunburst of TV light poured into the newsroom so abruptly then that reporters cried out as they covered their eyes. Tim Penn was in the lead, impatiently snapping a microphone cord behind him to tug it free of the trailing stumblers he was tied to. His blue blazer gleamed; it matched his eyes, Danny Fain noticed.

"Timothy Penn," he said to Dan. "You want to do this in your office or out in the hall?"

"I'm not talking to you," Danny said. "Get the hell out of here."

Tim Penn turned to the cameraman, who was poised on the balls of his feet, legs flexed, his off-eye squeezed shut, the other aimed. "You running, Hans?" Tim asked.

"Running," the cameraman nodded.

"Chicago *Bugle* Associate Metro Editor Daniel Fain was riding the Chicago and North Western train to work this morning when he witnessed the hit-and-run death of young Ralph Mustain," Tim Penn said into the camera. Like a trained seal, Dan remained in place, remained cooperatively framed. "Yet rather than report to Chicago police what he had seen, he sent a reporter out to try and locate the boy's body. Dan," Tim Penn said, turning, mike to mouth, "share with us your motive for such a decision."

"Beat it, Penn. I'm not talking to you."

Facing the camera, Tim Penn continued, "Danny Fain and all the other employees of the *Bugle* learned upon arriving for work this morning that the paper was ceasing publication in two weeks. Dan, did that distressing news lead you to believe you might improve circulation by sensationalizing this child's tragic death?"

"Tell your viewers that you were the reporter I sent out," Dan said into the camera.

Tim Penn pressed on, "Did it occur to you that Ralph Mustain's family would be paralyzed with fear for his safety . . . yet *you* withheld what information you possessed in order to improve the circulation of your dying paper?"

"Tell them you found the body and then negotiated with Channel Eight for a job before telling the police," Dan said.

Tim Penn turned to the cameraman. "Edit that," he said.

"Tell your viewers you planted three joints on the body."

"Even *I* am not that low, Dan," Tim Penn said.

"Tell your viewers Ralph's parents were so paralyzed with grief they accepted ten thousand dollars for the mom's exclusive story."

The cameraman murmured, "Is that right?"

"No, it's not right," Danny Fain interjected. "But it's true."

"Who're you working for?" Tim Penn snarled.

"I'm just running film," the cameraman said. "You ask the questions."

"Let's get Derringer's thoughts on this," Tim Penn said, turning away from Dan. "He's too stupid not to talk."

Bernie DeVille, a man with standards, a stalwart defender of employee loyalty, stepped into the frame just then and deposited a yellowish gob of phlegm on Tim Penn's tie. "Get out of our newsroom," he said coldly, reloading with a wet glottal scraping.

"Edit that," Tim Penn said to his cameraman.

"Go back to work, Bernie," Dan ordered.

"Not until he's gone."

"You'll be chasing me all night on this, Bernard," Tim Penn taunted, dabbing with a handkerchief. "I've got *tit*bits on this you and your sorry rag can only dream about."

Les Burkin then let fly from the left, a shot that hit Tim Penn in the sideburns. Becky Fudge was there, and Puncher Mudd had wandered over with a contingent from Sports, and Lawrence K. Mock had seen the bubble of artificial illumination go past his office and Dwight Spang and Nan Fullwood were there and all the newsroom saw in Channel Eight's Timothy Penn a blatant version of the disgraced and spit-dampened Alexandra Jones, and they closed around him to exact their retribution.

"Cover me," Tim Penn commanded his cameraman.

The crew exited backing out. The lens barrel swept across the gathering, getting on tape outraged faces, gaping mouths, undignified poses, pursed lips caught as if in the midst of blowing a kiss, and everywhere the camera touched there was a moment's pause in the emotion as the finality of being videotaped occurred to the people. In this moment came rational consideration of what they were doing, and then regret, so that when Tim Penn, only slightly shamefaced, and the cameraman got to the hall door they had lost their harassing escort and Tim Penn felt serene enough to pause, posing in the doorway, to touch up his tie knot and sweep a hand through his hair.

"Later, losers," he said and departed, camera guarding his retreat.

A congratulatory hubbub ensued; an invader had been repelled. Danny Fain slipped free of the merriment to enter Derringer's office.

"I need a minute of your time," Dan said. "I want to run at least a short on what happened in the pressroom today."

Derringer grimaced. "That's over, Dan. And it's private. With all the mess going on around here, is that all you've got to worry about?"

"We need to present a complete picture of what is happening," Dan said. "Those three guys are part of the picture."

"I even got a couple of calls about you," Derringer said. "You put the paper in a bad spot and I stood by you."

"Who called you?"

"Media types. The *Quill*. The wires. This has been an extraordinary day and the sooner we get it over with the sooner we can go on to tomorrow," Derringer said.

"A brief? A cop short?"

"No story."

"But—"

"What is this, Dan? We *negotiated* with those three for well over an hour," Derringer explained. "They were adamant in their refusal to listen to reason. We were coming up on firm deadlines that the presses needed to meet. They were lawbreakers and we were civil enough to let our inside security force handle matters. We saved them from jail and a criminal record."

"It could've been done without violence," Dan said.

"Were you there? You don't know how *unrealistic* those men were. They refused our every offer," Derringer said. "It was keep the paper running or nothing."

"What did you offer them?"

Derringer turned away. "I didn't memorize the terms of the negotiations," he said. "I gave our people an hour to talk sense into those three . . . if that didn't work, then they had my authority to remove them at whatever cost."

"What would it cost to keep the paper running?" Danny Fain asked.

Derringer fixed him with a bloodless glare. "Do you remember the day I interviewed you?" he asked abruptly.

"Vaguely," Dan said, though the session was an indelible sliver of memory.

"Do you remember the little test I gave?"

"It was a word on a piece of paper," Dan said, remembering perfectly well, but unwilling to help Derringer along.

He took a pen from his inside coat pocket and wrote on one of his notepads MANSLAUGHTER.

"Remember?" Derringer prodded, holding up the word.

Danny Fain nodded that he remembered.

"It was a test I gave to everyone I interviewed," Derringer said.

"I know," Dan said.

Derringer scowled. "They talk about me, do they? They think I'm worthy of their derision?" He glanced out the windows of his office. Everyone had gone back to work after routing Tim Penn; the view from Derringer's was of a kingdom smoothed and efficient, people on the phones, people typing, talking, passing notes, the room having entered the phase that lasted from a half hour to three hours, depending on the amount and importance of the news, when even goofs and incompetents could concentrate on the task of producing a newspaper.

Derringer said, almost dreamily, "I wouldn't have reached the level of being able to tell people their lives as they know them are over if I didn't have *some* ability."

"Those people deserve a story in their own paper," Dan said. "They deserve validation of their fate."

"You were the only person who looked at that word and didn't see MAN SLAUGHTER. You saw MANS LAUGHTER," Derringer said. He studied Danny Fain like a bug. "I didn't know how to interpret that. I still don't. Was it weakness? A sensitive nature? A creative turn of mind? But you know what? I didn't want to hire you because of it. Muff talked me into hiring you. She said you had the best clips she'd ever seen. So I thought, as a reporter, what threat would you be to me? Then you became a city editor, then associate metro editor. And now you're the new Lucy. It's lucky we're closing. If we stayed in business you would have been after my job. Yet today you let a kid die in the street while you pursued him as a news story."

"What did *you* see in that word?" Dan asked.

Derringer smiled contentedly. "I didn't have to see anything," he said.

Dan went to pester Bernie DeVille. "Write faster," he ordered jovially. "I want to go home."

"So go," Bernie responded. "I can finish and someone city side can edit it."

"I want to do it," Dan said. "It's my story."

"It's Tim Penn's story."

"Timothy," Dan corrected.

He phoned Dana Viola from his office. "I didn't picture you as Tim Penn's type," he said.

Dana Viola laughed hoarsely. "I'm not. He's mine."

"A pretty boy? Shallow as spilled decaf?"

"Don't underestimate the power of a beautiful face," she said solemnly. "TV gospel: If the face is fair, the rest is there."

"He'll let you down," Dan predicted. "He's all over this story because it's new and he wants to impress you but one day soon he'll go out on an assignment and disappear into the afternoon sunshine."

"We've discussed that," she said. "You don't think we didn't look into this one? We've been prepping him for almost eighteen months. Ever since he hit on me at a party while holding his wife's hand. I thought: He's handsome, he's heartless, he's perfect for TV. I started to tag his career right then. We would've moved on him ourselves in another month or so but then he came to us with this kid story."

"Did he find the body, then call you?"

"Of course he did. He wouldn't tell us where the body was until he had a signed contract."

"And you *hired* him?" Dan said.

"That's initiative, Danny. That's maximization of power. He had one piece of information we needed badly and he made the best use of it," Dana Viola said. "He's a legend in the newsroom and he hasn't even been *in* the newsroom yet."

"What about the ten thousand for the mom?"

"Talk to *her* about that," she said.

"I'd love to, but you bought her off."

"That's *your* answer," Dana Viola said. "What about you? Are you ready to talk on the record about your part in this?"

"I have no part in this," Danny Fain said.

"Sure you do. You're a star," she teased. "You're going to be all over the news tonight. At least Channel Eight."

"I've kept my responses purposefully disjointed and vague," Dan said.

"That wasn't hard for you to do, was it? My people are busy piecing together a montage of vague and disjointed Danny Fain footage," Dana Viola said like a murmurous threat. "By tomorrow morning you'll be the embodiment of everything people find callous and loathsome and cruel about the media. A newspaperman."

"Lucky for me I'll be out of the business soon," Dan said, hanging up, chilled by her prophecy.

Bernie DeVille came to his office with notebook and pen. "I've reached that point in my story when I have to interview you," he said.

"Why do you need to talk to me?"

"Because you are *in* this story," Bernie said. "Tim Penn may have the mom. *We* have you. You're a walking scoop. You're ours alone. Be proud and tell me what happened."

Dan sighed. "I was on the train this morning. I was spending the ride critiquing the *Quill* and not really paying any attention to anything when I very idly looked out the window and saw a kid dressed as a ghost get struck from behind by a car. He was in midair, *flying,* when a freight train traveling in the opposite direction blocked my line of sight."

"Color of the car?"

"Red."

"Make? Model?"

"A sedan. Boxy. Nothing memorable," Dan said.

"And you're *positive* the car didn't stop?"

"My last image of the event was the ghost in midair," Danny

Fain said. "Struck from behind and launched into the air . . . and in just that instant the train cut off my view. But the car was moving with the speed and the *attitude* of a car not planning to stop."

"You checked for witnesses on the train?" Bernie DeVille asked.

"Yes. Nobody saw anything."

"People in the cars behind you might have seen something."

"I was in the last car," Dan said. "Even as I was witnessing this hit-and-run the cars in front of mine had already had their vision obscured by the outbound train."

Bernie DeVille took notes. He said offhandedly, "Be forewarned that Abe Skinback called me to get a quote from you for his column. He got a call at home from someone asking about you and he was mystified. He'd never heard of you. Much as mystification is his normal state, he hates to have it made apparent to him and so he called me, his vacuum tube, so to speak, to the little people in the newsroom. He asked me, also, if I'd heard of any job openings."

"If Abe wants the goods on me, have *him* call," Dan said.

"Exactly what I told him," Bernie DeVille said. "Now, Dan. Let's reconstruct your thinking after witnessing this hit-and-run and then deciding not to report it to the police. You said you weren't sure of the kid's location?" he prompted.

"Yes."

"So you sent Tim Penn out to look for him."

"Yes."

"Did you give him coordinates? A place to start?"

"I had a general idea where he should start," Dan said. "When we reached the station I tried to call Stan Mansard at headquarters. He wasn't in."

"What would you have said to Stan?"

"I don't know. Ask him if he could be of help," Danny said. "I wanted to clue someone in, but not too well."

"What did you expect to accomplish?"

"It's creepy in retrospect."

"Tell me," Bernie DeVille urged.

"To work a story before it was a story," Danny Fain said. "To shape a scoop before anyone else was aware it existed."

Bernie DeVille looked away. "You do that with a crooked judge or a bribery story," he said. "Not a kid hit by a car. Maybe he lay there for a while before he died. Maybe they could've found him in time to save him."

Dan said stubbornly, "He was in midair when I saw him last. It's a decision I'll have to live with."

Bernie DeVille shook his head. "Whatever you do, don't repeat any of this on tape."

"It's no great shakes having me alone?" Dan winced.

"Have you worked up a standard apology statement?" Bernie DeVille said.

"I'm sorry?" Dan said.

"Not heartfelt enough. It should run a couple lines, at least, and you should come just short of accepting blame for the boy's death," Bernie DeVille said.

"Send Dwight Spang in here," Danny Fain said. "I want *your* story in fifteen minutes. I'm determined to be on the eight o'clock train."

He made a call to the composing room one floor down and casually identified himself as, "Hawkins, Financial." He inquired into the status of Page Forty-four. The type had been pasted in, the page approved by Reese Donkins, the Financial makeup editor, and the flat shipped to the pressroom. "Let me speak to Reese," Danny Fain muttered, sounding bored with the routine, a tad exasperated with a late snafu. He was informed that Reese had cleared all his pages and left for the night.

"We need Forty-four back," Dan ordered. "New story and dummy TK."

"We'll need kill sheets. Twelve copies."

"I'll fill them out when I bring down the new dummy." He hung up without another word.

What price would the *Bugle* put on their embarrassment? He

had been warned, emphatically and provocatively, and yet there was a hole on Forty-four, just the proper understated page position that with a twenty-four-point head would make a perfect display for a statement of conscience that Derringer would not even see until it was pointed out to him. Pinning blame would be rapid. Could they can him sans severance? Was Dwight Spang's informative little piece worth the risk that they would?

"Are you willing to print this without authorization?" Dan asked when Dwight Spang brought his finished story over.

"Sabotage the paper?" Dwight Spang asked, mildly bug-eyed.

"I guess it's sabotage."

"Hell, print it."

"You may lose your severance."

"No one's talked to me about severance."

"They'll bounce you immediately when they find out it's you," Danny Fain said.

"What do you mean 'when'? Is it inevitable?"

"Once you create a slug, even if you delete it a second later, a record of its being created will remain in the computer for twenty-four hours," Dan said. "You created it, wrote all over it, stored it, sent it to me. Probably even made a printout. Your name is all over it. Mine, too."

"There's nothing we can do to hide?"

"We can *not* run it," Dan said.

"What about going to the *Quill*?" Dwight Spang said. "I know people over there who would be glad to take my information and put it in their paper."

"You don't really want to do that," Danny Fain said.

"No," Dwight Spang said.

"I'll tell you this much," Dan said. "*I'm* willing to print this."

"No offense," Dwight said, "but you're company meat. You've done their bidding every day of your career . . . and I'm not faulting you for that. But you've accumulated a residue of good feelings. You're *respected.* Me, I'm a troublemaker. Muff Greene hates the sight of me. Derringer won't look at me. I'm always complaining. They might stretch a little to keep you covered. They'll stretch as far the other way to skin my bone, seeing as how I'm gone regardless."

Danny Fain fixed a misspelling in Dwight Spang's story. He had hardly absorbed a word of Dwight's speech after that phrase *done their bidding.* "I'm still willing," he said in a low voice.

"I guess I am, too."

Dan looked up. "Do you want a byline?"

Dwight Spang laughed. "No byline, thanks."

The hole on Page Forty-four was three columns wide, twenty-two lines of type in each column. He wrote a twenty-four-point headline: BUGLE TO CEASE PUBLICATION; 3 HURT IN PROTEST.

"What do you think?" Dan asked.

"I never could write headlines," Dwight Spang said. "Yours is good enough to get readers into the story."

Dan then inserted the sizing commands to fit the story into the hole. The computer hyphenated and justified the type, taking it out of sight for several seconds. The story returned in the width it would appear in the paper, three legs cut into even blocks of twenty-two lines, with a double line to show where the story ended and any type that broke beyond that length; in the case of Dwight Spang's story, eleven lines.

"That isn't much room," Dwight complained. "Couldn't you find a bigger hole?"

"I'll bet you said that to your mom the day you were born," Danny Fain said.

"This is important."

"A minute ago you were afraid to run it."

"I don't want to butcher it," Dwight said. "There aren't eleven lines of trim in it. I'd rather not run it at all than cut the heart out of it."

"You've got this long description of the pressroom and the newsroom," Dan said. "That can go."

"That's *atmosphere.* You've got to give an idea of what the interiors look like," Dwight said.

"Not in sixty-six lines. You need boom-boom-boom. A lack of fanciness. The reader doesn't care that the gallery windows were covered with paper."

"That's *very* important," Dwight Spang countered. "It indicates the company had something to hide."

"A point," Dan said. He transferred an extraneous descriptive paragraph into notes mode, where the words could still be read, but not counted in the length of the story. "That's five lines," he said. "Six more."

"What about you? Should we mention your knife wound?"

"Why?"

"It's symbolic of the generally chaotic nature of the place," Dwight said. "A place run amok. Knifings. Spitting on people. Beating employees with sticks. I think it's important."

"Then you'll just have to trim something else," Dan said with a shrug. It was the irrefutable fact that defeated every reporter's grandiose plans to write long and memorably about the most trifling event: *Sorry, honey. No room.*

"So. Six lines," Dan said.

"Any widows or orphans? Any spare *that*s or *which*s?"

"We really should have a graph on the company position," Dan said reluctantly.

Dwight Spang grew exasperated, snarled, "Their closing the fucking paper *is* the company position, Dan. They've said volumes with just that one thing. This is the rebuttal to that." He grew businesslike. "I'm willing to give up these three lines here"—he jabbed at the keyboard, moving the cursor up through the type until it rested on the paragraph in question—"if you will agree to a smaller head that will allow us an extra line per leg."

Muff Greene came to his door. She looked quizzical. Dan hit a key and the story vanished. He typed a slug and Dwight Spang's crypt-liner story appeared, fragmented, unfinished, a maze of notes and abbreviated shorthand, a blur of unattributed quotes.

"What're you working on?" she asked.

"Dwight's grave-strike story," Dan said. He made a gesture of pushing the screen around so Muff Greene could read it, but she betrayed no interest.

She checked her watch; a thin gold band, a green face. "I'm about ready to go home," she said. "Have you read Bernie's story?"

"No," Dan said.

"KLM is the line, obviously," she said. "Goop's Green Years story is going across the bottom of One with color of the GREEN YEARS spelled out across Lake Shore Drive that we bought from a stringer. Bernie's story will go inside. Derringer said somewhere behind seven."

Danny Fain objected. "I think that's a big mistake, Muff."

She looked at him hard for a long time. "You lost valuable points not making that call," she told him coldly.

"I made the call," Dan said.

"You wouldn't call for the picture," she said. "You weren't willing to go far enough to be *productive* in the call."

Dan looked away. "I won't apologize for that. And that has nothing to do with the merits of the kid story."

"Two hundred fifty-four people in little bits in the sea," Muff Greene said almost dreamily. "And four of them from here."

"A hell of a story," Dwight Spang agreed. "Miles of profiles."

"You two should have a child," Danny Fain said. "It'd be a *proto*journalist."

Muff and Dwight looked at each other for an instant, perhaps imagining the event, and then Muff Greene, childless, ashen with fatigue at the end of a heartbreaking day, retreated to her office to get her coat.

"Can you imagine fucking Muff?" Dwight Spang murmured, watching her depart.

"I need that trim, Dwight."

"What about the smaller head? Eighteen point."

"Over three columns," Dan said, "you might as well just type the lede."

"It's not *that* small. Everything in the story is golden," Dwight Spang said. "*Un*trimmable."

Dan laughed mockingly. "Such words don't exist," he said. He downsized the head and typed BUGLE TO CEASE PUBLICATION; 3 HURT IN PRESSROOM MELEE. It was four counts short; he bumped the size up to 19.5 points to fill out the line.

"There you go," Dwight said, watching over Dan's shoulder.

Danny Fain looked up at him. "Last chance," he said. "Still time to kill it and slink home."

"No. Seeing as how you've lost favor with Muff, I feel better about this. You have as much to lose as I do." He slapped Dan on the shoulder. "Drop it."

The Page Forty-four flat was laying by itself on the pasteup bank. The night's news pages, with ads in place, were on the other side of the angled table; it was too early in the shift to have type or dummies for them. A short, rotund man in a printer's apron and ponytail stood awaiting instructions. He carried his X-acto knife in a protective metal tube in his apron pocket. Sometime in the past he had lost a chunk of his throat, and when he spoke the words came out tinny, hollow, and electrified through a small gauze-muffled hole at the base of his neck.

"You Hawkins?" he asked, with feedback.

"Hawkins sent me," Dan replied. He had seen the printer before and assumed the printer had seen him; he might or might not know Danny Fain by name, and probably didn't, but Dan decided to extend the lie as far down the chain as he was provided opportunity.

"Type dropped?"

"It should be out any minute."

The printer wandered off to another job. His ponytail flowed down to the small of his back, where it had become inadvertently snarled in the confluence of belt and belt loop. The room was nearly empty. Light tables glowed in the ad pasteup room, dry-ice-colored squares bearing nicks of wax, with no one working at them. The walls were papered with mug shots used in previous editions and stuck up on the walls for future emergencies, union postings, and a tool supply company's calendar: for October, a topless vixen in black-net stockings and witch hat astraddle an industrial broom.

A wide ribbon of film rolled like a curling tongue out of the developer. Danny Fain stepped near and read his headline upside down.

"Here you go," he said. He reached for the story in the catch basket.

"Don't touch that," the printer warned sourly.

Dan fought against a glance at the man's throat. "Sorry," he said.

"We're still a union," he persisted.

"Sure. Go ahead."

"Dead. But proud." He cut the excess film off around the type, then ran the type twice through the waxer. "Heard there'd be no story," he said, glancing at Dan.

"Change of plans," Danny Fain said.

The printer pointed to the names of the three injured pressmen. "I knew them," he said.

"What they did was admirable," Dan said. "But kind of dumb."

The printer raised his jaw proudly, exposing the flap over the hole; the material looked like you could weave it into a porch screen to mend a puncture. Something fizzed in the back of his throat. "Dumb?" he challenged.

"Nothing they did was going to make any difference," Dan said. "We're closing. They're in the hospital. What did they accomplish?"

"Years you print junk," the printer countered, hissing. "Princess Di. Madonna. Lottery. Murders. Phone polls. Auto accidents. Celebs. Richest people in the world. Contests. Movie quizzes. Giveaways. You ever say stop? Say this is garbage nobody dumb enough to take serious? You have courage like my three friends maybe you and me have job tomorrow."

"Not likely," Dan said.

"How you know? You never do it." He slapped the story into the Page Forty-four hole. He smiled disdainfully. "Perfect? This tell the whole story?"

"Enough," Dan said.

"You got kill sheets?"

While Dan did the paperwork on the page change, the printer went through a revolving door into a smoky lounge where his fellow printers relaxed on couches and sipped coffee. The hair snarled in his belt kept the printer's posture erect; he drank coffee with one finger pressed to his throat.

Dan wrote through carbons. He needed twelve copies. He initialed them GH, giving Hawkins just the hint of a first name. The printer turned his head like a horse being reined around and Danny Fain waved the sheaf of papers at him. He set down his coffee and came out.

"You want proof?" he asked.

"No."

The printer carried away the flat and as he disappeared Dan almost called him back. He was accustomed to having a future to consider, a time down the road to weigh against present actions and indiscretions—a conscience; it had kept him faithful to a number of institutions, and now it almost held against this gesture of truth and rebellion. But the printer's accusations had made him bold with guilt; there would be one story worth reading in the next day's paper.

Muff Greene had removed her coat. She had been on her way out the door when Dan went downstairs, but now she was back at her desk, on the phone, and she caught Dan's eye and waved him in. He reflexively scanned the room to guess at the person on the other end of the line. Derringer was using his phone, characteristically with his back to the room, tracing the autographs on his Cubs ball with a finger. Bernie DeVille was on the phone, too. His story was late. Nancy Potter was speaking into her headphones. Everyone was busy.

Dan heard Muff say as he came into her office, "He's here now." She pointed to a chair. "That's up to you," she said. Her smile to him was weak and distracted. She had a pale mouth that she made no effort to enhance, and light brown eyes that heightened the impression of a tired face receding in mist. "I can't make that decision for you," she said. "We're getting on deadline."

He tried to see over the low wall into Derringer's office, to see if there was a balance to Derringer's mouth working while Muff Greene was silent, but the chair was too low. Since planting the pressroom story he felt a surge of journalistic integrity, a desire to meet his obligations, and on any other night he wouldn't be sitting in Muff Greene's office when there were stories to be done.

She brusquely hung up the phone. Dan wished he'd been paying attention to her salutation.

"We're taking heat on this kid thing," she said immediately. "Specifically for your part in it."

"What heat?"

"Derringer has gotten calls. I have, too. A Lieutenant ter Horst called complaining about your unwillingness to talk to the police."

"He wanted to do it over the phone," Dan said. "How do I know he's a cop?"

"We think you should cooperate."

"I *am* cooperating. But I've got a job to do, too. I don't have a couple hours to wander over to the station."

"Traffic is a mess," Muff said. "They're shorthanded. I can see his point."

"Can't you see mine?"

"Channel Eight is doing a commentary on us," she said. "They called to alert us. Dana Viola was considerate enough to read the editorial to me. They accuse you of everything short of hitting the kid yourself. They call the situation a despicable act by a dying newspaper. *Derringer* is mentioned prominently. They're leading with thirty seconds of KLM because they've got no film; we've got the local tears locked on that, thank God—and Nancy Potter. Then they're devoting three full minutes to your hit-and-run. All this even before The Green Years. They've got great tape from this afternoon and still they're putting us—and *you*—before it. That's how hot for us they are. Capped by this commentary calling for your resignation."

Danny Fain realigned himself in the chair. He said nothing. A question, a bizarre request or assumption, stirred the words in his head.

"Derringer wants the appearance of punishment on this," she said in a low voice.

"Just the appearance?"

"He wants to work in this town again."

"So do I," Dan said. With a start he wondered if he could get back Page Forty-four. He said, "I'm losing my job—being fired, as it were—in a couple of weeks."

"So is everyone else."

"He wants *extra* suffering then?"

"He wants to leave the impression of being in power until the very end," Muff Greene said with a whiff of disgust in her voice.

"I've got work to do," Dan said, rising, afraid of what he was about to hear, but also wanting to get a look at Derringer, who seemed to be waiting for him to appear because he crooked a finger at Danny Fain.

"He wants me," he said.

"How are your savings?"

"What savings?"

"Pay yourself first," she admonished.

"That's easy to do when you don't have to pay anyone else."

"Go talk to him."

"You talk to him," Dan said. "I've got work to do."

He went to Bernie DeVille. "Done?" he asked.

"Are you?"

"Am I what?"

"We heard you're getting sacrificed."

"Have you finished the story?"

"The raincoat thing?"

"Not the *raincoat* thing," Danny said. "The kid story."

"It's a caption," Bernie DeVille said. "I was told to send everything I had to Pix."

He went back to Muff Greene's and she was waiting, pointing dismissively next door. "I told you to talk to him," she said.

"I'm just going up the chain."

"And I'm sending you along."

"If you recall, I ran this story by you at the meeting this morning," Dan said. "I didn't hear any contrary wisdom then."

She refused to be linked with him. "Did you? I remember I was preoccupied," she said, looking into the distance. "I remember you told this rather involved story about something you'd seen on your way to work. I think I told you to tread lightly."

"I got an OK from *you,* Muff. I got permission to send Tim Penn after it."

"Well, there you are. You chose the wrong man."

"Regardless, it deserves more than a caption."

"Talk to Derringer. *He* wants to talk to you."

"I've got work to do."

"Talk to Wally."

Derringer was again waiting to catch Dan's eye, and when he did he waved him over like a next-door neighbor. "Sit down. Want a Twizzler?" He held out a limp rod of red licorice.

Dan refused it. "I've got work to do," he said.

"Take a load off, Danny."

"Why kill the hit-and-run?"

Derringer bit off one end of the hollow candy, then the other, and through the rubbery tube thus opened he musically sucked air.

"TV is all over us for what you did today," Derringer said. "Muff tell you about the commentary? Combined with our closing announcement, your action today looks incredibly tasteless to the public—and the journalistic community. I made the decision to run a caption only."

"It deserves more," Dan complained.

Derringer turned frosty. "It does. We'd run the kid's mug, but you couldn't get it. Your team on this fell down all around."

"Bernie has the story."

"Timothy Penn has the *story.* Bernie has fragments. The kid's face would tell the *whole* story," Derringer said. "To be honest, under the circumstances we don't want to go big with this. It would be unseemly, under the circumstances. Luckily we've got the local ties to the KLM thing, and we've been able to get mugs of some of the victims involved. Another instance—Muff tells me—where you sort of fell off the horse."

"In her opinion," Dan said.

Derringer selected another Twizzler and ran it like a fine cigar under his nose.

"I can't change your mind?" Danny Fain asked.

"The picture's already dummied. Page Seventeen."

"Is it a good picture?"

Derringer shrugged. "You know Dunkirk. If the kid was run over in a stadium and the cops wore numbers, he'd get the shot. Otherwise, he's passable."

"So a whole team of fuckups on this one, huh?" Dan said, angling for some solace.

"Fuckups and one traitor," Derringer corrected.

Dan stood up. "Should I bother to come to work tomorrow?" he asked angrily.

Derringer, to his credit, did not lose the cool thread of his agenda. "We were hoping you'd be offended, Danny, and resign."

"I'm out a job in two weeks," Dan said. "Why resign?"

"Someone has to take a hit on this," Derringer explained. "I'm taking mine tonight on the ten o'clock news. I'm hoping you'll take yours graciously—like a pro—and resign."

"I need the severance," Dan said. "I don't feel I did anything particularly terrible."

"We need you to go out front on this," Derringer said.

"Can't do it."

Derringer sighed.

Danny Fain said, "I've got to catch a train."

"Resign and we'll talk settlement," Derringer said.

"Talk first."

"All right. Resign and we'll keep you on our health insurance rolls," Derringer said.

"Family, too?"

Derringer shrugged. "Sure."

"Now what will I do for money?"

"You'll get a new job."

"But when? This will taint me. The *Quill* won't hire me."

"Branch out. Leave town."

"I don't want to. I'll resign if you'll pay my severance—plus a ten-thousand-dollar resignation bonus."

Derringer smiled wickedly around his licorice tube. His lips looked dyed in blood. "Don't talk insane, Danny," he said.

"If I'm going to take the hit, I want to be paid for it. This is my death sentence."

"Then ten thousand is cheap," Derringer said. "You don't place much value on your career."

"You said it yourself. I'm a fuckup. But my severance and the bonus will get my family through until I find someone who'll have me," Dan said.

"Severance. No bonus. No family health insurance," Derringer countered.

"Severance and health insurance are nonnegotiable," Dan said. "We're quibbling only over the one-time value of my services."

"I couldn't get you ten thousand," Derringer said.

"Nine five."

"Maybe two."

"I'll see you tomorrow."

"We don't want you back, Danny. Take a long weekend."

"It's Monday," Dan said.

"Call me in the morning. Let things cool down overnight," Derringer coaxed.

"I want to finish this now. If I go home you won't take my call. You'll lock me out of the building and keep my money," Dan said, the scenario scaring him as he laid it out, the truth of what he said becoming evident as he spoke the words.

Derringer seemed impressed to have had his mind read. "Well, I can't give you a check this moment," he said with an embarrassed chuckle.

"I've been here nine years. I'll resign with severance based on Lucy's salary, health insurance for me and my family, and a two-thousand-dollar resignation bonus," Dan said. "You agree to those terms—and promise you won't fuck me over when I get outside."

"Security won't escort you out of the building, no."

Danny Fain held out his hand. "Then I resign?" he offered.

Derringer hesitated. "I need to get back to you on the bonus," he said.

"I can't leave until you do."

"It's eight o'clock. The money men have all gone home."

"Safe on the banks of the Edens?" Dan said.

Derringer smiled. "With traffic the way it is, they're probably still *on* the Edens." Now he put out his hand. "We've worked together too long for me to cheat you," he said. "We'll do a deal."

Danny Fain shook Derringer's hand, whose fingers were adherent with sugar.

"Try them on their car phones?" Dan suggested.

Derringer extracted his hand from Dan's grip. "That would be awkward. They have a budget for closing this joint—they'd have to examine that budget to find where your bonus would come from," he said.

"I'll bet they have it memorized," Dan said.

Derringer's back was turned. "I'll get an answer for you," he murmured.

"Why am I afraid to walk out of your office?"

Derringer said, "I don't know, Danny. But I'm leaving in a few minutes—so you can't stay in here much longer either way."

"I'm safe here. I still have your attention. You can't ignore me," Dan said.

"Go home, Danny. It's Halloween. You should be in costume with your kids."

The lights were off in Muff Greene's office and her door was locked. He unplugged his office TV with the orange personal property sticker and wrapped it in the cord. A train left at 8:30. He called home and got the answering machine, Stu's cracking voice reading from the script Dan had prepared.

"It's me. My train gets in at nine-fifteen. Can you meet me? If you can't, I'll get a cab."

Dirk Flester came to his door. "We've got a problem," he said.

"I'm out of here," Danny said. "Talk to Muff."

"We got a complaint about the job pool," Dirk said. "The prize money has been paid to Deb Foster, who drew Lucy. But now Doug Watts is claiming he should have won because he drew Tim Penn. In my estimation, he has a valid claim."

"So split the prize."

"Do you by chance know what time Tim officially went to Channel Eight?"

"He hasn't filled me in on the details, no."

"Lucy quit after lunch. And I can't imagine Tim could get a blazer and makeup and camera crew in place if he didn't take the job sometime in the morning," Dirk said.

"He'd been talking to them before today," Danny Fain said. "Maybe they followed him every day with a crew and blazer waiting for him to change his mind."

"I'm inclined to call it a tie, with this tiebreaker: who went to work first. Using that yardstick, clearly the winner should be Watts."

"Then get the money back and rereward it," Dan said. He looked around his office, stripped of his lukewarm personal touch, which consisted of the TV, a picture of Rita and a picture of Rita and the kids, and mementos (letter holder, paper cup inkwell, knitted bookmark, the Pretty One's scribbled art) contributed by his children.

"I'm gone," Dan said.

"We know. That's why we thought you might take an objective stand and play commissioner on this contest," Dirk Flester said.

"*What* do you know?"

"That you tendered your resignation."

"Who told you?"

"I heard it from Hatton. Or Melvin. Someone reliable who'd heard it from someone even more reliable."

"I'll bet you heard it before I actually did it," Danny Fain said. "Which I haven't done yet."

"It's bullshit either way. They just wanted your severance."

He pulled the door shut. "I'm late for a train, Dirk."

"Need a lawyer? I'm willing to start a practice from this moment forward with you as my base."

"Thanks, Dirk. I'll manage."

"Could you just make a ruling, Danny? We'll stand by it."

"I don't work here anymore," Dan said.

"That's why you're the perfect man for the job."

He expected pickets in front of the building, smoking effigies of himself, a media crush. But the avenue was quiet; pedestrians in the last moments of heading home, a lunch truck parked in front of the *Bugle*'s loading bays to sell the evening meal to pressmen and mailers working nights at a dead paper. Some looked across at him with his cargo of portable TV and stuffed briefcase.

Fred Tobin was at the curb, raincoat thrown over his shoulder, his hat rakish.

"Where's your wife, Fred?" Danny Fain asked.

Fred turned, a wan smile in place. "I told her to stay home," he said. "With the expressways clogged it's better if I catch a train."

"Want to share a cab?"

"I'd be honored."

Danny raised his arm and a yellow cab from the stand across the street turned across the empty lanes and stopped for them.

Fred settled into his seat. "I was hoping to get out earlier than this," he said. "I've got a dozen people to call tonight for that piece on arsenic in the drinking water."

Danny Fain tried, but failed, to be interested.

"So what will become of us, Danny?" Fred Tobin asked.

Dan looked straight ahead. "We'll get new jobs."

"I'm retiring from the business. It's broken my heart twice now," Fred said. "My papers keep dying out from under me."

"I might run for political office," Dan joked.

Fred Tobin laughed. "Maybe *I'll* play major league baseball," he responded.

No trick-or-treaters downtown, no children anyway; he did see glimpses in passing traffic of people costumed for the evening's sugary revels, and at a light he was startled by a nude woman with a star-tipped wand and red high heels who could not get her arm fully extended before three cabs were jockeying for position and her business.

"Is she in a bodystocking?" Danny Fain asked.

"Who?"

"I thought I saw a naked woman."

Fred Tobin smiled. "Those were the days," he said.

"You used to see a lot of naked women in the past, Fred?"

"Just my wife. Now I have to use Braille on her," he said. "She seems to like that better."

Most of the benches they passed along the river were staked out for the evening, a cool evening with a damp cast and a threat of rain. Those occupying the benches alone stretched out their length and slept beneath soiled blankets and coats, their shoes ripe for stealing. Women with men, however, tried to imprint a grim domesticity on their surroundings: a flashlight for a lamp, their bags of rags neat and trim at their sides, their stoical faces turned toward the pitying passersby. The couples slept upright to foster the appearance of alertness; they looked like two heaps of dirty ice melting into one.

Fred Tobin was looking at Danny. "Don't think I don't appreciate what you've done," he said.

"I haven't done anything."

"You warned me when I was off a letter," Fred said.

"I was just spying on you," Danny Fain said. "It was purely self-interest. If you came in a letter off, I had to decode."

"Hey—let me say thanks."

"No need."

They arrived ten minutes early for Dan's train and he stood in line to buy a ticket. Fred Tobin waited patiently with him.

"You go north, don't you, Fred?"

"Zion. If you could direct me to the proper train I wouldn't have to bother an employee."

"Will you be able to find your stop?"

"They announce the stops. If I can get off the train at Zion, my wife should be able to find me."

The train north was three trains down from Danny Fain's.

"Could you seat me, Danny?"

"Sure, Fred."

"Put me in the smoker, please. I can get in three or four and then blame the train for the smoke smell when she complains," he said. He had a cigarette out and fired up almost before he sat down.

"I've got to go."

"How about your wife? She meeting your train?"

"That's my dream. But I've got to be on it for her to meet me."

Fred Tobin blew smoke into the air. "Go then," he said.

Dan took a seat on the upper level of a nonsmoking car. The train departed moments after he was in place. It was not an express. In the brief time that they paralleled the Kennedy Danny saw that the traffic was pumping along nicely, The Green Years merely an echo of an irritation, only the media to keep them alive in the public's memory.

At each station he looked for children in costume, but the hour was nearing nine, an hour when kids would be in the bath or already in bed. After the Edison Park stop he leaned hard into the window glass, framing his hands around his face to cut down the glare. The conductor looked in from the end of the car to announce that Park Ridge would be next. Danny Fain began to replay in reverse a string of landmarks he didn't realize he had remembered until then: the shape of a building, a succession of signs, a busy highway crossing the tracks at an oblique angle, and then the train glided through a cloud of artificial light thrown out by TV trucks, a half dozen police cars, camera flash, all congregated along a narrow street whose focus was the skinny outline of a boy sketched on the pavement in signal-yellow tape. And crowded at the outer rim of this spectral light were children decked out for the evening's ceremony, their postures respectful, their masks mute. Danny Fain passed back through the scene. He remembered as little as when he went through the first time. The flying ghost was replaced by that static yellow boy: a stick figure named Ralph Mustain, three joints in his pocket, less-than-ideal parents at home. Everything Dan knew about the story had been told to him by one person or another during the day. None of the facts were his own. He had made one personal observation that he had hidden so well it amounted to nothing.

Park Ridge's streets were wet with police-car light. Beams were shined in the faces of people disembarking from the train. Then the train gained speed in its sliding away and in eighteen minutes he was home. Stu, his face of death pressed to the car window, was the only one of his children still awake. Clark and Tracy were both collapsed within their restraining belts, their mouths agape, a stuporous sugar glow to their skin.

Stu put a hand to the auto glass in greeting. He'd been

chewing his wax talons. His makeup needed repair: Skin with a distressingly healthy sheen had begun to emerge in cracks around his mouth and eyes. One green fang had snapped off, giving his horrific mouth the lopsided dentition of a moron.

Rita reached across to unlock his door. Stu was still of an age when his father's return was an event, an end to strangeness, and he followed Danny's every move as he came to the door and slid in, draped a hand around Rita's warm, slim neck, pulled her to him, and kissed her. Her mouth broke open in an instant's promise before she pulled away, aware of their audience.

"Dad. Check it out," Stu beseeched. He presented the bag on his lap for his father's inspection. The bag sides were bulked out with bounty. Candy a foot deep coated the bottom. "Can we just do our block before we go home, Dad?"

"They're asleep," Dan said.

"Just you and me."

"He's waited all night for you," Rita said, nearly an aside.

"Mom can drop us off, then go on home," Stu said. "They'll never know."

"He's right. They won't," Rita said.

"I guess we can."

Rita squeezed his leg. "It's only a half dozen houses," she said.

"I'm taking the fall for this kid story," Danny murmured to her.

"What do you mean?"

"They killed the story. They asked me to resign. TV has it all to themselves."

"I hope you didn't agree to resign," she said.

"We worked out a deal."

"What kind of deal?" Rita asked suspiciously.

"Severance. Insurance. A quitting bonus."

"In writing?"

"I don't have to go to work tomorrow," Dan said.

"It's *not* in writing."

"Nothing's in writing," Dan said.

"What makes you think they'll honor this then?"

"I considered that. The money men had all gone home," Danny said. "I didn't want to spend the night in Derringer's office."

"Couldn't he give you a note or something?"

She pulled the car to the side of the road at the start of their block. The houses were set back from the road, porch lights burning more for protection than in welcome, and smeared down the center of the road were the spaced remains of four exploded pumpkins. No children were about.

"They'll wash their hands of me in public and that will be the end of it," Danny Fain said. "They'll give me my due under the table."

"Who will hire you then?" she asked.

"We'll find out, won't we?"

He opened his door, a signal to Stu, who exited the other side dragging his burden of candy.

"I'll take him to the houses on our side of the street, then come home," Dan said.

She drove away, and when she was gone a Channel Eight van came immediately around the corner, lights on high beam, and stopped by Dan and his son. A panel door rolled open in the side of the van and Tim Penn emerged. He was generously back-lit. A radio squawked in the truck behind him. A cameraman and a soundman followed, and trailing them was a young girl in white pants and green smock carrying a tackle box and a folding director's chair. She snapped the chair into shape in the center of the truck's glow. Tim Penn took a seat. She opened the tackle box and commenced to apply his makeup.

He winked at Danny Fain. "Timothy Penn, Channel Eight. Getting camera-ready," he said. "Tell him what you told me this afternoon, Blossom."

The makeup girl stepped back appraisingly. "That you were good-looking?" she said.

"Quotes are everything, doll. Remember what you say. You said, and I quote, that I set an impossible standard for TV hunks."

Stu pulled on Danny's sleeve. "Come on, Dad."

"Chico," Tim Penn said. "Run that last snippet on the monitor for Mr. Fain here. Come closer, Danny. Look at this."

Not quite unwillingly Dan crossed to where Tim Penn sat. The makeup girl was crouched to his left chiseling his jaw. Stu came along.

"Did you know Muff fired you?"

"They asked me to resign."

"Run it, Chico."

A monitor in the truck came on and there was Muff Greene squinting outside the *Bugle* building, her coat on, her hair combed.

"Leave the 'e' off the end of her name," Danny said. "She'll be so mad."

"Listen," Tim Penn said. "Turn it up, Chico."

Muff Greene spoke, "Although the situation at the *Bugle* might be considered desperate, we in no way condone the heartless and sensationalistic brand of journalism practiced today by Mr. Daniel Fain. Our editor, Walter Derringer, has asked for and received Mr. Fain's immediate resignation and we extend our sincerest apologies to the family of Ralph Mustain. We wish to take this opportunity to assure them that our association with Mr. Daniel Fain is at an end."

"*Woo!*" Tim Penn whistled. "She cut you off at the *root.*"

"What did she mean?" Stu asked.

"Yeah. Explain it to him, Dad."

"I had some problems at work," Dan said. "They're over now."

"A lot of things are over now," Tim Penn said. "Want to see it again? Rewind it, Chico."

"No."

"Your kid want a tour of the truck? We can get cartoons on

here any time we want. Show him around, Chico."

Stu started to go along, but Danny held him back. "We've got trick-or-treating to do," he said.

"I'm doing my report from in front of your house, Dan. I'd appreciate it if you would tape a stand-up with me beforehand," Tim Penn said.

"No, Tim."

"In light of Muff's remarks, I thought you might want to appear just in rebuttal. Try and put a little shine back on your career?"

"I'd just whimper."

"Muff's lying, isn't she? They didn't cut you loose."

"You heard her," Dan said.

"You're not cool enough to be this cool," Tim Penn said. "You're not acting like a guy freshly minced."

"Take it up with Muff."

Tim Penn turned to the cameraman. "Fire it up, Hans." The lens and its attendant illumination swung up into Danny's face. A dash-shaped red light came on atop the camera.

"I'm not talking to you, Tim."

He turned to the girl. "How's the face?"

"Beyond gorgeous," she said.

Tim Penn spoke into his mike: "So you're saying Muff Greene is not being totally sincere in her casting you off like a leper?"

"Talk to Muff."

He was moving now, Stu old enough to read the situation and follow along, understanding enough not to complain about missing this last take of candy. The camera team, quick, accustomed to this sort of treatment, got in front of Danny and began to scuttle backward, taping. The truck followed along at a Green Years pace; the makeup girl carried the director's chair and her tackle box of cosmetics. Dan angled out toward the middle of the street, hoping to steer the cameraman into a slick of pumpkin goo, get him to fall, break his camera, erase the footage. But he was young, wore running shoes, and the sound man had the responsibility of watching the cameraman's backward path.

"This won't look good on tape, Dan," Tim Penn said, keeping up easily. "You'll look like a mobster leaving court. Stop and talk to me."

"No."

"What deal have you struck with your former employers?"

"They were your employers this morning," Dan said.

"This is all editable," Tim Penn said.

"So why should I talk to you? Construct your own conversation," Dan said.

"Are you bitter about how the *Bugle* treated you?"

"No comment."

"What is your response to the report there will be no severance for *Bugle* employees?"

Danny Fain stopped in the street. "Who told you that?"

"That's the rumor. They didn't have a severance breakdown ready because there isn't going to be any severance."

"I had a severance formula quoted to me," Danny said.

"Nothing in writing, though. And why *should* they pay you?"

Danny had an answer for this: because they said they would. The silliness of his logic frightened him into motion again.

"If you could go back to this morning and see Ralphie Mustain get hit by a car all over again, what would you do differently?" Tim Penn asked.

"Send a different reporter," Dan said.

"So you're comfortable with your actions today?"

"Would you pay Ralph's mother ten thousand dollars if you had it to do over?"

"Editable, Dan. Remember that word. Can I ask your kid a couple questions?"

"Of course not," Stu said.

"A media-savvy kid! A no-comment kid at—what? Ten? Eleven?"

"Keep him out of this," Dan warned.

"I've got to talk to someone," Tim Penn said.

"Put me on live," Danny Fain said. "I want to be able to watch myself on *my* TV while I talk to you. That's my only condition."

"I can't do that," Tim Penn said. "You're too volatile."

"Then leave us alone."

"Can we do the Harveys once more?" Stu asked. "They were giving out malted milk balls."

"A trouper," Tim Penn cried. "Kids put things in perspective, don't they?"

"Shut up, Tim."

"In the morning the sun will come up, you'll look through the want ads," Tim Penn rhapsodized. "You'll have a vague memory of all this happening—and then the next day you'll find a great new job and forget this ever happened. So why don't you talk to me?"

"I've given you my one condition for talking to you," Danny Fain said.

"I've kicked your butt downtown on this story."

"On *my* story," Dan said.

"It's in the public domain."

"Who put it there? Who handed it to you?"

"Cut tape, Hans." The red light went out. Tim Penn lowered his microphone. "This is why I can't talk to you breathing, Danny. I've *got* a great new job and I don't want to lose it. You sent me out on this story after I'd just learned I'd be out of work in two weeks. If you expected my loyalties and my energies to remain true to the *Bugle,* then you're terminally naive. You'd do the same in my situation."

"I'd have finished out my time," Dan said.

"You say that because you've got nothing to offer anyone," Tim Penn responded. "It's easy to be loyal when no one else wants you."

They were in front of the Harveys' house, a trim little cottage set back in a birch grove, the driveway unpaved, the front lawn looking kicked about and trod upon. The Harveys' only son was a colonel in the Marines. He arrived in government cars, the driver remaining outside during the brief visits.

"Come on, Stu," Danny Fain said, steering his son off the road and down the Harveys' driveway. The camera light was back on. Tim Penn started to follow.

"I can't keep you from reporting your story from the street in front of my house," Dan said. "But I can order you to stay off my property. You *are* so ordered."

"But, Dad—" Stu said.

"Just talk to me," Tim Penn said.

They went around the side of the house and into the Harveys' backyard. Danny saw Mr. and Mrs. Harvey sitting side by side on the couch in their family room, watching a black-and-white TV. The bygone light washed around their delicate paired skulls like a mild abrasive.

Danny guided his son to the shadows under the trees at the tip of their driveway and from that hiding place they watched next door, where Tim Penn stood fidgeting in an impeccable bubble of unnatural light. The camera was on him. He pressed a button in his ear like a man monitoring a ball game in church. He checked his watch. Chico in the truck called, "First story running. Fifteen seconds."

Tim Penn turned to his makeup girl for a last bit of reassurance, but she had moved the chair to the side of the truck, out of the unforgiving light, and sat reading a magazine and smoking.

Chico suddenly said, "Wait. Shit. This is the wrong damn house. We're looking for 706."

Tim Penn took two steps up the street.

"Stay put," Chico warned. "No time. They can't see you out there in the dark. Get back in the light. Hurry now. It's coming to us. It's here."

Tim Penn jumped back onto his mark and immediately began to speak.

Dan heard his name uttered almost immediately and felt the newsman's perverse pride at being the lede. Then his front door opened and Rita called his name. Tim Penn stumbled over the unexpected echo but did not betray himself by looking toward the sound, even when Rita said, "You're missing the news."

—30—

About the Author

Charles Dickinson's work has appeared in *The Atlantic, Grand Street, The New Yorker,* and *Esquire.* His stories "Risk" and "Child in the Leaves" were included in O. Henry collections. He has published three previous novels, *Waltz in Marathon, Crows,* and *The Widows' Adventures,* and a collection of stories, *With or Without.* He has been a newspaperman for sixteen years, including six years at the *Chicago Sun-Times.* He is currently an Assistant Metro Editor for the *Chicago Tribune.* He lives near Chicago with his wife and two children.